CRITICS RAVE

"Cosmic chaos and lau... ...n the always wonderful ... s paranormal fun with lo..."
— RT BOOKclub

"Nina Bangs has written a truly fascinating romantic tale with *Night Bites*. It has everything from trickery, sorcery, sizzling sex, intrigue, and danger all rolled into one explosive package just waiting to be devoured."
— *Romance Reviews Today*

"Ms. Bangs is an extremely talented author who expresses such wit and humor in her writing that I found myself giggling more often than not. *Night Bites* is most definitely a keeper!"
— Coffee Time Romance

NIGHT GAMES

"A look into a future where sex is the only game worth playing showcases Nina Bangs's talent for witty, irreverent eroticism.... A sensual time travel that at once titillates and satisfies...a tempestuous fantasy with scintillating details."
— *The Midwest Book Review*

"Nina Bangs has to be the imagination queen. Who else could come up with...a humorous satire poking fun at the games people play?"
— Harriet Klausner

MASTER OF ECSTASY

"Is there any author who does humor, horror, and romance in one blending better than Nina Bangs does it? ...An amusing romance that will lead the audience to read in one enchanting bite."
— *The Midwest Book Review*

"Bangs...mixes in several different paranormal elements and equal measures of passion and humor to create her latest wonderfully creative, utterly unique romance."
— *Booklist*

MORE RAVE ABOUT NINA BANGS!

NIGHT BITES

MORE PRAISE FOR NINA BANGS!

THE PLEASURE MASTER

"Sizzling! ...A remarkable blend of extremes, including charming, endearing, and exciting, *The Pleasure Master* lends a new definition to the word 'tease' as it titillates the reader."

—Wordweaving

"An irreverent, sexy and hilarious romp... Nina Bangs has done a fabulous job of creating a funny, sexy and off-beat romance that time-travel aficionados will absolutely relish."

—Writers Write

"Plenty of laugh-out-loud moments...if you're looking for fun and fantasy, you will find it here!"

—*Romantic Times*

AN ORIGINAL SIN

"Ms. Bangs has written a fun comedy of people out of time. It is a romp and should be enjoyed in large gulps."

—CompuServe Romance Reviews

"If you're looking for a funny, heart-wrenching and truly lovely romance to read, try this one. You won't be disappointed."

—All About Romance

"Nina Bangs has come up with a completely new and unique twist on the time-travel theme and has delivered a story that is both humorous and captivating. No one is exactly what they appear in this clever tale."

—*Romantic Times*

BIGFOOT SIGHTING

As suddenly as the play began, it ended. She lay in the snow with him leaning over her, and his gaze was hot enough to melt all the snow on the mountains. Some time during their wrestling, he'd returned from vampire to human form.

Not knowing what to say in the face of his naked desire, she asked a stupid question. "Ever seen Bigfoot around here?"

Daniel looked blank for a moment and then smiled. "No, but I've seen Big…" He took her hand and drew it lower. "Bigfoot, Big-whatever, any body part gone wild can be dangerous."

"Hmm." Kisa tried to look serious. "Is it ferocious?" She massaged him through his jeans.

He groaned. "You bet. And hungry." Daniel slid his tongue across her bottom lip. "And impatient."

Kisa grinned as the tugged at his T-shirt. "I've seen about all I want to of this. Take it off." She wanted him naked, a powerful animal in his own hunting ground.

Other books by Nina Bangs:

NIGHT BITES
NIGHT GAMES
PARADISE (anthology)
SEDUCTION BY CHOCOLATE (anthology)
UNWRAPPED (anthology)
THE PLEASURE MASTER
AN ORIGINAL SIN
FROM BOARDWALK WITH LOVE
MASTER OF ECSTASY

A Taste of Darkness

Nina Bangs

LEISURE BOOKS NEW YORK CITY

A LEISURE BOOK®

May 2006

Published by

Dorchester Publishing Co., Inc.
200 Madison Avenue
New York, NY 10016

If you purchased this book without a cover you should be aware
that this book is stolen property. It was reported as "unsold and
destroyed" to the publisher and neither the author nor the publisher
has received any payment for this "stripped book."

Copyright © 2006 by Nina Bangs

All rights reserved. No part of this book may be reproduced or
transmitted in any form or by any electronic or mechanical means,
including photocopying, recording or by any information storage
and retrieval system, without the written permission of the
publisher, except where permitted by law.

ISBN 0-8439-5634-8

The name "Leisure Books" and the stylized "L" with design are
trademarks of Dorchester Publishing Co., Inc.

Printed in the United States of America.

Visit us on the web at www.dorchesterpub.com.

For Gerry Bartlett

*Thanks for always being there to read my books,
offer suggestions, and listen to me whine. You've helped
make my stories better. Good luck with the release of
your own vampire romance series in 2007.*

Chapter One

Werewolves—furry pains in the butt.

Werecats—sneaky, whisker-twitching manipulators.

Werejerks—every freakin' loser with a *were* in front of its name.

Reinn hated them all. But most of all Reinn hated his job. Guardian of the Blood. What a crock.

He'd been a warrior in some form or another for most of his thousand years of existence. When he'd finally decided to walk away from that life, he'd bought a house and property in the Colorado Rockies, and then settled down to be alone. That was it. He. Wanted. To. Be. Alone. No friends, no emotional chains, no *vulnerabilities*.

Yeah, he was a cold bastard. But he was one cold bastard who was still alive. So how had the clan's governing council rewarded him for surviving longer than any other Mackenzie? They'd made him the official clan exterminator. In other words, he was a glorified Weedwacker. He lopped off the head of any member of the almighty Mackenzie clan who was crazy enough to mate with a shape-shifter or demon. Dumb asses. Who'd want to do that?

He climbed off his bike—the classic Harley was the only possession he'd allowed himself to care about—and grabbed his pack. Reinn left the back scabbard that held his sword right where it was, strapped to his back. He didn't give a damn what anyone thought about him toting a weapon into the inn. Not that he needed a weapon. He was the oldest and most powerful of the Mackenzie vampires. But the sword was a symbolic thing, a nod to the condemned, who was always allowed to fight for his life. Stupid clan law. If you were going to kill, just do it and get out. He stared at the Woo Woo Inn.

The old Victorian mansion surrounded by forest looked spooky beneath the summer full moon, but Reinn knew from last year's visit that what was inside was a lot weirder than what was outside.

There were three kinds of guests who stayed at the inn: nonhuman entities, idiots who liked to pretend they *were* nonhuman entities, or humans who were paranormal junkies, the ones who hung on every UFO report or ghost sighting. Together they turned happenings at the inn into supernatural suckfests. Wouldn't catch him dead here if he didn't have a vampire to off.

He tried to push aside his distaste for the inn's Amityville-wannabe commercialism and climbed the wooden steps of the old-fashioned wraparound porch. Yanking the door open, he stepped inside.

Okay, if he had to stay here for a few days, he

might as well find something good to say about the place. He thought about that as he headed for the small registration desk. The inn was air-conditioned. The cool hall felt great after the humid New Jersey night. And he'd have a chance to get caught up on things when he talked to Thrain and Cindy. Not that they were friends, because he didn't have friends.

When he reached the desk, though, all positive thoughts vanished. The woman seated there crossed her long legs, making her short, tight black skirt ride high on her smooth thighs, and leaned toward him, assuring that he got an eye-popping visual where her black top gaped open. She ran her fingers through her long red hair as she smiled at him, a predatory smile repeated in the gleam of her strange amber eyes. Sparkle Stardust, in the flesh. Bare flesh. *Hell*.

"Well, hello, gorgeous." She slid her gaze the length of his body. "You have no idea how I've looked forward to seeing you again." Emphasis on the word *seeing*. Sparkle was the kind of woman who could make a compliment sound threatening. "Ganymede, Trouble, and I have so many things planned for you."

Ganymede. That would be the fat gray cat sitting on the desk staring at him with avid interest. So Trouble must be the brown dog wagging its tail as it watched from beside the desk. Woman, dog, and cat all had the same amber eyes, and they were all going to be tacks on his road to the quick completion of this job.

He'd seen firsthand what kind of havoc the

woman and cat could cause between them. What had Thrain called them? Cosmic troublemakers. If they were here, then bad things were going to happen. *Great. Just great.*

Reinn didn't know anything about the dog, but if he was with the other two, then Trouble was probably a good name. "So you guys are using your real names this time?"

Sparkle blinked at him. "Of course. Sparkle Stardust is who I am."

"Yo, Reinn, what brings you to Jersey?" Behind the good-old-boy fat-cat persona, something powerful and dangerous shone in the cat's eyes. *"Bet you didn't know that all the shifters and demons in North America went on high alert as soon as word came down that the Guardian of the Blood was back from Australia. You scare them shitless."* Ganymede paused as if savoring the thought of scaring someone shitless. *"And they don't have a clue what your name is or what you look like because of that can't-take-a-vampire's-picture thing. All they know is that you're a ruthless killing machine. You're the man!"*

"Mmm. Powerful vampires are soooo sexy." Sparkle's sensual drawl hinted at where she'd like to direct all that power. "And you're the biggest and baddest of all the Mackenzies. It makes me tingly just thinking about you."

"Every man makes you tingly." Ganymede sent Reinn a belligerent stare. *"Just remember, hotshot, that you might make her tingly, but I'm the only one who lights her fire."* He stood, stretched, and then sat

down again. *"Have to keep the old body limber. Oh, since the place is overrun with humans, I decided I'd better do the telepathy crap again. I thought about taking a different form this time, but cats are best for sneaking and spying. I live to sneak and spy."*

Ganymede yawned. He was probably ready for a nap after that tough stretching exercise.

Reinn searched for a believable reason for his presence here. "I had a few free weeks, so I decided to get some R and R." Yeah, like he'd choose the Woo Woo Inn for a relaxing vacation. "So where're Thrain and Cindy? And why are you here?"

Sparkle studied her nails. "Cindy and Thrain are in Scotland. They're celebrating their first wedding anniversary by visiting Cindy's dad and stepmom."

Uh-oh. This didn't sound good. "And?"

Sparkle didn't answer. She seemed enthralled by the light shining off her nails.

"We told Cindy we'd run the place until she got back. Sparkle got someone to take care of her candy store in Texas while she's here." Ganymede watched a woman walk by eating a doughnut. *"I could get down with a doughnut right now. When's breakfast?"* He stared at Sparkle until she looked away from her nails.

"What?" She looked from Reinn to Ganymede. "Oh, breakfast. I'll check to see if Katie's done once we get Reinn settled."

Reinn glanced at his watch—nine P.M. He'd forgotten that everyone at the Woo Woo Inn slept during the day and played their supernatural games at night. So breakfast was after sunset and dinner

5

was sometime in the early hours of the morning. Not that he cared. All Reinn wanted to do was go to his room, drop off his stuff, and then do some mingling.

"Look, no one knows my name, but just to be safe, call me Daniel . . ." He glanced at the painting of the Woo Woo Inn on the wall behind Sparkle. Wrapped in night shadows, it was one creepy house. "Night."

"Oh, yesss." Only Sparkle could make approval sound like an orgasm. "I like it. Daniel is a strong, masculine name, and strong, masculine men are incredibly arousing. What can I say about Night? It makes me think of hot sex in dark, erotic places."

"*Oh, brother.*" Ganymede looked long-suffering. . Trouble just looked confused.

Sparkle stood and then stretched much as Ganymede had. "You're in the Werecat room, second floor, turn left. You'll find a brochure on your night table listing mealtimes and activities. Right after breakfast everyone gathers in the parlor to talk about what happened the night before. Any questions?"

Reinn was suspicious. "Any particular reason you put me in the Werecat room?" He didn't believe in coincidences.

Sparkle gazed at him from wide, innocent eyes. *Uh-huh.* And he was supposed to believe a being whose sole purpose in life was to mess with people's sex lives ever had an innocent moment? No chance.

"I always try to match guests with rooms that are symbolically significant to them. If I remember correctly, your job as the Guardian of the Blood is to keep members of your clan from getting it on with werecreatures and demons." She shrugged. "The Demon, Werewolf, and Vampire rooms were taken."

Made sense, but Reinn still didn't trust her. But then, he didn't trust anyone. "Right. Give me my key, and I'll head on up to my room."

Sparkle handed him a big old-fashioned key. He turned toward the stairs.

"Whoa, there, bloodsucker."

Reinn paused to look back at Ganymede.

"We're having a big wedding in a week. A vampire and a werecat. Now, I'm not saying you're here to take off the groom's head." That was exactly what he was saying. *"But since we have lots of guests here who're looking forward to that wedding, I'll keep your sword nice and safe. You can pick it up when you leave. Oh, and if you try to do the job without your sword, you'll have to answer to me."*

"And if I don't give up my sword?"

Ganymede offered his version of a cat shrug. *"You don't stay at the inn."*

Reinn narrowed his gaze on Ganymede. The gloves were off. He didn't for a minute underestimate the cat's power. But he'd do what he had to do, and to hell with Ganymede, Sparkle, and Trouble. Without comment, he took off his back scabbard and handed it to Sparkle.

Tail wagging, and mouth open in a happy doggy grin, Trouble stood and trotted over to Reinn. He looked up and woofed.

"What's with the dog?" Anything with sharp teeth, that looked that happy, made him suspicious.

Sparkle had returned to a contemplation of her nails. "Trouble doesn't say much. We gave him to Thrain and Cindy as a wedding gift, and they're the only ones he's warmed up to. But he seems to like you. Strange." She seemed to realize how that had come out, because she looked away from her nails to smile at him—a smile filled with wicked intent. "Not that you aren't supremely lovable."

"Sure." He'd never been lovable. Never wanted to be lovable. And he'd bet Ganymede had ordered the dog to stick with him so he couldn't take the head of the dumb vampire groom when no one was looking. The dog was a snitch, but no drooling pooch would stop him when he decided to make his move. "Will he keep quiet about who I am?"

Sparkle did her pouty act. "Cosmic troublemakers know how to keep their mouths shut."

Yeah. Right. Reinn climbed the stairs with Trouble beside him.

"When you were a baby vampire, did you—"

"I was never a baby vampire. I was born human." Trouble's voice in Reinn's head was the voice of a little kid. Okay, a young cosmic troublemaker. He'd have to simplify his explanations. "Listen up, because I'm only going to say this once. I was human until I was twenty-eight years old and then I became vampire. Don't ask me why, because I don't know. That's just the way things work in the Mackenzie clan. Got it so far?"

"No." Trouble looked up at him from wide puzzled eyes.

"Good. I was a Viking until the clan decided to settle in Scotland. Then I became a Highlander. We took the clan name Mackenzie so we'd sort of fit in."

"Did you?"

"Sometimes. Okay, not so much. But hey, we were vampires. Anyone gave us a hard time, we invited them to dinner. We just didn't tell them they were bringing the drinks. Everything clear now?"

"Uh-uh."

Reinn patted him on the head. "Give it a few years, kid, and it'll all make sense." Turning left, he searched for the Werecat room.

"Why do you want to kill, Alan? He's a vampire, but he's nice to me. Julie feeds me under the table, and she's going to marry him. She's a shape-shifter. Don't you like shape-shifters?"

"I don't have anything against shape-shifters." Besides wishing the earth would open and swallow them all. "But my clan has a law that shape-shifters and vampires can't . . . marry each other. So I'm like a cop enforcing the law."

"Wow, a cop. I'd like to be a cop when I grow up." Trouble looked at him with hero worship shining in his brown doggy eyes.

"Sure, kid." Reinn was an antihero, but he wouldn't tell Trouble that. Let the kid keep his illusions for a few more years. He knew what it was like to have those illusions stripped away too soon.

Reinn stopped in front of the Werecat room. He put the key in the lock and turned. Nothing happened. Putting down his pack, he fiddled with the key. He was just getting ready to use his power to open the damned door when the sounds of voices stopped him. He'd have to wait until they went past.

As the voices drew nearer, he wrapped his mental shields around him. No being could touch his mind or even identify him as a vampire now. A thousand years of building his defenses, both psychic and physical, had made him untouchable when he chose to be.

In the Woo Woo Inn, you never knew who or what you'd meet. Reinn glanced at the three people who'd stopped to look at him—two women and a man. All werecats. He scowled at them.

"Need some help there? The guy who had that room before you always had trouble with the key." One of the women smiled and moved to his side.

Warm. That was his first impression. Warm brown hair falling almost to her waist, large, warm brown eyes, and a warm, friendly smile. He'd bet that in her cat form she was a cute, cuddly tabby.

"That's okay, I'll get it." He didn't trust warm and friendly from werecats. They were sly and untrustworthy in both human and cat forms.

Her smile widened. "No, you won't, not for a while, at least. Come on, let me try. I know exactly how to wiggle it." She glanced at the man and woman, who'd paused to watch. "Oh, and these two are Wendy and Jake, my sister and brother. We're here for our sister's wedding next Saturday."

Wendy and Jake offered a friendly hi. Reinn smiled at them. No fangs this time. He shifted his attention back to Ms. Warm and Cuddly. "And you are?"

"I'm Kisa Evans." She reached for the key, and he let her have it.

"Kisa? A little more exotic than Wendy and Jake." So far, so good. He'd met the bride's family right away.

Now all he had to do was meet the groom and separate his stupid head from his body if he didn't agree to walk away from his werecat honey.

Reinn had been Guardian of the Blood for only about a year, and this was his first job. He'd thought he had a job in Australia, but when the groom heard that the Guardian of the Blood was in the country, he'd left his werebunny bride at the altar.

Reinn thought the council needed to get a life if they were all bent out of shape over a werebunny. He hadn't seen any fanged bunnies lately, so he didn't think the lop-eared bride was going to chomp down on a Mackenzie neck and suck his powers from him.

He didn't expect to have any dealings with demons. Demons weren't into loving relationships. Which was all good, as far as he was concerned. A few random sexual encounters wouldn't do a lot of damage. It was when a Mackenzie decided to get into a long-term relationship that the Guardian had to step in.

Luckily the previous Guardian was a vicious bastard, so Reinn didn't have to build a scary rep. His predecessor had gotten his jollies by not only offing the guilty Mackenzie but also every shifter within a five-mile radius. He'd claimed the carnage was necessary so no shifters were left alive to ID him. He'd also believed in practice, practice, practice—whacking werecreatures wherever he found them. But that was okay, because the more the weres feared Reinn, the less whacking *he'd* have to do.

Kisa wiggled the key, and the door slid open with a muted click. "Mom was probably feeling exotic when she named me. Kisa means kitty in Russian. Mom loves cats." She offered him a triumphant smile as she gestured toward the open door.

I just bet she does. "Sounds like you have a large . . . family." He'd almost said litter.

"No kidding. Three sisters and four brothers. So what brought you to the Woo Woo Inn?" There was no suspicion in her eyes, just friendly curiosity.

By the time he finished with her family, she'd have a healthy dose of suspicion for everyone. Something about that thought didn't amuse him as much as it should. "I've always had an interest in the paranormal, so when I read about this place, I had to take a look." A lie. He'd gotten an anonymous tip that Alan Mackenzie was going to break clan law by marrying a werecat. He'd never met Alan, but the jerk had to be really dumb not to know that the Guardian of the Blood would get wind of his marriage. The Mackenzie clan wasn't that big, and news traveled fast.

Personally, he didn't give a damn if the clan's blood mixed with the blood of every freakin' demon, werewhatever, or as-yet-undiscovered supernatural being sneaking around looking to improve its gene pool. But the clan didn't ask for the opinions of its guardians before ordering them into battle. He'd been tempted to turn the council down, but then they would've set loose their hunters to destroy him. Mackenzies didn't say no to their council.

"We're gonna run, sis." Jake speared Reinn with the unblinking stare cats were so good at. "And your name is . . . ?" He waited for Reinn to plug in a name. Jake didn't look quite as trusting as his sister.

"Daniel Night." Reinn tried to ignore his usual reluctance to give away any part of himself, even a false name.

"Nice meeting you, Dan. See you downstairs, sis." Jake nodded at Reinn before he and Wendy continued toward the staircase.

"Daniel, not Dan." But they were already out of hearing range.

Kisa looked puzzled.

He offered her his friendly and nonthreatening smile—the one he'd had to practice in front of a mirror for three weeks before he got it right. "Sorry, I don't like nicknames." Nicknames suggested familiarity, like someone really knew you, was your buddy. He never wanted anyone to know him, and he wasn't anyone's buddy.

Kisa nodded, but her expression said she thought his response was kind of weird. "Okay, Daniel, let me show you how to wiggle the key so the door opens."

He leaned forward. Up close, her eyes had the

same mysterious quality he'd noticed in the eyes of other werecats.

But somehow *her* eyes didn't immediately make him think of slyness and deceit. They just made her look sexy. That he could think any positive thought about any shifter made him uneasy.

Kisa pulled the door closed again so she could demonstrate even as she tried to maintain her cool. Wow, talk about a seriously sexy male. He was hot in a totally primitive way that made a woman want to do the tangled-sheets tango with him. There was masculine and then there was the capital-M kind. He was masculine with a huge gothic capital. Tall, dark, and so sensual it made her teeth hurt. Not like when you bit into something too sweet, but the kind of hurt you felt when you sank your teeth into hard-frozen ice cream. The potential for sweetness was there, but not until a lot of softening took place. But then, she'd never liked mushy ice cream.

He had to be about six-two, with broad shoulders and the promise of a bare body women would love. Just the thought of wrapping herself around that body as she slid her fingers across all that muscular expanse of smooth, warm skin—

Stop it. She took a deep, steadying breath. She was like a cat in heat. Oh, wait, she *was* a cat in heat. Kisa smiled at him while she tried not to whisper, "Meow." She hated it when her cat nature intruded on her human self.

"I'm impressed." He smiled, his full, sensual mouth softening the blue eyes that had triggered her frozen-dessert image.

She'd bet he hated the thick, dark lashes that made his blue eyes a breathtaking wow. He didn't seem like the kind of man who wanted to stand out in a crowd. Too bad. Even if he cut off the tangled glory of his long dark hair and wore contacts, his very *being* would make people—mostly women—turn for a second look.

"What do you do when you're not planning a wedding?" His gaze was direct and his expression said he was just making polite conversation.

Kisa pushed aside her instinctive werecat mistrust of anyone who wasn't family. This was 2006, and no one had killed her kind for decades, except for a few rogues like the Mackenzie clan's Guardian of the Blood. But Kisa, even at twenty-eight, had enhanced senses powerful enough to identify a vampire. Daniel was safe. Well, maybe not safe, but definitely not a vampire.

"I'm a food critic. I tell the public what's hot and what's not in the restaurant world." Hot, definitely hot. It wasn't just that he was a great-looking man; it was the feel of primal dominance rolling off him in waves. He'd always be king of the pride. Of course, she wasn't a lion, so he wouldn't be her king.

No one would ever be her king—or mate. The thought leached some of her joy from the moment. In the rigidly male-dominated culture of werecats, females could mate only with males more powerful than themselves. Kisa hadn't found anyone who qualified yet. Probably never would. Dumb rule.

His smile never reached his eyes. "Interesting."

The master of small talk. Not. "Watch while I

unlock your door." She moved the key in the lock slowly so he could memorize each twist. And when the lock clicked, she pushed the door open, pulled out the key, and handed it to him.

"Thanks." He stilled, watching her from those cold blue eyes.

She resisted the urge to squirm. His stillness made her uneasy. It was the stillness of a cat right before it leaped onto its prey. That completely focused attention when danger vibes sang in the air and death circled the unwary.

But she wasn't prey, would never be prey. "You might want to mention the lock to Sparkle." She paused at the thought of the inn's hostess. "Sparkle Stardust. Unusual name." For an unusual woman.

His smile warmed just a bit. A woman would have to work hard for a sincere smile from him, but it'd be worth the effort.

"There's power in a name. It can make people remember or forget you. Sparkle wants everyone to remember her. A lot." His smile turned enigmatic. "I've been here before. And I guarantee no one forgets Sparkle Stardust."

Hiding secrets? Could be. She didn't want to know. "Maybe I'll see you downstairs later tonight." Because she had her own secret, and she'd bet hers trumped any he might have by a mile.

He nodded and then disappeared into his room. As he closed the door behind him, she held the memory of his cold eyes and sexy mouth. She wondered what it would take to make those eyes warm. Shrugging, she headed for the stairs.

16

Kisa had reached the bottom of the stairs when she heard the shouting. Curiosity—a sometimes unfortunate werecat trait—drew her to the kitchen. Katie the cook and Sparkle had faced off across the table, with Ganymede as an interested observer.

Katie stood with hands on hips while her broom sort of hopped up and down behind her. Katie practiced Wicca, and Kisa thought Sparkle had better keep one eye on Katie's attack broom.

"What's wrong with bacon, sausage, steak, and eggs for breakfast? You've got lots of carnivores here. They want protein, so I'm giving them meat. I'll have toast, muffins, bagles, cereal, and fruit for the ones who want something different." Katie glared at Sparkle. "What's wrong with that, boss lady?" The cook sounded ticked, and her broom bounced higher.

Sparkle's expression said she was trying to explain the secrets of the universe to a five-year-old. "We're feeding sensual beings here. Sausage and bacon are so not sensual foods. Did you make any oatmeal?"

Katie's narrowed eyes signaled a potential-for-violence broom warning. "No one here eats it when I make it."

"Well, make it anyway." Sparkle was into bossy mode. "Oats encourage testosterone."

"More than enough testosterone already in this place." Katie was starting to breathe hard.

"Put walnuts in the oatmeal. The Romans thought they improved fertility." Sparkle was ignoring all danger signals.

"Anything else?" The fewer words Katie used, the more frantic the broom became.

"Oh, lots." Sparkle pulled out a list. A very long list. "No more fried foods or rich cream sauces. They make people feel sluggish, not sexy. And cut down on sugar, salt, saturated fat, and highly processed foods. They're linked to frigidity, difficulty reaching orgasm, and lack of interest in sex. And—"

"I quit." Katie ripped off her apron and threw it on the floor. She grabbed her broom just before it dived at Sparkle.

A bearded giant of a man interrupted whatever Katie had planned to say next. "Hey, cook, where's the grub?" He looked past Katie at the stove. "Make sure you fry extra bacon and sausage for me. Don't want to run out like yesterday." Then he lumbered out of the kitchen.

"Ha!" Katie pointed dramatically at the doorway where the man had stood. "Tell *him* he can't eat fried stuff." Then she grabbed her purse and marched from the room.

Sparkle turned a bemused look on Ganymede and Kisa. "Okay, so maybe I should've left werebears off my list of sensual people." She widened her eyes. "Did Katie just quit?"

"Um, I think so." Kisa intended to store up lots of fat grams with this meal, because things didn't look promising for future ones.

Ganymede panicked. *"What're we going to eat? Katie was a good cook."*

Sparkle grew quiet. Too quiet. "I'll take over the cooking."

Ganymede's panic escalated. *"But you don't cook, sweet cheeks."*

Sparkle cast him an impatient glance. "Well, how hard can it be? And I'll use all sensual foods. By the time I'm finished, the inn will be a seething cauldron of sexual frenzy."

"Oh, shit." Ganymede's input.

"I'll fix my plate now." Kisa's input. And after she ate this plate, she'd come back for a second one to store in her room's minifridge. Just in case.

Sparkle studied her perfect fuchsia nails. "I'll have to get gloves before I cook my first meal. Chipped nail color puts me in a vile mood."

Ganymede sidled up to Kisa. *"Want to make a covert run to the nearest McDonald's for me?"*

Kisa sighed. *Oh, boy.*

Chapter Two

Reinn shut down his laptop. It hadn't taken him long to order another sword online. The council was big on every clansman having his sword handy in case he needed to do a little skewering, maiming, or decapitating. Talk about medieval mentalities. A clan courier would deliver the sword to him tomorrow at dusk just beyond the tree line behind the inn. Then he'd find a place in the woods to hide his weapon until he needed it.

He glanced at his watch. Time to go down and meet the dumb-as-dirt groom. Reinn decided the occasion called for a change of clothes. He hadn't brought much with him, since he'd be here for only a few days—a couple of extra pairs of jeans and T-shirts along with something a little more special if he felt getting noticed would further his agenda.

Agenda furthering was in order tonight, so he put on his black pants and black silk shirt. He paused before pulling open his door. Okay, so he didn't know what agenda the black pants and shirt would further, but if he felt like wearing them, he'd damn well do it. And he definitely wasn't trying to impress Ms. Kisa the kitty. He didn't play those kinds of games. Ever.

Now that he had that straight, he went downstairs and made his way to the parlor. Reinn felt as if he were drowning in werecats, but once he settled into a big easy chair and looked around, he realized the inn did have other guests.

A big guy with a beard sat in the chair beside him. "Just got here tonight, huh?" He stuck out his huge hand. "Seth Clemmons."

"Yeah." Reinn shook the man's hand. "Daniel Night."

A werebear. Jeez, the man was as big as a continent. Reinn was kind of glad Seth wasn't one of the happy bride's brothers. No matter how many vampiric powers he had, if good old Seth connected with one of his giant paws, Reinn would be a permanent stain on the inn's shiny wood floor.

Seth nodded. "Lots of weird people come here, but I like to get away from Philly once in a while and just enjoy the woods."

I bet you do. There were more werecreatures sitting around that Reinn hadn't noticed at first. He figured nights in these woods were a real howl . . . or growl, or yowl.

But he forgot about everyone else in the parlor when Kisa came in. And here he'd thought she was warm and cuddly. How about hot and sexy enough to make his body tighten in response to dozens of fantasy possibilities? He followed her with his gaze

21

as she swayed past him, all that curvy body wrapped in what looked like an oversize clingy handkerchief. Heels made her bare legs go on forever, and . . . *And she's the enemy, pal.*

She sat on one of the couches near the fireplace. When she caught his gaze, she smiled.

Reinn returned her smile, but purposely didn't let it reach his eyes. He'd stayed away from women too long if a werecat looked good to him.

Sparkle Stardust entered the parlor with Ganymede and Trouble padding beside her. Trouble trotted over to him and sat next to his chair. *"Can we go for a walk tonight, huh? I'll show you all the neat places around here."*

"Yeah, sure, kid." Not Reinn's first choice for a partner on a walk in the dark. Without his permission, his gaze drifted back to Kisa. Now *there* was one hell of a hiking partner.

Reinn quickly looked away, and instead scanned the rest of the people while Sparkle got ready to talk. A few werewolves along with a scattering of other shifters, a harpy, some vampires he didn't recognize, quite a few regular humans, and one being he couldn't make. The rest of the guests were werecats. If he had to guess, he'd say the older man and woman sitting on either side of Kisa were her mother and father.

Sparkle held up her hand to get everyone's attention—an unnecessary gesture, since her slinky black dress with the slit up to her armpit and the plunge that stopped just short of her navel got her plenty of attention.

"Just a reminder, folks. The inn's rules. Werecats, werewolves, and werebears are to stay off the furniture in your animal forms. It's the pits trying to vacuum your hair off the cushions. And—"

"Excuse me, Ms. Stardust." A small man with a not-so-small nose and thinning blond hair stood up. "Don't you think that's a little discriminatory?"

"What?" Sparkle blinked at him.

"Uh, well, you're denying a segment of your population the right to sit where they choose based solely on what covers their skin." The man fidgeted under Sparkle's glare.

Sparkle looked puzzled. "And your point is?"

The man looked like he didn't know what to say to this kind of attitude. Reinn could've told him arguing with Sparkle was a losing proposition.

Sparkle brightened. "Now I remember. You're Bernie Fetzer. A wereduck." Payback gleamed in her amber eyes. "And you're absolutely right. I was picking on our furry-butted guests." She looked around. "Okay, anyone who turns into something with fur, feathers, or anything else that sheds, keep your ass off the furniture." She beamed at Bernie. "Satisfied?"

Quelled for the moment, Bernie sank back into his chair.

"One more thing before we share last night's adventures. Please be careful in the woods. Make sure you're with another person, and try to control your . . . more primitive natures. The Woo Woo Inn will remain a safe haven for everyone only if we all cooperate." She cast a meaningful glance at all nonhuman entities.

Finished with her thinly veiled warning, she smiled at her guests. "So what kinds of exciting things happened last night?"

One of the werewolves raised his hand. "Melissa and I saw a whole bunch of rabbits."

"Where?" All the werecats spoke in unison.

Melissa grinned, glad to share the good news. "Over by the cemetery."

Reinn smiled at the confused looks on the humans' faces. Even the ones who were way into role-playing hadn't a clue what sat in the same room with them.

Sparkle frowned down at her silver stilettos. "How exciting. Anything else?"

A human stood. "I'm Celia, and last night while I was having an out-of-body experience, I drifted high above the forest." Celia thrummed with excitement. "And guess what—I saw the Jersey Devil. It had a big horsey head with really sharp teeth, and glowing eyes, and huge bat wings, and—"

"Fascinating, Celia." Sparkle fingered the silver chain around her neck and made a valiant effort not to look bored. "No one has to worry, though. He stays clear of people. I'd only worry if you're a small feathered creature." She threw Bernie a vindictive glance.

"Well, I guess we've heard all the exciting tales we can take for one night, so I'll wish you happy hunting. I don't mean that literally, of course." Her warning glance was aimed at werecats, werewolves, and vampires.

Everyone stood and began moving toward the

inn's front door. Reinn sifted through possible excuses that would get him out of his walk with Trouble.

"Um, Ms. Stardust?" Bernie again.

Well, damn. You couldn't keep a good man down. Reinn felt grudging admiration for the wereduck.

"He's either very brave or very stupid." Kisa's amused comment right behind him was accompanied by the faint scent of vanilla.

She had a low, sensual voice that his sexual self thought was eminently growl-worthy. *Ignore it.* He resisted the urge to turn and fill his senses with the scent, the sight, and the sound of her. Because Reinn had the sinking feeling it would only trigger two other senses. And no way could he afford to taste or touch Kisa Evans.

"I noticed that no one served breakfast, Ms. Stardust. Uh, we had to go into the kitchen and help ourselves. Will all of our meals be buffet style from now on?" Bernie at least had the good sense to look wary.

Sparkle's smile was a slow, sensual slide of seduction. "My cook quit, and I was all on my own in that big hot kitchen, Bernie. I mean, sweat made my dress cling to every part of me. *Every* part." She sighed and then put her hand over her breasts just in case he didn't get what body parts *every* included. All the men still in the room paused to enjoy their mental kitchen images.

"And I would've done anything, I mean absolutely *anything*, to have someone strong and assertive help me serve breakfast." She slid her tongue across her lower lip and moved in for the kill.

"Would you help me serve the meals? I would be oooh, so grateful, honey." She threw in a touch of a Southern accent to seal the deal.

A clamor of male voices offered to help her serve whatever she cared to serve.

Ganymede looked at Reinn. *"You gotta love a woman who can work a room like that. Once a man gets stuck in her web, she reels him in, wraps him up, and stores him away for future use."* The cat sniffed the air. *"Wonder if there's any bacon left over. I feel a snack attack coming on."*

Bernie stared at Sparkle with wide, adoring eyes. "I'd be honored to pitch in and help a lady."

"Now he's done it. He's insulted her. Men have died for calling her a lady." Ganymede padded toward the kitchen.

Sparkle frowned. "Thanks. We'll talk at dinner. Lunch will just be soup and sandwiches until I get a feel for the kitchen." She dismissed Bernie as she glanced toward Reinn and Kisa.

"Well, hi." She slid her gaze the length of Reinn's body and smiled her approval. "I love a man in black. It makes me feel all savage and primeval."

Reinn met Kisa's gaze. Something in her eyes said she agreed with Sparkle. He fought the need to give his savage and primeval nature its head. *The job.* He had to remember the job.

He smiled his blandest smile at Kisa. "Were your sister and her fiancé here tonight?" He already knew Alan wasn't here. He'd recognize a Mackenzie.

"No. They're off somewhere in the woods." Kisa smiled. "They need some private time away from family hordes."

26

Sparkle wasn't about to let the conversation veer off course. "Love the outfit, Kisa. A scarf-print handkerchief dress in silk chiffon. Turquoise is you. Incredibly sensual in a casual, playful way. And the sandals—yum, yum. Manolo Blahnik." Her glance turned sly. "Someone told me that Reinn and Trouble are going for a walk in the woods. Bet they'd love some company."

"No." Kisa said it at the same time Reinn did, and illogically he felt disappointed.

Sparkle dug in for the long haul. "If you don't want to go, I'd appreciate some help in the kitchen, Kisa. I have a few new recipes I'd like to try for dinner. You could give me your expert advice."

Reinn took pity on Kisa's hunted expression. "Come with Trouble and me. You can make sure we don't get lost." Okay, lame. He didn't really want her along anyway. She was just a complication. Without her, he could scout out a good place to hide his new sword.

Kisa bit her bottom lip in indecision, and when she released it, the wet sheen woke something long asleep in him.

The beast stirred. And it shocked the hell out of him. After a thousand years he didn't feed often. And when he did, he took very little blood. He became vampire while he fed, but he was always in control of the change. His need to change never rose unless he called it, and he didn't call it very often anymore. He hadn't called it now.

But something else had. Sexual hunger ripped through him, and he fought his desire to feel the slide of his fangs filling his mouth, the craving to taste the hot life that flowed in her veins. Hell, he'd better get control fast or Kisa would be doing a Little Red Riding Hood rerun with someone a lot scarier than the Big Bad Wolf.

Kisa smiled at him, but he sensed secrets behind her smile. Well, that made two of them.

"Wait here while I go up and change into flats." She hurried from the parlor.

Trouble wagged his tail. *"Goody. I like Kisa. I'm glad she's coming. If I bring my ball, will you throw it?"* His back end wagged in time with his tail. *"Will you, will you?"*

Reinn exhaled deeply. "Go get the damned ball."

He watched Trouble race toward the back of the inn, his paws slipping on the floor in his haste to fetch his ball. Reinn scowled at Sparkle. "Happy now?" Werecats weren't the only manipulators. But Sparkle would find she couldn't sidetrack him with sex. And he never for a moment doubted that was her goal.

She reached up and slid her hand along his tightly clenched jaw. "Lighten up, hot bod. No one's going to think you're any less dark and dangerous if you have a little fun once in a while."

He knew his expression was grim. "I stopped having fun about a thousand years ago."

If he hoped to intimidate Sparkle, he failed. "Sorry, but I don't buy what you're selling. Being an old grouch isn't a badge of honor. Break out and use up some stored fun time. Who's it going to hurt?"

Me. The thought came unbidden, a truth he knew without having to reason it out.

He was saved from answering Sparkle because Kisa returned at the same time Trouble skidded to a stop in front of him with a ball clamped in his jaws.

Kisa walked with Daniel to the door, and they stepped into the night. She controlled her eagerness to sniff the darkness, searching out the small scurrying things that were her natural prey. Whatever else happened, she had to deny anything that encouraged the change. Instead she allowed Daniel to lead her onto the wooded path leading to the old cemetery.

"Feel the need to scope out a few spirits at the graveyard?" Kisa teased him just to see if she could coax some warmth into his smile.

"It's somewhere to walk." His smile was many things, but warm wasn't one of them.

Well, she was feeling enough warmth for both of them. Kisa sensed an aggressiveness in him that excited her, that hinted he might match her in many ways. But he was human, so she could forget that. No human would ever be powerful enough to pass muster in the werecat world, so unless she wanted to cut herself off from her people, she'd better keep her hormonal surge in check.

Talking about warm—summer in Jersey was a hot, humid affair. A trickle of moisture trailed between her breasts. And when she saw his gaze fixed on the trickle's journey of discovery, areas a lot lower took notice.

"I stayed here for a few days last year." Reinn threw Trouble's ball far down the path, and the dog galloped after it. "This place can be seriously creepy sometimes." He didn't sound like creepy bothered him.

Kisa let the night's silence wrap around her for a moment, enjoying the smooth flow of Daniel's muscles beneath the black silk as he threw the ball. What she could see of his broad chest exposed by his partly unbuttoned shirt hinted at an amazing expanse of warm skin and hard body. She didn't drop her eyes any lower for fear she might make a few excited cat sounds. Hard to explain to a human.

"What do you do when you're not here?" She was going to have to dig for every morsel of information.

He shrugged, bringing impressive shoulder muscles into play. "I have a pilot's license, so I fly some charter flights. I'm sort of a bounty hunter off and on, too."

Kisa frowned. She didn't know if she liked the bounty hunter part. "What did you think of the people you saw tonight?" No, she was *not* sounding him out to see how open he'd be to nonhuman entities.

Trouble raced back with his ball and Daniel took a moment to heave it into the darkness again. "I believe my senses. When I hear Bernie quacking and I see him flapping his wings, I'll believe. Same with all the others."

She nodded, disappointed. "I guess so. But I'm open to lots of possibilities." Kisa knew many humans were too arrogant and blind to see the world of unique beings living right under their noses. She frowned. Even she didn't have a handle on all of the inn's occupants. For example, what the heck was Ganymede? Sure, he was probably some kind of shifter, but she sensed a lot of power packed into his chubby gray body.

Kisa watched Trouble return with his ball. He dropped it and then flopped onto the ground, panting. Daniel stood staring into the darkness, and she stood beside him, comfortable with the silence between them. So many times when she was with people, she felt the need to fill the quiet with meaningless words. Her true nature was here in the forest and the silence.

In the distance, the first howls of the werewolves echoed eerily among the trees, followed closely by some really funny fake howls. The moon was full tonight. She hoped the werewolf wannabes had enough sense to stay away from the real deal. Of course, they hadn't a clue that Melissa and Jared were authentic.

The roar of a lion sounded much closer. Uncle Ed. Rustling noises in the bushes told her that other members of her family were doing a little spying on her. She'd have a few things to say to them when she got back to the inn.

Kisa had expected Daniel to register surprise at the sounds, but his smile didn't waver.

"The guests really take this stuff seriously. Very realistic." His smile widened. "Haven't heard any quacks yet."

"The predators make Bernie nervous, so he paddles in the pond during the day." She kept a straight face when she said it.

He didn't comment, but his expression said, *Yeah, sure.*

What was it about Daniel? Once she got past his mind-numbing magnificence, something about him didn't ring true. His reactions were a little bit off. Whatever revelation she was reaching for stayed just out of reach. Maybe there was no revelation. Maybe the night and the man were messing with her head. And other body parts.

They continued walking until they got to the cemetery. Five or six humans were scattered among the old tombstones that tilted at crazy angles. She recognized the people as the ghost-hunter group that had checked in two days ago. They had their equipment ready to search out any ghostly activity.

"Have they seen anything?" He seemed only mildly interested.

She shook her head. "I feel sort of sorry for them. They have all that equipment, and they're trying so hard."

He turned to her in the night, and those incredible blue eyes seemed darker, not quite the same as they'd looked in the inn's parlor. "You'd like them to see some spirits?"

She smiled. Why not? A few ghosts might distract her from the man standing beside her. "Yeah, I would. They paid a lot to stay at the inn, so I'd like to see them get their money's worth."

He didn't say anything as he returned his attention to the hopeful ghost hunters. Absently he reached down to scratch Trouble's head.

Startled gasps and a few cries made her forget

Daniel for the moment. She turned to stare at the cemetery, and did some gasping of her own.

A shape materialized over one of the old tombstones. "Oh, my God, do you see that, Daniel?" Kisa watched the image become more distinct. It was a woman in a long pale gown. Her equally pale hair floated around her face in the sudden breeze that swirled among the tombstones. Blood dripped from her outstretched hands.

Daniel said nothing as the ghost hunters frantically worked to photograph the spirit. One of the men edged closer to the ghost, a recorder in his hand. "Uh, is there anything you'd like to say? We're here to listen." His rapt expression held the intensity of a true zealot.

The ghost's light laughter blew away into the night. "My William cheated on me, and so I ripped out his heart with my bare hands." She held her bloody hands up for all to see and admire. "No one cheats on Lily LaGrand." She slowly disappeared on another ghostly trill of laughter.

Kisa squeezed Daniel's hand. She didn't even remember grabbing it. "Did you see that? I can't believe I really saw a ghost." She stared up at him as the ghost hunters packed up their equipment amid excited chatter.

He stared down at her, and for the first time she felt a slide of unease along with the ever-present sensual awareness. Shadows highlighted lips that seemed fuller than she remembered and eyes that looked larger, darker, *hungrier*.

He didn't smile, and she felt herself being pulled

into his gaze, deeper and ever deeper. She tried to blink, but nothing happened.

"Hey, sis. I didn't expect to see you out here." Julie's voice dragged her back from the brink.

The brink? Yeah, like that made a lot of sense. She dropped his hand. Gratefully she looked past Daniel to where her sister and Alan were weaving through the tombstones to reach them.

Kisa had always thought her baby sister looked like a fairy queen, and she'd been a source of much envy during Kisa's younger years. Julie was slender with delicate features and long blond hair that framed her face. She had big blue eyes and knew exactly how to use them to best advantage.

"Hey, there." Kisa smiled. Alan had been a worthy catch. Tall and broad-shouldered, he had blond hair that was tousled by the wind, and his blue eyes were as potent as Julie's. All in all, they made beautiful bookends.

Kisa stood close to Daniel, and so she felt him tense. His gaze skimmed over Julie and then fixed on Alan. She couldn't read his expression.

"Daniel, this is my sister Julie and her fiancé, Alan Mackenzie." She smiled to ease his tension. Maybe he was the kind of guy who was uneasy around strangers. *Uh-huh, and you believe that.* "Julie, Alan, this is Daniel Night. He's here because he's interested in the paranormal."

"Hi, Daniel." Julie offered him her patented I'm-too-winsome-for-my-wings smile.

Alan nodded. But Kisa sensed his wariness. He was checking Daniel out. A vampire who intended to marry a werecat never knew when the Guardian of the Blood would come for him. But the killer vampire wouldn't find a group of frightened and helpless werecats if he showed up. Her family would protect Alan.

Kisa told Julie and Alan about the ghost while Daniel added nothing. And whenever she glanced his way, he was watching Alan. Did he suspect Alan wasn't human? Some people were sensitive to non-human entities. She was probably imagining things, because he sure hadn't seemed suspicious of her.

Finished with her ghost story, Kisa decided she'd walked far enough. When she stayed out too long, the night called to her and the change got harder to resist. "I'm heading back to the inn. The ghost was my big excitement for the night." *Daniel* was her big excitement for the night. "The rest of you can keep walking. I know the way back."

"We'll walk back with you." Julie linked arms with Kisa and dragged her ahead of the two men. "So what's with tall, dark, and gorgeous?"

Kisa shrugged. She glanced back. The men seemed to be talking. Trouble had wedged himself between the two of them and wasn't budging. Strange doggy behavior. "I think we were both victims of a Sparkle Stardust matchmaking blitz. He seems like a great guy, but you know he doesn't qualify."

Julie looked outraged on her behalf. "It's not fair. Where are you ever going to find someone more powerful than you are? Nowhere, that's where. You deserve your shot at happiness. I think the whole stupid rule is just something to pump up our males' egos. They always have to feel like they're stronger than the 'little woman.' Jerks. I'm glad Alan isn't a werecat. He'll treat me as an equal."

Kisa tended to agree with her sister. At the rate she was going, they'd be able to carve "Here Lies the Oldest Virgin in the World" on her tombstone. Werecats really did live the proverbial nine lives. So she could be a nine-hundred-year-old virgin when she died—an old, shriveled-up, sexually frustrated biddy. *Unless you walk away from all the stupid rules and find your own happiness.*

She'd be lying if she said she didn't want to have hot sweaty sex with a man. Werecats were sexual creatures. But to abandon her people, her whole way of life, and go out into a human world where she'd always have to hide her true nature? She glanced back at Daniel, who was now deep in conversation with Alan. Maybe. For the right man.

Chapter Three

Reinn slowed his pace until the women were too far ahead to hear his conversation. "No doubts about the marriage thing, huh?"

"None." There was a finality to the word that made Reinn wince.

Alan stared at the gentle sway of his beloved's hair, clearly visible beneath the full moon. Reinn's gaze would've been a little lower, but that was just him.

This job might be more complex than he'd expected. The council, in its infinite stupidity, had ruled that the Mackenzie who was about to lose his head should be given the chance to use his sword to defend himself. It would be a lot less complicated if they could just fight each other using their powers. But it wouldn't change the outcome.

Now he'd have to wait for his new sword to arrive. Then he'd have to arrange a scenario that would bring Alan to the woods with *his* sword, where they could go at it without the interference of every shifter at the inn, not to mention a pissed-off Ganymede.

Reinn refused to admit he didn't really mind spending a few more days here, maybe even looked forward to it. Sure, he liked being with Kisa, but when the time came, he'd do his job and walk away without any regrets.

Meanwhile he could float a few dark clouds over Alan's sunny view of wedded bliss. Not that Reinn had any personal experience. He'd enjoyed a lot of women, human and vampire, but never enough to spend a lifetime with any one. Besides, women might love what he brought to the sexual table, but they weren't standing in line to share the danger that was part of the package deal.

Reinn glanced at the man walking beside him. He'd liked it better when Alan was a faceless stranger. He didn't want to hear how much Alan loved Julie. He didn't want Alan to share his marriage plans. He didn't want to *know* him.

"You might want to think twice about going through with this marriage." Reinn tried to sound experienced, whatever the hell that sounded like. "Marriage means"—okay, he had to make this something any guy would hate—"sitting in front of the TV each night watching home-makeover shows."

Alan brightened. "Julie and I are fixing up this old farmhouse. We're doing it together. Those shows are great."

Right. Reinn tried to think of something else. "Women make men soft. They use emotion to keep

guys from doing things women think are dangerous, like skydiving or mountain climbing."

Alan looked puzzled. "I don't skydive or climb
mountains. I like to stay home and work around the
house. Maybe take in a game or a show once in a
while." He grinned. "Besides, I'll have all the excitement I need in bed."

Reinn shook his head and tried to look wise.
"That rush you get from sex sort of fades after a
while, and then you're just left with each other."

"The sex will always be good between us." Alan
sounded so sure of himself, Reinn lost his temper.

"Dammit, man, she'll make you put down the toi-
let seat." Okay, that was stupid.

"You divorced?" There was a note of sympathy in
Alan's voice.

Reinn took a deep, calming breath. Angry dia-
tribes wouldn't do him any good. "Yeah. Five years
of hell." He used his best heed-my-warning-or-die
expression. "Women change after you marry them,
Alan. And they try to make you into their image, all
civilized and sensitive. Just think about that."

Alan nodded and then switched his attention back
to Julie, who'd stopped on the inn's porch to wait
for him. His gaze softened. Reinn shook his head.
Alan *wasn't* going to think about it. Too bad.

Reinn joined Kisa in the inn's foyer. "Going up to
your room?" *Can I come with you?* That was his primal beast talking. It thought about sex with Kisa at
five-second intervals. His brain was standing behind
the beast wildly semaphoring an emphatic, *Not a
good idea*.

Kisa nodded. "For a while. I need some time alone. Maybe I'll read for a few hours. I haven't had a chance to do that with all the wedding plans going forward."

"I hear there're some great discussions going on. Think I'll sit in on one of them. Guess I'd better go up to my room and get a pad so I can take notes." He'd walk her to her room and then go back out into the forest. He had to find a hiding place for his sword before dawn.

Reinn followed her up the stairs, his attention riveted on the sensual sway of her behind in that dress. Spectacular female body parts never made him lose his focus, but he couldn't concentrate on anything while her incredible bottom led him up those stairs like the Pied Piper of tempting asses.

Once in the hallway, he moved up beside her so he could at least think again. She stopped at her door and turned to smile at him. "I enjoyed the walk. And the ghost was awesome. We'll have to do it again."

When? Reinn shut that thought down fast. He was getting too anxious to be with her. And that wasn't what his stay here was about.

He watched her unlock her door and was starting to walk away when he heard her gasp. Turning, he saw her standing just inside her room while fine grains of something drifted over her from above the doorway. *What the . . . ?* He moved toward her.

"No." She held up trembling hands to stop him. "Go away. Leave me alone." She tried to close the door in his face.

He pushed past her. "No chance, lady. What's wrong?" Because something *was* very wrong. Her eyes widened with horror, and as he watched they seemed to change shape and color. *Cat eyes.*

"Catnip. That stuff was catnip." She staggered across the room toward her bed. "Get the hell out of here. *Now.* Lock the door and tell everyone to get out of the inn."

"Uh-uh. Isn't going to happen." He slammed the door shut. What did catnip have to do with anything? But he wasn't leaving. For some reason, Kisa's change terrified her. Probably because she didn't seem to be in control of it. That had to be scary. He'd stay until the change was complete; then he'd hold her in his lap while she was in cat form. Once she was safely back in human form, he'd assure her he'd survived the shock, and then he'd leave.

"No! You don't understand. You won't be safe." Kisa ripped at her dress, dragging it from her body along with her bra and panties.

Reinn's beast did more than just stir this time. It raised its head and roared. Even with her ragged emotions washing over him, he felt the slide of his fangs. Her body was all smooth, warm skin, high, full breasts, and long, slim legs.

I—" She got no farther as the change took her.

"My God." Reinn realized fast that no cute, cuddly kitty was taking shape.

She was enormous. About six feet long and four feet tall, with powerful front legs and a short bobtail. But that wasn't what widened his eyes and backed him against the closed door. The cat turned her huge head toward him and opened her enormous mouth in a snarl, showcasing what had to be at least eight-inch-long serrated canines. Kisa Evans was a freakin' saber-toothed tiger.

And he was in big trouble. Nothing of Kisa and everything of a ferocious predator gleamed from those cat eyes.

Reinn reacted. He called his beast to him and became vampire. He felt the slide of his fangs filling his mouth and the subtle shift of his facial muscles and eye shape. Reaching behind him, he locked the door. Not that a door would stop this remnant of Earth's last ice age. He had to make sure, though, that Kisa didn't get out of the room. There were humans in the inn, and Kisa in her present form would make a werewolf look like a playful puppy.

The cat tensed to spring, and Reinn loosed his power, wrapping a mental shield around the animal just as it pounced. The shield shuddered and bent, but didn't break. Reinn didn't know how long he could hold it, though, as the great cat thrashed and snarled.

What the hell had caused her to change? He remembered the small particles falling around her. And then she'd said something about catnip. *Catnip.*

Someone knocked on the door behind him. *Great.* "Go away. We're busy."

There was quiet on the other side of the door for a second before someone spoke. "I'm so sorry. I'm Felicia Carter, the wedding planner. I needed to speak with Kisa about the food."

Step inside this room, lady, and you'll be the food. "Come back later. A lot later." He didn't have time for politeness.

Reinn wasn't going to be able to hold Kisa much longer. And if she got loose and attacked him, he'd have to hurt her. He needed someone else with strong mental powers to join with him. Reaching out with his mind, he found Ganymede in the kitchen. Figured.

"Get your butt up here to Kisa's room. Now. She's changed. Oh, and have someone leave a vacuum outside her door." Ganymede was smart enough to realize that her change mustn't be a good thing if Reinn needed his help.

Reinn had barely finished his thought when the door swung open and Ganymede padded into the room. A few seconds later Sparkle hurried in, dragging a vacuum behind her. The door swung shut behind them.

Ganymede looked at Kisa. *"Holy crap. Make sure she doesn't claw the furniture. Cindy'll be pissed."*

Ignoring the saber-toothed tiger, Sparkle rushed over to pick up Kisa's dress. "Thank heaven she had enough sense to take this off first. It's a one-of-a-kind designer creation. Must've cost megabucks."

Reinn scooped Ganymede up and held him so they were eyeball-to-eyeball. "You're going to join your mind with mine to hold her or else Cindy won't have an inn to come home to."

Ganymede evidently got the message, because Reinn felt an instant surge of energy reinforce the shield he'd built.

Reinn turned to Sparkle. "Vacuum up all that catnip by the door."

Sparkle cast him a puzzled look. "Was the catnip part of some kinky foreplay?" When Reinn didn't answer her, she shrugged and then turned on the vacuum.

They waited, and waited, and waited. Sparkle spent the time going through Kisa's closet, making small sounds of pleasure as she rooted. Finally, an hour later, Kisa began her change back to human form.

"*Jeez, about time.*" Ganymede sounded tired.

Reinn's thoughts exactly. "Here's a chance for your fifteen minutes of fame. I doubt she'll remember anything that happened during the last hour. She wasn't in control of the change." He kept a close eye on Kisa as her animal form flowed back to human. "I don't want her to know anything about my part in this. Does she realize you're not just a cat?"

"*Yeah, I've talked to her.*" Ganymede glanced at Sparkle. "*For crying out loud, leave Kisa's nail polish alone.*"

Sparkle threw him an annoyed glance. "I was just checking out the color."

"Tell her I called Sparkle on the phone. When you and she got here I was outside the room trying to hold the door closed. You used your power to control her until she returned to human form. You'll be her hero." The twinge of jealousy he felt surprised Reinn. Dammit, *he* wanted to be Kisa's hero. It was only a momentary stupid thought, though, because he'd never been anyone's hero—

not his family's or anyone else's for a thousand years.

Without waiting for Ganymede's reply, Reinn slipped from the room and went downstairs. He met the couple he assumed was Kisa's parents in the foyer. The man was about five-ten, stocky, with brown hair graying at his temples. And his wife was everyone's mother—short, comfortably round, with a smile that could warm even Reinn's soul. Their faces lit up when they saw him.

"Mr. Night, just the man we've wanted to talk to." The man smiled at him. "I'm Bill Evans, and this is my wife, Helen. We're Kisa's parents, and—"

Reinn held up his hand. "Nice to meet you, but we can talk later. You need to get upstairs to Kisa. She changed and—"

He was talking to empty air, because they were already rushing up the abstairs.

As he left the inn to find a safe place to hide his new sword, he thought about who might've planted the catnip in Kisa's room. Because it *had* been planted, and by someone who knew what would happen. He'd leave Kisa to her family tonight, but tomorrow night they'd talk.

And as he faded into the darkness, he drew his lips back to expose his fangs. Whoever it was would be very sorry.

Kisa lay in bed with her eyes closed, trying to make sense of what had happened. Her mom had told her to rest till morning, but the few hours of sleep she'd gotten had already made her feel better. She couldn't hide in her room forever. Besides, she was hungry.

Opening her eyes, she glanced at the clock. The night was almost over and Sparkle would be serving dinner. Kisa shuddered at the thought of what might be on Sparkle's "sensual" menu. But the change always left her starving. That she felt hungry now was a good thing, because it meant she hadn't eaten anyone in her saber-toothed form.

Daniel had seen her change. That was the one thing that had stuck in her mind as Ganymede and Sparkle tried to explain everything and her parents hovered and fussed over her. Lord, what had he thought? Thank heaven he hadn't stayed in the room trying to help her.

Kisa climbed from bed, took a quick shower, threw on a pair of jeans and a T-shirt, and headed down to dinner.

She entered the dining room to complete silence. Everyone's attention was riveted on Sparkle, who sat at the head of the long communal table. Kisa slipped into the empty seat next to her mother.

Bernie hurried over to her with a salad and a bowl of soup. She didn't have a chance to investigate it because Sparkle was talking.

"Celia had a question about the salad. You'll notice there are carrots in it." Sparkle waited while everyone duly noted the carrots. "The ancient Greeks ate carrots before an orgy."

Everyone looked back up at Sparkle.

"And I had to include avocados. The Aztecs

called them *ahucati*, which means testicle. When the Spanish took the news back home about the arousal power of avocados, priests ordered their parishioners not to eat them." She sighed. "Poor deluded souls."

"Can we eat now?"

Kisa smiled. Her brother Jake didn't sound particularly impressed with the sensual properties of his food.

Sparkle glared at him. "No. You'll only reach your full sensual potential if you understand which foods lead to the greatest sexual pleasure."

All the males at the table perked up at the word *sexual*.

"I've chosen asparagus soup to go with the meal." Sparkle was on a roll. "What a wonderful sexual stimulant. In nineteenth-century France, a bridegroom ate at least three courses of hot asparagus before his wedding night."

All the carnivores at the table looked as green as the asparagus.

"Bernie will be serving oysters marinated in vodka in a few minutes. Make sure you slurp them provocatively." She paused to let the erotic implications of oysters sink in.

"Oysters make me throw up," observed someone at the end of the table.

Sparkle chose to ignore the comment. "And for dessert we'll have strawberries topped with whipped cream and almonds." She stared down someone who looked as if he were going to interrupt. "Strawberries, also known as fruit nipples, are powerful aphrodisiacs. And the smell of almonds excites a woman."

"What would excite me is a big steak. Rare." Melissa looked like her werewolf sensibilities were offended.

"Katie promised me salmon for dinner tonight." Seth was as sulky as a bear could be.

"The dessert sounds pretty good." Nothing could dampen the happy bride's spirits. Julie smiled at Alan, who looked relieved not to be involved in the oyster slurping.

Kisa didn't think either of them needed any more sexual stimulation than they already had going for them. Her mom was eating her salad right now, but Kisa knew as soon as she finished, she'd start grilling her daughter again about why she'd changed. Then she'd worry, worry, and worry some more about what would've happened if no one had been around. Maybe coming down for dinner hadn't been such a good idea.

Sudden awareness touched her, and she glanced around the room. Daniel was standing in the dining room doorway, his broad shoulders propped against the door frame as he watched her. When she met his gaze he smiled at her, a slow, sensual lift of his lips that made her forget all about slurping oysters.

And when he hooked his thumb in the top of those black pants and nodded toward the door, she didn't think twice about pushing back her chair and excusing herself.

Kisa met him at the front door. He held it open for her and she walked onto the porch. There was a

Piney Woods Steakhouse take-out box resting on the seat of the inn's porch swing.

His smile widened to a grin. "I ate in town and then picked up a take-out order for a guest who wants to remain anonymous because Sparkle would kick his furry butt if she found out he didn't like her meal. I thought you might enjoy a big steak and a baked potato. Sorry, not a sensual bite in the whole meal."

"Thank God. Hand it over." Sensual was in the eye of the beholder, and right now that steak and its donor made her want to purr.

He sat watching her eat for a few minutes before asking the question she'd been expecting. "What happened tonight, Kisa?"

She had no lie big enough to cover up what he'd seen. Kisa was surprised he even wanted to be alone with her. She wasn't sure *she* wanted to be alone with herself. But he deserved the truth. What he did with the info was up to him. She wasn't really afraid he'd blab to the press or anything. After all, who'd print the story other than a tabloid?

Kisa finished the last bite of steak and put the take-out box aside. A gentle breeze kept the mosquitoes away, and the full moon lit up the inn's lawn. The solid blackness where the forest began still called to her, but she turned away from it to look at Daniel.

"I become a saber-toothed tiger in my animal form. I'm the only werecat who's ever done that. No one knows why, but I'm a throwback. *Way* back. I'd changed only one other time before tonight's . . .

incident. That was one time too many, as far as my people were concerned. I scare the whiskers off the rest of the werecats. Up until tonight, only werecats knew about me. Now you, Ganymede, and Sparkle know." She paused to study him. "Why aren't you scared silly? I would be if I were in your shoes."

Daniel shrugged. "I told you before. I believe what I can see, hear, or touch. You weren't hard to see or hear, and I suspended my need to touch for health reasons." He speared her with an intense stare. "Was I scared? You bet. Will the fact that I now have solid proof shape-shifters exist send me screaming into the night? No. I'm interested in the paranormal. That's why I'm staying at a place called the Woo Woo Inn." He shook his head. "They need to do something about that name."

As she studied him, a sudden flash of memory came and went—Ganymede watching her out of amber eyes, Sparkle rooting through her closet, and Daniel . . . He was there, too, but he was different. The thought was gone too quickly for her to make sense of it.

"Well, add me to the list of the scared silly. Someone not only knows what I am, but knows catnip will trigger the change. And the scariest part of all? They wanted me to change badly enough to sneak into my room and plant the catnip over my door. Why?" She rubbed at a rash of goose bumps on her arms that had nothing to do with the temperature.

Daniel moved closer and put his arm across her shoulders. "We'll figure it out."

We'll? Something about that one word brought

her the first warm and safe feeling she'd had since she'd walked into her room and found it was raining catnip. Kisa sensed Daniel's unease with his role as comforter. This wasn't a man used to being close to others. That he was clumsily offering comfort now was so endearing, she wanted to cry. Okay, so she wanted to cry over the whole damned night.

"Maybe I should go home. I could kill a lot of people if I changed, say, at dinner." Kisa mulled over that idea. Of course, she could kill a lot of people no matter where she changed. Because even if she was out in the middle of the forest somewhere, her cat form would go hunting to feed its voracious appetite.

His smile almost, not quite, warmed his eyes. "I'm thinking Seth would choose you over death by oyster slurping."

She knew her smile was a weak imitation of the real thing. "Maybe here is the safest place for me after all. Ganymede is probably the only being powerful enough to control my cat."

He nodded. "And the person who did this to you is here. So while they're stalking you, I'll be stalking them."

His eyes gleamed with a savagery that made her swallow hard. Even knowing he was on her side, she felt ripples of fear touch her heart. Kisa forced herself to relax. She needed someone ruthless watching her back now. And if he was volunteering for the job, she was accepting.

"Any ideas on how to find the person responsible?" Pushing with her foot, she set the swing gently swaying back and forth. "I'll have to let Mom or Dad check every room for catnip before I go into it. Whoever did this might try again." She bit her lip as she thought out the ramifications of what had happened. "I'll have to make sure Ganymede is always close by."

She cast him a startled look. "Wait. I didn't even think about Ganymede. You have to know now that he's not just a cat. So you've had a double whammy tonight."

"Yeah. Ganymede was a shock."

Kisa frowned. She heard what he was saying, but why didn't she believe him? Her intuition was telling her he wasn't shocked at all. But that didn't make any sense. He had to be shocked. Maybe she was making this into a big deal when it wasn't. Probably her intuition was out of whack tonight.

"Did you ever try to purposely change forms?" The night cast his face in shadow, making him seem almost sinister.

"Are you crazy? Why would I want to do that?" Sinister? She had to lighten up. Daniel was just an ordinary man trying to help her. Fine, so he would *never* be ordinary.

"You have to learn to control your cat form, and you'll never do it if you don't practice." He gazed toward the woods, and she had the feeling other thoughts were distracting him.

"Uh-huh. And who's going to volunteer to be my teacher when they know there's a good chance I'll eat them?" But the thought intrigued her. If she could control what she did in her tiger form, then she wouldn't be so panicked when something like today happened.

A smile tugged at his sexy mouth. "You're not the only one who's been keeping secrets. I have one, too." He glanced away from her so she couldn't see the expression in his eyes. "I'm telepathic. That's one of the reasons I'm here. I hoped I could find a few people willing to discuss telepathy."

"An impressive gift." Kisa tried not to show any surprise. If he could be Mr. Cool in the face of a saber-toothed tiger and Ganymede, she could accept his revelation without gasping and going all wide-eyed on him. "So what does that have to do with me learning to control my cat?"

"If I were in your head when you changed, I could help you deal with the primitive animal brain." He looked back at her, and something in his expression said he wasn't sure his offer was a smart move.

Too late. His idea was the first one anyone had come up with to help her, and she was going to grab it. "I'm willing to try anything. I don't want to live the rest of my life in fear of crossing paths with a few leaves of catnip." In spite of tonight's horror, she smiled. "Since it would be a real downer to find out I ate my teacher, maybe Ganymede should hang around during the lessons."

"Makes sense." Once again he was staring at the forest.

He definitely had other things on his mind, and she'd monopolized too much of his time.

"It's been a long night, and I'm tired. Thanks for

dinner. I think I'll head to my room." She stood and stretched.

He followed her into the inn. "I'll see you up to your room and then come down to do some mental eavesdropping. Never know what thoughts I might scare up."

Kisa started to tell him he didn't have to follow her to her room, but then stopped. Okay, so she wanted him to walk up with her. She was into self-indulgence right now. So she just nodded.

All the way up the stairs and during the walk down the hall, she was aware of the man beside her. Some men started out looking big, but shrank when you really got to know them, their pettiness and egos diminishing them an inch at a time until they just disappeared. But right now Daniel filled the whole hall and was getting larger each minute she spent with him.

This walking-her-to-her-room thing was a mistake. She needed to put a lid on her interest in Daniel Night. Because no matter how she felt, he'd never be more powerful than she was.

The scary part? Right now she didn't give a damn. She just wanted him to ki—

He stopped in front of her door, lowered his head, and covered her mouth with his.

She reached up to wrap her arms around his neck and pull him closer. He traced her lips with his tongue, and when he deepened the kiss, she opened to him. His lips were firm but surprisingly soft for such a hard man. His tongue was a tireless explorer, and he tasted of hot, erotic places.

She'd spent too much time thinking tonight, so she abandoned all mental activity and gave herself over totally to her senses: the smooth, wet heat of his mouth, the sound of his low, hungry murmur, and the faint scent of something tempting and dangerous that brought out the sexual animal in her.

Just when she was thinking about pushing open her door and dragging him into the room with her, he broke the kiss and stepped back. *Damn.*

"That was incredible, but our emotions are too close to the surface tonight. Things need to cool down a little." He sounded like he was delivering the message more to himself than her.

She sighed and raked her fingers through her hair. He was right. Sure, she wanted to make love with him, but she could reason that away. It was a lot of things coming together at once—years of sexual denial, a close encounter with her primal self, and the hottest guy who'd ever orbited her personal sun. She'd even bet that Mercury was in retrograde. That was the kind of night it had been.

"Yeah, cooling down would be a good thing." She started to open her door, but he reached out and took the key from her.

"I'll take a look first and make sure you're not walking into another catnip attack." He opened the door and went in.

While he was searching, she was thinking. She wanted to make love with him. The werecat society would say no to that. Did she want him enough to cut herself off from those of her kind? No, but . . .

And as she stood in that hallway, a devious

thought slithered in through the door her lust had left open. Kisa had always been honest, forthright, and all that good stuff. If her people said she shouldn't make love with someone less powerful than she, a good little werecat should accept their decision without question.

Except this time she didn't want to. This time she'd found a temptation too great. As of right now, she was no longer a "good little werecat." Kisa knew the smile spreading across her face was all about slyness, deceit, and all that bad stuff. She was *not* going to spend all nine of her lives without even one big O racked up beside her name. The werecats couldn't condemn what they didn't know about.

She should be feeling tons of guilt now, but instead she felt . . . free. For the first time in her life she felt really free.

"Everything's clear. Lock your door. I don't think the person responsible will attack you openly. I'm sure whoever it is doesn't want to be caught in the same room with you when you change." Daniel joined her in the hallway. "If you need me, you know where to find me."

She nodded before stepping into her room and closing the door behind her. Then she just leaned against it. Why did she get the feeling that she'd just leaped from a cliff so high she couldn't see the bottom?

Chapter Four

Why the hell was he helping Kisa? On his way down the stairs and into the parlor, he thought about that. Okay, he wanted to have sex with her. A lot. But he'd never let his cock rule his head before. Besides, he sensed her interest. He didn't have to offer to help her to get her into his bed.

Reinn stood in the parlor doorway and glanced around the room at the small discussion groups in progress. He was getting ready to root around in a bunch of human minds and probably be bored to death. Most people didn't think interesting thoughts. He'd leave the nonhuman entities alone. They'd sense his intrusion, and he didn't need any of them outing him. He had to keep his cover in place.

Reinn was doing this for a werecat when he didn't even like werecats. Unfortunately he couldn't get past Kisa as a woman to think of her in terms of Kisa as a werecat. And that was just plain stupid. Because tonight he'd seen that he ignored her cat

side at his own peril. So he was helping her because . . . He didn't have a clue.

Reinn stood close to the first group of people and
tuned in to their minds. Past-life regression. Interesting. Three of them thought they'd been
Napoleon in a past life. Tough to do unless
Napoleon had one hell of a split personality. What
he didn't get were any thoughts of where they were
going to plant the next batch of catnip.

He moved on to another group, and another, and
another. Nothing, nothing, nothing—other than a
growing wonder that so many people could believe
so many stupid things.

The last group included a few zoologists. They
were discussing legendary creatures—read Nessie
and Bigfoot. Even though he didn't pick up on any
suspicious thoughts, he'd keep these people in
mind. A saber-toothed tiger would do a lot for any
zoologist's career.

"Mr. Night?"

Reinn turned to find Kisa's parents behind him.

"Could we speak with you in private for a few
minutes?" Bill Evans sounded excited.

"Why don't we go into the room next door. It's
the inn's library, but no one's there right now." Helen Evans clutched a covered plate in her hands.

"Sure." They probably wanted to make sure he
wouldn't tell anyone about what he'd seen tonight.

Once seated in the library, Reinn waited.

Bill Evans leaned forward. "We know who you
are, Mr. Night."

Reinn had honed his instant reaction to danger

over centuries—the slide of his fangs, the gathering of his power, the automatic assessing of his best escape route. Unlike his predecessor, he wouldn't wipe out all the werecats to get at one vampire. He'd simply pull back and wait for another opportunity.

"Are you okay, Mr. Night?" Helen sounded puzzled.

Finally Rein looked at their expressions. They were smiling. Every few moments Helen would cast a nervous glance toward the door. These weren't two people facing their worst nightmare.

"I'm fine. And it's Daniel, not Mr. Night. Who do you think I am?" Mistaken identity. Talk about an adrenaline rush. He felt every muscle in his body relax.

"You're the Protector." Bill held up his hand. "Don't worry. We'll keep your secret."

Helen beamed at Reinn. "We saw you at a wedding a few years ago. It was just a glimpse, but I'd never mistake your eyes."

Well, hell. "I'm sorry, but you have me mixed up with someone else."

Bill shook his head. "You were in shadow that night, but Helen and I agree. You're the Protector. The Guardian had the groom on the floor when you challenged him. The Guardian's back was to us, but we got a quick look at your face." He shooed away any comment Reinn might make. "We understand you want to keep your identity quiet. Don't worry; your secret is safe with us, boy."

Boy? Reinn's vampire sensitivities were offended.

He hadn't been a "boy" for at least a thousand years. "Okay, humor me. Who's the Protector?"

Helen winked at him. "We get it. You can't admit who you are. But we're so glad you're here. The thought of the Guardian of the Blood showing up had me scared silly." She put her plate down on a table so she could hug him. "Julie would never recover if that savage killed her sweet Alan."

Reinn stood shocked as Helen wrapped her arms around him and squeezed. She'd *hugged* him. *No one* hugged him. He wasn't huggable, and he was damned proud of it. Then Helen's words registered and he grinned. Sweet Alan? He couldn't wait to see Alan's face when he found out Helen was calling him sweet Alan. He'd . . .

Reinn stopped smiling. He wouldn't be telling Alan anything. He'd be facing the other vampire over a sword in a few days. And Helen would never talk about sweet Alan again. He shouldn't care. But he did. *Dammit!* These people were making him soft.

Helen picked up the plate she'd abandoned and shoved it at him. "Here. I got Sparkle to let me bake you some of my chocolate-chip cookies. Just a little something to let you know how important you are to us. And don't you worry; we'll keep your secret."

They walked from the library, leaving him holding a plate of chocolate-chip cookies and wearing a bemused expression. And feeling an unfamiliar emotion: guilt.

Cookies. He lifted the end of the foil to take a look. He got no nourishment from food, but over the centuries he'd used his power to allow him to eat a few solids when he needed to mingle unrecognized as a vampire. He'd eat one of the cookies just to enjoy the taste. Sure, he'd have a stomachache tomorrow night, but he'd live. No danger of death by cookies. And he knew exactly who would finish off the rest and not rat on him to Helen.

Reinn found Ganymede in the kitchen with Sparkle. Big surprise. "Hey, Ganymede, how about sharing some cookies with me?" He took off the foil wrapping.

"You know, bloodsucker, you're okay." Ganymede leaped onto the table and pulled a cookie off the plate with his teeth.

Sparkle wandered over to get one.

Reinn smiled at Sparkle. He'd done a lot of that lately. Had to watch it. Smiling said you were a friendly guy. He wasn't. "You sure cookies are sensual enough for you?" Teasing? This was serious. Reinn didn't tease. Ever.

She offered him her you've-gotta-be-kidding look. "Brother, anything with chocolate in it has my sensual seal of approval."

Now might be a good time to find out about this Protector character. Reinn had been Guardian for only a short time, and before that he'd stayed out of the clan loop. The council should've clued him in to anyone out to stop him. He hated the council. "I heard a couple of the cats talking about someone they called the Protector. Know anything about him?"

Ganymede stuffed another cookie in his mouth. *"Mmm. Better than sex."*

No help there. He turned to Sparkle.

She aimed her death glare at Ganymede. Reinn figured he'd pay for that sex comment. How could someone so powerful get so stupid over a plate of cookies? He could ask himself the same question, because his stupidity rating was off the scale when it came to Kisa's sweet, sexy behind.

Sparkle shifted her gaze to Reinn and shrugged. "He's the one who shows up at weddings when a cat is marrying a Mackenzie. He protects the vamp from you. He saved a few vamps from the guy before you. Guess your council never heard about the last guy's failures. Everyone covers his own butt."

"How long has he been around?"

"No one knows for sure. Eight, maybe nine hundred years. Of course, there might've been more than one Protector, just like there was more than one Guardian of the Blood."

Interesting. "Then the Protector can't be a werecat if he's been around that long."

Sparkle looked like she was getting bored with the subject. "Werecats live longer than most people think. The nine-lives legend is true. They live nine consecutive life spans, a life span being one hundred years. So Kisa will live nine hundred years, barring anything catastrophic."

"Why would I care how long Kisa will live?"

Sparkle smiled her low-down, conniving smile. "You tell me, hot bod."

Reinn didn't honor that comment with a response. Her info about the Protector had given him a lot to think about.

She peered at a list she'd been working on. "What

do you think about oatmeal and bananas for breakfast? Legends say the serpent that tempted Eve hid in a bunch of bananas. Not that I believe stuff like that. But bananas do have bufotenine. Boosts the sex drive. And God knows this group needs all the boosting it can get."

"The bear's going to be pissed. Don't think the cats are big on oatmeal and bananas either." So he looked something like this Protector. Maybe he could use the similarity to his advantage. And if the real deal came along, he'd take care of the problem.

"Cookies, cookies, cookies. Can't get enough of them." Ganymede was going through that plate of cookies like a vampire through a blood bank.

Sparkle frowned. "Guess I'll have to throw in some food with no sensual value. Sausages would be okay. They're phallic symbols." She stared down at her stilettos. "My feet are killing me."

"So take the damn shoes off." Ganymede.

She closed her eyes and put her martyr expression firmly in place. "A sensual woman should be willing to suffer for her erotic image."

Lethargy was starting to creep up on Reinn. He didn't have to look outside to know dawn was close. "Did *you* fix all that stuff for dinner?"

"With my own two perfectly manicured hands." She opened her eyes to offer him wide-eyed honesty.

"Ha!" Ganymede had cleaned the plate. *"She called this catering place in Atlantic City, told them what she wanted, and they delivered."*

She didn't deign to even look at the snitch. "But that was just for dinner. Breakfast will be simple. I'll tell Bernie what to cook and forget about it." Her smile was slow and sly. "Men are such marvelous creatures. Useful in so many ways."

Reinn had taken all he could of the two cosmic troublemakers. As he dragged his tired predawn body up the stairs, he wondered briefly where Trouble was.

He found out as he stumbled into his room. The dog was stretched across the foot of his bed.

Trouble's tail beat a tattoo of happiness. *"Sparkle yelled at me because I chased the ball instead of listening to what you and Kisa said. She told me I had to stay here all day and then follow you around."*

Great. Just freakin' great. But he was too tired to throw the dog out on his furry ass. So he dragged off his clothes and fell into bed.

His last thought before sleep took him should've been about his job. It wasn't. It was about Kisa. A major danger signal.

Kisa wondered where Daniel was. Even allowing for eight hours of sleep, he should've been up a long time ago. She'd been up since midafternoon and had already put in hours of helping with the wedding plans. Not that there was much to do. It was going to be a simple ceremony held in the inn's parlor with a reception afterward. But her mom managed to make simple into we'll-never-get-it-all-done.

The sun had set, and the three vampires staying at the inn had just come downstairs. They kept to themselves, so she didn't know much about them. The only important thing she needed to know was that none of them was the Guardian of the Blood. The Guardian worked alone.

"Hi, there, Kisa." Felicia Carter stopped beside her. "I'm sorry I didn't get to talk to you last night." Her smile widened. "Sounded like you had company."

Kisa nodded absently at the wedding planner. "Why didn't you talk to Julie or my mom about the food?" She tried to pay attention to Felicia while she kept an eye on the stairs.

"Hey, you're the food critic. I thought you might want some input. But that's okay. Your mom took care of it." Something flickered in her eyes and was gone. "Are you going to hang around here tonight?"

Kisa shrugged. "Haven't decided yet." There. Daniel had finally come down the stairs. Worn jeans, scuffed biker boots, and shirt hanging open. Sexy-scruffy, yum.

"Oh." Felicia turned to see who'd caught Kisa's attention. "Hot guy. Did he check in last night?" She smoothed her hand over her short blond hair, a reflex action for any woman when Daniel was in the room.

"Yeah. Daniel Night." Kisa watched, puzzled, as Daniel didn't even pause to look around before walking out the front door. Disappointment warred with curiosity. "Look, I've got to go. If the caterer has any questions I can answer, let me know." She was pretty sure the caterer could handle everything without her input.

She didn't wait to hear Felicia's response before following Daniel out the door. Darkness wrapped around her, but she had great night vision, a perk from her cat side. He was just disappearing into the forest.

Should she or shouldn't she? Okay, so she'd made her decision even before she asked the question. Curiosity. A weakness. Stepping off the porch, she followed him into the night. Once she reached the forest Kisa went into stealth mode. She grinned. Slinking and sneaking came naturally to her.

Kisa didn't know what she'd expected, but it definitely wasn't to see Daniel meet another man. She had to stay out of sight, so she didn't get a look at the man's face. He handed Daniel a long, wrapped package, and then faded back into the darkness.

She frowned. Why couldn't the man bring it directly to the inn? All the possible reasons were bad. This would teach her. Sneak around spying on people and you saw things you didn't want to see. Now she'd be suspicious until she knew what was in the package. Kisa stepped back and got ready to run so she could reach the inn ahead of him, then winced at the faint crackle of a dry leaf beneath her shoe.

Daniel turned his head to stare at the spot where she hid, and Kisa held her breath. He was a large, dark shape in the night, and she was out here alone. Prickles of fear danced over her skin. Talk about an intimidating presence. If you could change into a saber-toothed tiger, no human should be able to scare you. But she was afraid to change, so yep, he scared her.

Kisa turned away, and when she glanced over her shoulder to make sure he wasn't following, Daniel was gone. Uneasiness touched her. Where was he? Well, this time she wouldn't try to follow him. She retraced her steps back toward the inn.

She'd almost reached the porch when she heard a terrified quacking. Bernie? He didn't swim at night. The sounds were coming from the small pond just inside the woods on the other side of the inn. She glanced around. No one else was out yet, so if it *was* Bernie, she'd be the only one riding to his rescue.

Kisa sprinted across the inn's back lawn and into the woods. She was puffing by the time she reached the pond. Riveted, she tried to make sense of the scene. The duck—she could tell it was Bernie by the black spot on one wildly flapping wing—was held fast in the talons of a nightmare creature.

The monster's chest and head were human. In fact, Kisa recognized the face. It . . . she . . . whatever was a guest at the inn. Not a pretty face, but Kisa had never judged by externals. These externals, though, were too gruesome to ignore.

Beyond the human chest and face, everything else was bird. Vicious bird. It was all deadly claws and huge wings. And it was lifting Bernie into the air. Bernie was trying to change back to human form, but panic slowed down the process. Kisa didn't think his human form would help him much anyway against this creature.

Kisa splashed into the shallow pond, but knew she'd be next to useless in her human form. The creature was too big, too powerful.

Decision time. She could change into her animal form and risk laying waste to the whole area, or let

Bernie die. Panic washed over her. What if she shifted and then ate Bernie? Maybe after chowing down on Bernie she'd go on to the inn and kill everyone there. What if she was inside her cat and had to watch the slaughter but couldn't do anything to stop it? How would she live with herself?

"I'll be in your mind to help you." Daniel's quiet voice came from behind her.

Kisa didn't even turn around to look at him. Did she trust Daniel enough to do this for her? She'd better decide quickly or else all that would be left of Bernie would be a few feathers floating in the breeze. "What'll you do if both of us together can't control my cat?"

"I'm telepathic. I'll call for Ganymede. He can hold you." He laughed softly but without humor. "Then I'll get my butt up a tree and hope you can't climb."

She made her decision. For the first time in her twenty-eight years, she willed the change. It came with a breathtaking flow of muscle and bone as she shifted from human to animal. She felt no pain, only awareness that she was now something else—something primitive, ferocious, and hungry. Her tiger mind struggled with the outside force trying to control it, to remind it of something it should do besides rend and tear. And within her primal consciousness, her other self fought to be heard. The saber-tooth was confused.

"Kisa, speak to your animal; guide it. Your tiger has to attack the harpy. Make it release the duck." The voice

was low, commanding, and impossible for either of her selves to ignore.

She roared her unwillingness to listen, to obey. But slowly her primal self gave way to the human awareness blossoming inside her animal body. Kisa was back, and she was in control.

She launched herself at the harpy, claws unsheathed and massive jaws opened. The harpy screeched its alarm and dropped Bernie, who was somewhere halfway between duck and man.

Flapping its huge wings, the harpy rose just out of reach of Kisa's leap. It screamed its anger.

"Who are you, harpy?" Daniel's voice was calm.

He didn't sound afraid of her or the harpy. A brave man or just someone not clear on the concept of imminent death?

The harpy snarled at him. "I'm Ocypete. I work for Hades. This is the address he gave me. I checked the mailbox to make sure I had the right place. There's someone here who's about to die, and it's my job to bring that someone to Tartarus." It glared at Bernie, who was still doing his duck-man imitation. "Little bastards like him piss me off."

Then the creature's expression turned sly. "I thought it was the duck, because he must have a death wish to swim here at night in his animal form. But perhaps it's you. If the cat doesn't get you, I will."

Meanwhile Bernie had finally returned to human form—naked human form—and was crouched behind Daniel.

Kisa shook her massive head. Her control was slipping in and out. One minute she wanted only to kill, and the next her tenuous hold on humanity urged her to protect Daniel and Bernie.

The harpy cast Kisa a frustrated glare. "Well, I can't wait around forever. I don't know who I'm supposed to snatch, but Hades isn't picky. I'll take whomever I can get." It rose into the night and was gone.

Daniel turned his gaze to Kisa. *"I'm adding my strength to yours. Return to human form. Send your animal back to the strong, safe place you keep it in your mind. Make it obey you, Kisa."* The soft murmur in her mind held only calm confidence in her ability to change.

Kisa felt a surge of power so strong she rode its energy as she willed back her human form. Once again she felt the shift of muscle and bone.

She stood for a moment, shocked. The echoes of her animal nature faded as she reclaimed her humanity. Kisa closed her eyes as she waited for her heartbeat to slow and her breathing to even out. Then she opened them to the reality around her.

Triumph pulsed through her. She'd done it. With Daniel's help, she'd controlled her cat and saved Bernie. Her emotional high came to a crashing halt, though, as she realized something.

Holy cow! She and Bernie were naked. *Very* naked. This time she hadn't had time to strip down. Her short red dress, her red panties, and her red bra lay torn and useless. *Oh, my God, where's a fig leaf when you need one?* She scanned the immediate area. Nope, a maple leaf wouldn't cover squat.

Daniel's grin was a flash of white in the darkness. "It'll take lots of practice before you're at ease with your cat. I want to be there for every one."

Ack! Bernie didn't have it so bad. He had two hands to cover a few little thingies all crowded into one spot. She had two hands that weren't nearly enough to cover her strategic areas.

Okay, she had to admit it: she couldn't cover everything. Might as well stop acting like a crazed mime and go for some dignity. She dropped her hands to her sides and glared at Daniel. "Do something. Go get me some clothes. But before you leave, give me your shirt."

"No, no!" Bernie took a chance and removed one hand from coverage duty so he could wave it around. No problem. One hand covered everything. "If you leave, that harpy thing could come back, or Ms. Evans here might hiccup and turn back into Big Tooth."

Daniel's gaze never left Kisa. She felt the heated slide of it the length of her entire body. The places where his glance lingered ignited like dry tinder. He might have a forest fire on his hands any minute now.

"You need clothes, huh?" His expression said his words were incidental, just something to fill up time while he continued to contemplate her navel and other spots heretofore unseen by man.

"Well, duh." She leaned over to pick up her sandals and the remains of her clothes. "Maybe it's just me, but I think some people might notice if I walked into the inn wearing just my shoes. Because they're the only damn things still in one piece. Now give me your shirt."

"When you lean over and talk at the same time, I guarantee I'm not hearing you, sweetheart." Even in just the moonlight, Kisa could see the amused glitter in his eyes.

She'd had enough. Bernie looked too harpy-shocked to speak up, but Kisa didn't have any trouble giving as good as she got. "You give me your shirt and then go get me some clothes or else I'll whip your butt from one end of this forest to the other. And I think you've seen enough to know I can do it." As soon as she saw his expression, Kisa knew she'd used the wrong phrasing.

"Whip my butt? I love it when you talk sexy. You excite me, lady." He purposely gripped his bottom lip with his teeth, and then slowly released it.

The full, damp sheen of it riveted her attention, so she didn't realize he'd taken a cell phone from his pocket until he spoke. "Sparkle? I need clothes for Kisa. Don't ask questions, and come by yourself. No one else needs to know about this. We're out by the pond."

She was busy trying to arrange the remains of her dress to cover her hot spots when he put his phone away. Without comment, he stripped off his shirt and handed it to her.

Woo-hoo, would you look at that chest? Broad, muscular, with male nipples that just begged to be licked, nipped, and . . . *Halt, cease, desist.* Sure, she'd done a lot of creative erotic-imaging during hormonal surges, but now wasn't the time to go into lust mode.

"Thanks." After her butt-whipping remark, Kisa decided to keep her conversation brief and safe. She slipped on the shirt and then buttoned it. Huge relief. It came almost to her knees.

Bernie had evidently given up on protecting her virgin eyes from his male organ, because he was doing a frenetic dance as he slapped at his arms and legs. "Mosquitoes. Hate them. They're eating me alive. They don't bother me in my duck form."

Daniel exhaled deeply. "Where'd you leave your clothes?"

"I took them off in the woods on the other side of the pond. Do you think the harpy will get me if I run over and put them on?" He peered fearfully into the forest. "I took a chance swimming at night because I didn't think any of the carnivores would be out yet. I didn't know anything about a harpy staying at the inn. Who knew harpies were for real?"

Amen. Kisa knew that when she had a few minutes to think about Ocypete, she'd feel suitably horrified. She'd also have a few questions for Mr. Night. Like how he knew the creature was a harpy, and why he wasn't even a little afraid. Oh, and how did a human get the kind of mental power he'd demonstrated?

But right now she was letting it all roll over her. And she refused even to consider that she felt this way because Daniel made her feel safe. She could keep herself safe—from most things. Fine, so maybe she needed some help with catnip.

"Forget about the harpy and go get dressed. Sparkle will be here any minute. You want her to see you like this?" He sounded as if he was holding on to his temper by a thread.

Daniel had turned his back to her as he spoke to Bernie, so Kisa had some uninterrupted ogling time. His back was a broad expanse of smooth skin. How warm would that skin feel if she slid her hand across his shoulders and then traced the line of his spine? Mmm, what a stimulating idea.

"Oh, no. Ms. Stardust can't see me like this." Bernie's eyes widened a second before he raced away. He was already in the woods when Sparkle came into view.

Words couldn't express how much admiration Kisa felt for Sparkle. It took a tough woman to run all the way from the inn on her toes. But here she came, tiptoeing on her stilettos at the speed of light, clothes draped over her arm.

Sparkle stopped in front of them, cheeks flushed and eyes gleaming with excitement. She looked at the remains of Kisa's clothes and then turned her awe-filled gaze toward Daniel. "You wanted her so much you ripped off her clothes? You guys made passionate love here beside the pond?" She stared at Kisa. "You're wet. Even better. You made wild, kinky love *in* the pond?"

Kisa shook her head as she took the clothes from Sparkle. "I shifted. One of your guests is a harpy.

Bernie had changed to duck form and was swimming in the pond. The harpy tried to snatch him. I wasn't strong enough to challenge her in my human form."

Sparkle frowned. "You didn't make love?" She zeroed in on the only part of Kisa's tale that interested her. "Well, that's a big fat disappointment." She made a shooing motion toward Daniel. "As much as I'd love to gaze on your incredible body for hours, I need you to follow the duck to make sure he gets back to the inn in one piece." She glanced around. "Wait. Where's Trouble?"

A smile tugged at Daniel's sensual lips. "I told him Ganymede was waiting in the kitchen for him with a big juicy pork chop."

Not waiting for Sparkle to comment, he disappeared into the forest. Random thoughts. He'd gotten rid of the long package somewhere before he rode to Bernie's rescue. And Trouble was the brown dog. Why was he talking to the dog?

Sparkle frowned, evidently not pleased about Trouble and the pork chop. Then she crossed her arms over her generous chest and tapped her foot impatiently. "Dress. Now. I brought one of my own outfits—guaranteed to turn any man into a growling, lust-filled beast."

Kisa sighed as she turned away from Sparkle and began putting on the clothes. She could tell Sparkle that she was already a charter member of Lust-filled Beasts, Inc.

Finally dressed, Kisa looked down at herself in horror. "Jeez, you've gotta be kidding." The short black skirt rode low on her hips, and the dangly red beads sewn to the hem did *not* make it longer. If she bent over, God and the rest of the world would get an eye-popping view of her panties, the ones with BAD GIRL printed all over them. The hem of the black, clingy top wasn't even within shouting distance of the waistband of her skirt. Once she slipped on her red shoes, she'd officially morph into Slut Woman, able to seduce thousands of men at a single glance. *Sheesh*.

Sparkle nodded, satisfied. "*Now* you look sexy. I'll walk back to the inn with you. We're going to talk sex, sister—why you're not getting any, and what I'm going to do to change that."

Kisa swallowed hard. She looked at Sparkle. She looked at her new outfit.

Oh, boy.

Chapter Five

Sparkle linked arms with Kisa as they walked back to the inn. "So how much sexual experience do you have?" She shot from the hip at point-blank range.

Kisa considered lying, but then rejected the thought. It was no big deal. All the werecats knew. "None."

Sparkle stopped walking and dropped her arm. "Like, just a few times? Like, they were so ho-hum you don't even want to mention them? Like that?"

Kisa sighed. Sparkle was making this tough. "Like never. I'm a virgin."

"Virgin?" Sparkle spit the word with the same loathing she'd use for things like chipped nails, flat shoes, and vanilla pudding.

Kisa shrugged. "No biggie. In the werecat culture, a woman can't have sex with any man less powerful than she is. You saw my cat form. Haven't found any man who can go one-on-one with that. Probably never will. So, yes, I'm a virgin."

Sympathy shone in Sparkle's eyes. Kisa almost expected her to tear up.

"You poor thing. And you bravely suffered so long in silence." Sparkle put her hand over her heart to emphasize how stricken she felt for Kisa's plight.

Kisa suspected that Sparkle was into the drama of the moment. "Never in silence. I've complained long and loudly, but no one listens too well in the werecat community. I guarantee, though, my thoughts aren't virginal. I want to make love, and someone will damn well know he has a tiger in bed. Werecats are comfortable with their bodies and are aggressive lovers. Probably a perk of our animal natures." Okay, why was she blabbing all this to Sparkle? She almost felt compelled to share. What was that all about?

"I'll help you break free of your chains." Sparkle looked totally committed to the chain breaking. "Daniel will be perfect for your first time. He's gorgeous and . . . Well, I guess that's the important part." Sparkle held up her hand to stop Kisa from answering. "I saw the way you looked at him. Don't deny it."

"But that was just lust." Why was she arguing? Kisa thought Daniel would make a great first time, too.

Sparkle blinked. "And your point is? Sister, it's always about lust. You can love a man for his mind later."

"Doesn't he have any say in it?" Kisa had to put up some kind of a fight, because Sparkle was a steamroller wearing Casadei sandals and a Barely

Basics silk halter dress. Sexy and stylish, but a steamroller nonetheless.

Sparkle's expression said that such naïveté would be endearing if it weren't so stupid. "Let me see, I'd guess that Daniel would think about it for, oh, say, five seconds before dragging you off to bed. All men are hot-wired for sex."

Kisa frowned. Sparkle's take on men and sex was realistic, but it hosed down Kisa's enthusiasm. She'd sort of hoped for more than an any-woman-will-do attitude from Daniel. She wasn't looking for love, but she wanted at least a hint that she was a little special. They'd almost reached the porch. Maybe Sparkle would find something else inside to distract her from Kisa's pitiful sex life.

Oblivious to Kisa's mood change, Sparkle rattled on. "You have good clothes sense, but from now on you have to dress for effect. Every piece of clothing has to whisper, 'I'm a sensual woman on the prowl.'"

Kisa didn't have a chance to comment on Sparkle's vision of her new sensual self, because at that moment the five-second man strode from the inn and stood, still shirtless, waiting for them on the porch. He looked grim. And gorgeous. She couldn't forget gorgeous.

"What happened? Who's hurt?" Kisa Evans, Ms. Always Positive.

"Catnip." He nodded toward the door. "All the werecats were in the parlor when your mom saw me come in. Bernie got here before me, and I guess he told her that you were with me. So she said to everyone, 'Here's Kisa now.' Then all hell broke loose. Someone had put catnip in the parlor air-conditioner vent and then turned on the air at exactly that moment." He shook his head in wonder. "Right now there's a roomful of grown people rolling around on the floor giggling and acting stupid. We can go in the back way."

No matter how scary it was to know the attack had been aimed at her, Kisa couldn't help smiling. "That's the way catnip usually affects werecats. Lots of rolling and giggling, but nothing else. It doesn't make them shift." Lucky her. She was the unique one.

After handing his shirt to him and waiting while he slipped it on, Kisa walked with him to the back entrance. His very presence made the summer night a little warmer, a little more humid. The hollow between her breasts grew damp, along with . . . other places. When she was near him, the scent of dangerous male and the low, husky temptation of his voice made her think that maybe she should just let the lust rip.

Sparkle huffed and puffed all the way to the kitchen. "Okay, this nonsense has to stop. How can I concentrate on important things"—meaningful glance aimed at Kisa—"when some loony is launching catnip attacks?"

Since Kisa didn't want to go up to her room, and she couldn't go into the parlor until the catnip had been cleaned up, she trailed along behind Sparkle. Daniel followed her toward the kitchen.

Just before they entered the room, he leaned close, and she could feel the touch of his warm breath on the side of her neck almost like the slide of fingers across her skin. "Those clothes that Sparkle loaned you are . . . stimulating. If I drop my jaw, will you lean over to pick it up?"

Kisa had forgotten about Sparkle's outfit. She should glare at him, but her lips refused to turn down. Against her express orders, they kept tipping up. *Traitors.* Fine, so she liked the feeling of being a sex object. So sue her.

She didn't have to think of any sexy and clever retort, because they'd entered the kitchen. Sparkle took center stage.

Her scowl should've turned Trouble crispy and well-done, and with all the pork chop grease smeared over his furry muzzle, he would've browned nicely. He rolled his eyes toward Sparkle in an attempt to look both sorry and apologetic. Kisa didn't buy it. She'd bet he'd sell his doggy soul for another pork chop.

Sparkle narrowed her eyes to evil slits. "You've failed me, Trouble. I need to be able to depend on those I entrust with a job."

Jeez, she sounded like a mob boss. Kisa hoped she wasn't planning on fitting Trouble with paw-sized cement boots and dumping him in the pond. "Uh, maybe it's just me, but has anyone noticed that people are talking to a dog? Have I missed something here?"

Laughter gleamed in Daniel's eyes, and once again Kisa felt the falling-in-an-elevator sensation she got every time she really focused on him. He'd reclaimed his shirt, but it still hung open. She was surprised not to actually hear a ripping sound as she tore her gaze from the exposed strip of muscular chest.

"Oh, good grief." Sparkle threw up her hands. "Do I have to explain everything? Mede, Trouble, and I are all cosmic troublemakers. We're exactly what our name implies. And if you put your tongue into that ice-cream container one more time, Mede, I'll cut it off. I'm planning a special dinner, and if you keep pushing food into your fuzzy face, you won't have room for my meal." This to Ganymede who was crouched on the floor beneath the table with both front paws wrapped around the container.

Kisa stood awestruck at Sparkle's ability to segue from one thought to another without taking a breath.

The cat lifted his head and stared at Sparkle. *"Exactly, honey bunny."* He looked down at the container regretfully. *"All gone."* His expression would've been truly pathetic if his whiskers weren't dripping melted ice cream. *"What're you planning for dinner?"* He didn't look hopeful as he sat up and began cleaning his face with one paw.

Daniel interrupted. "Forget dinner, Ganymede. Someone has tried to force Kisa to change twice now. If they try again, and she's inside the inn when she shifts, two things could happen. First, a saber-toothed tiger tearing through the inn would not only wreck the place, but if she managed to catch any of your guests, she'd eat them. The Woo Woo Inn would lose its five-star rating, and Cindy would never climb out from under the mountain of lawsuits. Might put a little strain on your friendship with Cindy and Thrain. Second, if anything bad happens to Kisa, I'll be really pissed."

About her? She was special to him in some way? She tried to stomp out the glow his words triggered, but it kept right on shining.

That was all he said, but Kisa got the feeling bad things happened when Daniel got pissed. Strange. How could a human cause the feeling of dread she sensed in the room?

Reinn smiled. He'd delivered his message, and he hoped Ganymede understood its implications.

Ganymede met Daniel's gaze and then nodded. *"We know none of the cats put the catnip in the vent. They were all in the parlor when the air went on. Sparkle turned the air off a few hours ago because the temperature outside had cooled down enough to open the windows. Someone turned the air back on."*

Reinn thought about that. "So we can eliminate the cats, unless one of them has teamed up with a partner. I don't think it's the harpy. She's pretty straightforward." That left the vampires, werewolves, humans, and the guy he couldn't make. He kept this to himself, because a human wouldn't be expected to know anything about the other entities.

"I'll find the bastard. And when I do, I'll eliminate the problem." Ganymede's amber eyes glowed with

menace. *"I'll start listening to everyone's chatter."*
Translation: he'd be doing some mental eavesdropping.

That was good, because Ganymede could monitor the nonhuman thoughts without consequences.
You'd have to be crazy to challenge anyone with his power.

"Hi, everyone. I just popped in to find out what we'll be having for dinner tonight." Helen and Julie stood in the doorway. Kisa's mom looked determinedly cheerful.

Sparkle seemed distracted. Reinn figured dinner wasn't at the top of her priority list tonight.

"Dinner? Oh, I was just about to start the veggies. We're having turnips cooked in milk. In Iran they're served to anyone whose sex life is dwindling. Then I'll prepare—"

Julie waved her hand at Sparkle. "I'm so sorry, Sparkle, but Alan and I will be going into town to eat. There's an all-night restaurant he wants to check out. I hope you'll have some leftovers that I can eat tomorrow."

Reinn figured that as soon as the word got around about the turnips cooked in milk, there'd be a convoy of cars leaving the inn for town. Sparkle wouldn't expect him to eat her dinner. Sometimes being a vampire wasn't half-bad.

Meanwhile, he'd better get his butt out of here. Kisa had moved closer to him, and her woman's scent along with all that smooth skin exposed by her skirt and top were making mush of his brain. That left his cock in control. And his cock thought that having sex with Kisa would be a good thing. It wouldn't. Because he still had to off her sister's husband-to-be.

"Daniel, didn't you tell me you were thinking of going into town to eat? Why don't you and Kisa go with Alan and Julie?" Helen's smile was overbright as she stared at him. Her eyes begged him to keep Alan safe. *Hell.*

Kisa glanced at him. "Really?"

"Yeah." The Fates were laughing their asses off over this one.

Her smile warmed him from the inside out. "I'll go up and change and then meet you out on the porch." She glanced at Julie. "Okay with you?"

"Sure, it'll be fun." Julie wouldn't be so happy if she knew death would be riding with her.

He hated his job. And he hated the council for being such hard-asses and Alan for thinking he could cheat death. It would serve them all right if he stayed at the inn and chowed down on turnips cooked in milk.

But one glance at Helen's beaming smile convinced him that he didn't have the guts—not heart, because he didn't have a heart—to wipe that smile from her face. After all, in a few days she wouldn't be smiling at all. He nodded. "I'll be on the porch."

A short time later, he and Kisa were sitting in the backseat of Alan's car. Alan had lowered his window, and Julie and he were singing. My God, *singing.* He knew now that he'd been right never to fall in love if it made you do stupid things like that.

Julie was almost in Alan's lap—would've been if not for the center console. But Reinn was barely within shouting distance of Kisa in the backseat. *Good.* Closeness with her made him hard, and he didn't need one more thing to distract him from his crappy job.

Kisa hadn't said anything for the last few minutes, and Reinn could only think about laying her down on this backseat and stripping her dress—he'd liked Sparkle's outfit better—from her lush body. He didn't think that was a great conversational opener, though.

So instead he stared out the window at the forest, nothing more than black tree shapes in the darkness. This strip of road had no streetlights. It wound through the forest without any houses to break the monotony.

Alan was busy talking to Julie. Reinn was busy thinking about why he shouldn't be imagining hot sex with Kisa, when he noticed headlights behind them growing brighter and brighter. This was the first car they'd seen since leaving the inn, and he waited for it to pass.

It didn't pass. As the car pulled even with them, someone in the darkened interior pointed what looked like a long tube at them through the passenger-side window. *What the . . . ?* Reinn had just opened his mouth to shout a warning at Alan when a whirlwind of what smelled like catnip exploded into the car through Alan's open window.

"Hell!" Startled, Alan jerked the wheel. The car veered off the road into a deep ditch and rolled over.

For a moment Reinn felt disoriented, and then he reached for Kisa. She wasn't beside him. A thousand years of training kicked in. He shut down all panic and looked around. Kisa's door was hanging open. He quickly crawled to her side and out of the car.

An ominous growl confirmed his worst fear. Kisa was changing. At least she was alive. Julie stood crying beside the car. Okay, she wasn't injured. "Where's Alan?"

"He's under the car!" Julie's voice shook as she pointed to the open driver's-side door. "He wasn't wearing his seat belt, and he got thrown from the car when it started to roll." Her voice was getting louder as panic set in.

The growling grew fiercer. "Julie, can you climb a tree in your cat form?"

"Yes, but Alan is—"

"I'll take care of Alan. Shift and then get your behind up the nearest tree. Your sister's running on all fours, and she hasn't had dinner yet." They should've stayed for Sparkle's meal. Turnips cooked in milk sounded pretty good right about now.

Reinn didn't look to see if Julie had obeyed him. He hoped her survival instinct would kick in, and she'd realize she couldn't do a damn thing for Alan if she were dead.

Reinn had a split second to make a decision. He could either help Kisa control her cat or get Alan from under the car. The accident alone wouldn't kill him, but smoke was starting to rise from the wreck. Fire would do the job as surely as separating Alan's head from his shoulders.

Let it happen. No more wedding. Problem solved.

Uh-uh. Reinn didn't work that way. Alan deserved a chance to defend himself.

If he was going to save Alan, he'd better do it now, though, because the fire was spreading. Reinn would have to trust in Kisa's inner strength, because he couldn't help both at the same time.

Might as well accept the inevitable. He'd have to change forms to deal with Alan and then chase after Kisa—something he'd wanted to avoid. But the best-laid plans, and all that crap.

Gathering his power, he became vampire. The familiar sensations rolled over him—his eyes growing larger, elongating, and the slide of his fangs pushing against his lips. His body bulked up, his shoulders and chest widening, his muscles expanding. Then came the real rush—a surge in sensory awareness that allowed him to hear the rustle of a tiny animal scampering through the grass, see in perfect detail an insect clinging to the bark of a nearby tree even in the darkness, and smell the scent of distant rain in the humid air. He could taste the night.

Along with all of this came preternatural speed and strength, plus a whole bunch of other powers he rarely thought about. But it was his enhanced mental power that he'd need now. Barely aware of the small leopard Julie had become crouched on a branch high above him, he focused all his power on the burning car.

With a mental surge, Reinn envisioned invisible hands reaching for the car, lifting it into the air, and shifting it away from the ditch where Alan lay, before setting it down gently on the side of the road. Then those same hands cupped the fire. And even as the leopard shifted back to human form, the fire died, leaving only the darkness.

Reinn exhaled deeply. Now to hunt down a saber-toothed tiger and hope to hell none of the locals saw her. Cindy and Thrain didn't need the media nosing around the area. Not that he cared about them, because they weren't really his friends. And he certainly wasn't doing this for Kisa. She was just a great-looking woman he wanted to have sex with, who was fun to be around.

Once he'd reaffirmed his complete independence from all human ties, he lifted his face to catch Kisa's scent. "Can you take care of Alan while I look for Kisa?" He glanced at Julie, who was staring wide-eyed at him as she tried to wrap the remains of her dress around her.

She nodded but didn't seem capable of speech yet. *Good.* He didn't need anyone wasting his time with useless chatter. Without hesitation, he raced into the forest.

Kisa sensed him coming, and her cat snarled its defiance. She was stalking a deer while *he* stalked her. First she would kill the deer and then she'd kill him. Everything was clear in the cat's mind.

Within that mind, Kisa the person fought to gain control. She'd managed to steer her animal away from those she knew she shouldn't kill, but now help was coming. Kisa's human side struggled to stop her cat from abandoning the deer for the easier kill it sensed at a nearby camp.

When the one who'd been pursuing her finally separated himself from the darkness, Kisa's humanity rose to help him battle her cat. And if he looked familiar but not the same as the cat remembered, Kisa was too busy to notice.

"I'm here, Kisa."

The words in her mind were like coming home. He was strength, caring, and safety. She moved toward the words. But her cat wouldn't be denied. It crouched and then sprang at the one who would deny it the night and its kill.

Nooo! Kisa's silent scream went unheard as the cat hit him squarely in the chest with teeth bared and claws unsheathed. But instead of crumpling beneath the immense weight and ferocity of the saber-tooth, he wrapped his arms around the cat and threw it to the ground.

"Control it now, Kisa. I can't help you mentally because I've sort of got my hands full."

Kisa fought her way through layers of primal rage until she finally reached the cat's mind. With a will she'd never pushed to its limits and strength drawn from a place inside she'd never explored, Kisa wrested control from the cat and changed.

She kept her eyes wide-open during the shift, and as her humanity returned, so did the realization that Daniel was straddling her. She recognized those hard thighs encased in soft, worn jeans and, as she moved her gaze a little higher, the black shirt he'd buttoned before their trip to the restaurant. The shirt would hang forever open now because all his buttons were gone. She tried to concentrate on the why of that but couldn't.

She was naked. Not unexpected, but it still startled her. Add shock to the list as her gaze at last reached his face. A vampire was straddling her naked body. *Holy cow!*

Kisa bucked and fought. "Let me up, bloodsucker, before I . . ." *Whoa, back up and put brain in motion.* Vampire or not, he'd just saved her from creating some really bad karma in the neighborhood.

As she watched, he returned to the man she knew, or rather, the man she *thought* she knew. "You're vampire. Why didn't I know?" He'd lied to her. Why? She pushed away her need to cover herself, along with the remaining primal urges of her cat, who thought that naked underneath a hot-looking guy was a great place to be.

"Because I didn't *want* you to know. It causes a whole lot less fuss if everyone thinks I'm human." He made it sound so reasonable.

But only a very powerful vampire could've cloaked his presence from all of them. The first prickle of suspicion touched her. The Guardian of the Blood would have that kind of power. Even as the thought formed, she felt the prod of Daniel's mind. Too late she remembered to block her thoughts.

"Don't worry; I'm not the bad guy here. Your mom told me about the Guardian. Hey, I just saved Alan's butt. Would the Guardian do that?" His gaze warmed as he stared down at her.

She knew exactly why his gaze was warming, but she had another question to ask before she addressed the warming thing. "Why would Mom tell you anything?"

"She thinks I'm the Protector. She caught a glimpse of him once, and she thinks I have his eyes. I told her I wasn't her man, but she didn't believe me." He shrugged. "That's why she wanted me to tag along while Julie and Alan went to the restaurant. Protection."

"Oh." That was the extent of her vocabulary at the moment, because the primal roar of her cat was becoming her own. Neither had ever had sex, and both thought it was about time. And she wouldn't even be cheating. She'd actually found a man stronger than herself.

The best part? She wanted him with a deep sexual hunger that made her clench her thighs around her need. All her adult life she'd longed to be with someone who could make her scream in uncontrolled completion. The uncontrolled part was important, because she'd never allowed herself to lose control in any aspect of her life for fear of triggering the change. She needed a man who could free her in the most elemental way. Daniel was the first male who'd ever made her want to scream before he even touched her.

His heated gaze touched her breasts, and it felt as though he'd slid his tongue across them, leaving the nipples hard, sensitive nubs. She arched her back, an instinctive invitation for him to put his mouth on her breasts and anything else he chose.

"Not a good idea. Your emotions are still running with the tiger, and I want you too much for just a few hot kisses." His voice was harsh with need.

"Yeah?" Kisa brightened. He wanted her. That had to be good. "Well, I think it's a great idea. I've waited my whole life to find a man stronger than me. You're the first."

"And?" He looked puzzled.

"In werecat society, a woman can make love only with a man stronger than herself." There. She'd explained it without saying the hated word *virgin*.

Kisa watched his expression as he put it all together. When he widened his eyes, she knew he'd reached the punch line.

"You're a virgin." His tone *didn't* say, *Whoopee, I get to deflower a virgin.*

Men liked being a woman's first, didn't they? Then why didn't he look even a little happy at the thought? "Would it help if I said I lusted in my heart?"

He shook his head, his smile wry. "I'm not the man you want for your first time." Something in his expression told her he had good reasons for saying that. "You need someone gentle, someone who'll take his time with you. I'm not gentle. Wouldn't have a clue where to start. I'm as savage as your cat, and I'd take you fast and hard. We'd blaze hot, but you'd be left with ashes. Trust me, it wouldn't be a good thing." His expression said he was trying to convince himself.

She didn't want gentle. She wanted him, and she was about to have the first full-blown hissy fit of her entire life. "Damn you." Kisa reached up and socked him in the jaw. "I should've eaten you when I had the chance." She bared her teeth at him. "You just don't get it, do you? I'll die a virgin because—drumroll, please . . . There. *Are*. No. Men. Stronger. Than. Me."

Kisa followed up her punch with a hard shove to the middle of his spectacular chest. And if her hand rested there a little too long, well, too bad. "I don't want a man who'll take it slow and gentle. I'm a saber-toothed tiger, for God's sake. I want a mating that'll shake the jungle, send brave men running for cover, and leave me knowing that my world has been officially rocked. And guess what? You look like a world rocker to me."

He jerked his head back, and something hot flared in those blue eyes. Slowly he peeled his shirt off, exposing the broad expanse of his muscular chest.

"Forget it. I don't want your damn shirt. Maybe I'll walk all the way back to the inn naked." That sounded childish even to her own ears.

"I didn't take it off for you, sweetheart." He flung the shirt away from him.

Startled out of her bad temper, Kisa stilled.

"Okay, maybe I didn't word that right, because I *did* take it off for you. Just like I'm taking everything else off for you." Standing, he stepped away from her, got rid of his boots, and then unbuttoned his jeans.

Kisa's eyes widened. It was really going to happen. Right here on the forest floor among the sticks and other prickly things littering the ground, and with a million mosquitoes feasting on their bare bodies.

Not even bothering to turn away from her, he yanked off his jeans and briefs. Could full-frontal nudity blind her? If so, her last sight would be one worthy of taking into the darkness.

She knew the glory of his broad chest and shoulders, knew the temptation of smooth skin stretched over hard muscle, but the perfection of the whole sucked all the breath from her lungs. His ridged stomach drew her gaze downward to his strong thighs and legs.

She'd saved the best till last. His sacs hung large and heavy, and his cock rose long and thick between his thighs. He was a hard man in all the ways that counted.

He made her feel . . . She closed her eyes. For just a moment, she'd felt self-conscious, maybe even a little vulnerable. Not emotions she'd expect. She'd seen male bodies before. But not *his* body. And there was something in the way he looked at her that made her aware of her nakedness and all that she hoped would happen between them. He was the catalyst. He made her aware of herself as a woman, not as a werecat with an unfortunate alter ego.

She opened her eyes. Whenever she was unsure of herself, she talked. Maybe he'd be so busy listening to her blab that he wouldn't see the uncertainty in her eyes.

"How about giving me your shirt to lie on. There're a bunch of twigs or something poking me in the back." She wiggled around to demonstrate her discomfort.

Heat flared in his eyes. "Who said you'd be on the bottom?" But he turned around and bent over to pick up his shirt.

"Oh, my God. Would you do that again?" He had an incredible butt. Strong, masculine cheeks that were so *there* they could bring tears to a woman's eyes.

He tossed her the shirt before lowering himself to lie on his side next to her.

She sat up and spread the shirt under her. All ready. But her mouth didn't think so. It kept on flapping. "I guess I should say something sexy now. Jeez, I don't know what's happening in the sexy-talk world. What about . . ." She wasn't sure about this, but she might as well give it a try. "Do me." She looked hopefully at him. "Do me? Maybe that wasn't a great choice. I mean, it's not too specific. It could mean scratch my back, or rub my feet." It was now official. She couldn't control her mouth or her cat. "What do you think would be a sexy thing to say?"

He leaned over her, his sensual mouth so close that if she stuck out her tongue, she could taste his lips. "Shut up, Kisa." And then he covered her mouth with those sexy lips.

Chapter Six

He was probably making one of the biggest mistakes of his life, but he didn't give a damn. Her mouth was warm, wet, and welcoming. She parted her lips for him, and he explored her mouth's sweetness.

Kisa tasted of the forbidden—sex with the enemy. The council would be in his face before dawn if they knew what he had planned for her. Mixing business with pleasure was probably number three hundred on their almighty list of things a Guardian couldn't do. Well, to hell with them.

It would take someone a lot stronger than he to resist those luscious lips and that wild tangle of hair begging for his fingers. *Yo, your common sense interrupting for a commercial break. She's a virgin. Virgins have expectations. You've never lived up to anyone's expectations. Leave her alone.*

Uh-huh. Like he was going to listen to the voice of his common sense. He was too far gone.

Reinn abandoned her lips to nibble a path down

the side of her neck. He paused to circle the spot with his tongue where her life force beat a rhythm of seduction. An erotic bull's-eye.

She made a little sound of pleasure. "Mmm. Your mouth on my body makes me feel all tight inside, like if you touch one more place I'll explode into a million pieces and have to spend the rest of my life searching for all of me. Don't stop. It'll be worth the search."

Kisa was quick to qualify that statement, though. "Warning. Sink your fangs into my neck, and my cat will leave permanent teeth marks on your magnificent butt." Her smile was slow and sexy as hell. "But the nibbling's excellent." She slid her palm over his jaw and traced his bottom lip with the tip of her finger. "Nibbling makes me want to do things to you."

"What kind of things?" Reinn grinned. "Whips, chains, honey, feathers? The possibilities are endless"—he paused to kiss the smooth skin above the swell of her breast—"and endlessly arousing."

She might be in human form, but her eyes gleamed in the darkness. Cat eyes. "Honey? I think warmed chocolate would be a lot more sensual. I'd spread it all over you here." She reached between them and circled the head of his cock with the tip of her fingernail.

He sucked in his breath. He'd told her he wasn't a slow and gentle kind of guy, but he was trying. She wasn't making it easy, though.

"Then I'd lick it all off. Yummy." Her voice a husky purr, she closed her fingers around him.

"Jeez, woman, you're killing me." He'd last all of five minutes unless he slowed down the action. Not giving her a chance to argue, he rolled onto his back and pulled her on top of him. "There. Now you won't have twigs sticking you in the back."

Kisa stared down at him, her eyes luminous, her position wanton as she straddled him with thighs spread. Her long hair framed the face of an angel, but that face lied. She slid the tip of her tongue across her bottom lip, tempting him. Then she arched her back, drawing attention to her full breasts with nipples hard and begging for his mouth. Yeah, this position was really going to slow the action.

"Having a naked man at my mercy has always been a favorite fantasy." Her smile turned teasing. "And here you are. I get to touch, stroke, and lick whatever I want."

He suppressed a groan. No use in encouraging her, because if she did any of the things she'd just mentioned, it'd be all over for him. "Ditto for me, sweetheart."

To emphasize his point, he buried his fingers in her long hair and drew her down to him. Her scent of cool pines and heated desire drew a growl from him. He circled one sexy pink nipple with his tongue. And even as he saw her shiver in reaction, he closed his lips over it—flicking it with his tongue, nipping and sucking. She moaned her appreciation.

"I imagined what it would feel like, but I was so far off I wasn't even in the same galaxy." She tightened her thighs and pressed down hard against his swollen cock.

He felt the damp readiness of her. Now it was his turn to moan. He transferred his mouth to her other nipple, but at the same time he lifted his hips to increase the pressure. The incredible pleasure-pain would end only when he buried himself deep inside her. But for now he'd suffer the anticipation.

Kisa wasn't so deeply lost in her own pleasure that she forgot her plans for his body. She flattened her palms on his chest and rubbed in a circular pattern, evidently enjoying the tactile sensation of flesh against flesh. He sure knew he was enjoying it. When she rolled his nipple between her thumb and forefinger, he jerked and gasped.

She leaned over him, her soft, shining hair trailing a searing path across his chest and stomach. And when she leaned even lower, her nipples scraped across his chest, leaving heat and desire and an unquenchable hunger for her body—a hunger he couldn't completely satisfy, since fangs were out, but one he was still sure would turn him into a glowing pile of orgasmic dust. He wanted her that much.

Straightening, she flung back her hair, and her breathing quickened, lifting her glorious breasts, which gleamed softly with a thin sheen of sweat. He smoothed his fingers over her stomach and along the outside of her thighs. Then he traced the spot where she pressed hard against his cock. She responded by rubbing back and forth, back and forth over his arousal. The friction of flesh against flesh drove him crazy. The heat she was generating spiraled to every nerve ending that had anything at all to do with sexual pleasure. Right now that included just about every inch of his body.

Enough. He'd reached his slow-and-gentle limit. He was ready for hard and fast. Had he lasted more than five minutes? Probably not. When had he wanted a woman so much that he couldn't even last five freakin' minutes? Try never.

But he couldn't take her with his brain fogged by sexual need. He might lose control and hurt her. That would be a titanic turnoff for her first time, no matter how much she claimed to want this.

Besides, a horrible realization had just slipped into his sex-obsessed brain: he didn't have any damn protection. Sure, he could tell her he couldn't get her pregnant or give her a disease, but she'd still worry about it once the passion ended, still wonder if he was telling the truth. Women seemed to have this sense that identified predators, and they made him every time. Women didn't trust predators. Smart.

Great. He could see a crappy ending for him. But it didn't have to be a total loss for her. Without explanation, he lifted her off him, moved so that his shirt was free, and laid her back on it. Then he nudged her legs apart and knelt between them.

Kisa glared up at him, her eyes flashing outrage, her lips, swollen from his kisses, looking sexy as hell as she pouted. "Who gave you the right to do that? I was way into the queen-of-the-mountain thing. I was sitting on the mother lode, for heaven's sake."

Reinn took a deep breath and lied. "Yeah, but you were doing most of the touching."

Her glare grew fiercer. "And your point is?"

"This is your first time. Let me touch you as you should be touched." He leaned over and swirled his tongue inside her navel.

"Oh." Her eyes widened and her stomach muscles tightened. Her glare faded.

"Making your body come alive would give me pleasure." Not as much pleasure as he'd get if he could slide deep inside all that heat and wetness, but pleasure all the same. His cock was pissed off, but he calmed it with promises of another time. Surprisingly, he knew he'd want this woman over and over again—a dangerous precedent in his line of work, but he'd worry about that later.

She smiled at him, an intimate smile between lovers, and guilt touched him when he remembered why he was really here.

"Knock yourself out, but I think my body's about as alive as it's going to get." She stretched, not trying to hide her enjoyment of the sexual adventure.

Kisa Evans was made for love and . . . No, *love* wasn't in his vocabulary. He might not be able to give her love, but he could compensate with tons of erotic play.

He kissed a path down her stomach even as he rubbed the pads of his thumbs over her nipples. There was nothing kittenish or sweet about her purr. It was rasping and rough with passion, and he could hear the tiger beneath it.

"Are we there yet?" Her laughter was husky with need. "Jeez, I sound like a little kid riding in the backseat."

"No. We have to take a few detours first." He pushed her thighs farther apart, and she bent her knees as she complied.

Still kneeling, he slipped his hands beneath her bottom and shifted her toward him. Her sweet cheeks filling his palms gave him a tactile rush. Side-tracked for a moment, he indulged himself by kneading the firm flesh of her ass. He'd give that particular part of her body more attention next time.

He quickly rejected the thought that if he had any decency there wouldn't be another time. He'd fight that battle with his conscience when he had a clear head and his cock wasn't dictating terms.

Lingeringly, he slid his tongue up the inside of first one thigh and then the other, teasing as he stopped just short of where she wanted him to be.

"You're a cruel man." She spoke between pants. "Do you need a damned sign? 'Vacancy: inquire within'? Don't make me wait any longer or I'll . . . Well, I'll do something we'll both regret."

He laughed softly. "I love surprises. Maybe I'll keep you panting and wanting so I can find out what evil act you'll come up with. Vengeful women excite me." Reinn leaned back on his heels and then pulled her tightly against him so that she was resting on his lap with her legs spread wide, her sex open to him. Her bottom rested on his rock-hard erection, a special kind of torture for him.

When he put his mouth on her, she screamed. Not a high-pitched shriek, but a low, guttural sound that was so sexual he almost lost it and replaced his mouth with his cock.

103

He slid the tip of his tongue back and forth over the small nub of supersensitive flesh in a motion he knew would push her to the brink. She writhed against him, lost in her pleasure. When he finally slid his tongue into her and began the in-and-out motion that mimicked his cock, she dug her fingers into the dirt and lifted her hips to pick up the rhythm of sex.

Her breathing came hard and fast; her cries grew more frantic, until she finally bucked and shouted his name as her climax rocked her.

He lowered her to the ground with hands that shook. Even though he was so hard he didn't know if he could walk, her release had touched him on a level he hadn't expected. He wasn't one for second-hand orgasms, but he'd been with her at the end. An unusual reaction for him, because he was always about his own pleasure.

When he'd controlled the shaking, he looked down at her. Her eyes were glazed, and she seemed a little disoriented.

"I don't know whether to kiss you or belt you. Words can't even describe what I felt, but as incredible as it was, I'm still a virgin." She pushed her hair away from her face and stared back at him. Her gaze was more focused now. "Why?"

He shrugged. "No protection. And maybe I decided you deserved somewhere more special than on the ground among the pine needles and bugs."

"Bugs?" She sat up with a jerk, her eyes wide and fearful. "Where?" She brushed at herself. "Get them off me."

He grinned. "You're kidding, right? You turn into almost five hundred pounds of killing machine and you're afraid of bugs?"

She scowled at him. "Yes." Her expression said, *Don't mess with my phobia.*

Okay, he'd leave her alone for now, but who would've guessed that a little spider could send her fleeing? He'd have to remember that.

Reinn thought he'd better clear up the protection thing before she asked. "No, I can't give you a child, and no, I don't carry diseases, but you'd be uneasy once the sexual glow wore off."

Kisa wasn't sure whether to hang on to her mad or not. He was right about the protection, though. Even at the moment she'd thought life as she knew it would end if he didn't push deep into her, she'd realized they hadn't taken precautions. Would she have had the will to stop him if he'd tried to enter her? She'd like to think so. And he'd given her the most spectacular physical experience of her life. But she'd wanted more. She'd wanted to feel him inside her, filling her, completing her.

Whoa, there. Completing her? She didn't need a man to complete her. All she wanted from Daniel Night was . . . What? Things were a little confused in her head right now. Once she was alone, she'd figure everything out. But first: "Thanks for giving me the confidence to lose control."

"Confidence?" He looked puzzled.

She watched as he pulled his jeans over those hard thighs and harder erection. It looked painful, but she felt a twinge of satisfaction knowing she'd made him that way. Too bad he wouldn't let her help with his release, but she sensed that wasn't an option now. Lord, he was a beautiful man. But she knew he'd hate it if she told him so.

"I've spent my whole life afraid to lose control of any situation because losing control could trigger the change. I knew you could handle my cat, so I felt free to lose myself in the moment. Simple." Not so simple. He had no idea what it felt like to finally be able to put her cat in someone else's care.

He didn't get a chance to reply. Suddenly he froze in the act of handing her his shirt.

"What?" She glanced around her. Werecats had enhanced senses even in human form. Those senses weren't picking up anything. But she slipped into his shirt just in case. *Mmm.* His scent of wild, dark places and aroused male took her breath away.

"Someone's coming." He buttoned his jeans, slipped into his shoes, and then reached out to pick twigs and leaves from her hair.

His action warmed her. It said he cared what people thought of her. Kisa could've told him she didn't give a damn if anyone knew she'd been with him. She, for one, was proud of it. The werecat community might disapprove of her hooking up with a vampire, but they couldn't deny he was stronger than she was.

Sure enough, a few seconds later she picked up the sound of someone drawing near. Whoever it was, he or she didn't have a clue how to move through the forest silently. Or maybe the newcomer just didn't care.

How amazing were Daniel's senses that he could hear what a werecat couldn't? What else could he do better than she? Kisa allowed herself a small, secret smile. She had proof of at least one thing.

She'd just finished buttoning Daniel's shirt when Felicia burst into view. For the first time since meeting the wedding planner, Kisa saw Felicia without every hair in place. Instead of her usual business suit, she wore jeans and a light jacket, despite the warm Jersey night. Wild-eyed, she looked around until she spotted Kisa and Daniel.

Felicia drew in a deep breath and stared. "Thank God. I was so afraid. I was driving back from town when I saw the wrecked car, with Julie kneeling beside Alan. Of course I stopped. Alan mumbled something about you running into the forest. I don't think he was too coherent, poor dear."

The wedding planner frowned. "Julie's dress was torn apart. She could barely hold it together. She said something about a fire and how both you and she had to rip off your clothes because they were smoldering. How awful."

Thank you, Julie. The excuse might not hold up under close scrutiny, but Kisa gave her sister full credit for coming up with anything under the circumstances.

"Julie wasn't too clear about where you'd gone, but I could see the crushed undergrowth. It was pretty easy to follow you. I didn't know you were with Daniel." Felicia didn't sound too thrilled to see him. *Strange.*

"Let's head back to the car." Daniel rested his

arm across Kisa's shoulders, lending his support. "Kisa got a little panicky, but she's fine now."

Felicia slapped at the mosquitoes. "Wretched insects. Aren't they driving you guys crazy?" She started back the way she'd come, not waiting to see if they followed.

Up until that moment, Kisa hadn't noticed the mosquitoes. Amazing how a great orgasm could block out everything. Now she swatted the blood-thirsty minimonsters away. She'd be an itchy mess by the time she got back to the inn. She glanced at Daniel. He was shirtless, his body unmarked by bites, his hard, muscular torso free of small stinging terrors.

Kisa mouthed, *how?*

He grinned and shrugged. But suddenly the mosquitoes abandoned her. Daniel evidently didn't care about Felicia, because she continued slapping and complaining all the way back to the road.

Once in sight of the car, Kisa felt Daniel tense. She looked around for the reason. Trees, trees, and more trees. Alan was on his feet, and Julie hovered next to him. There were serious perks to being a vampire. No lingering effects from cars rolling on you, for one.

A man stood next to Alan. Kisa recognized him from the inn. He kept to himself, but his spectacular looks made it hard for him to fade into the woodwork. She'd never caught his name.

She could still feel tension flooding Daniel as they joined the group at the side of the road.

Felicia huffed as she brushed twigs and pine needles off herself. "Well, since everyone seems okay, I'll be on my way. Do you need a lift back to the inn?"

Julie smiled her thanks. "We appreciate the offer, but Mason said he'd drive us back. He called a tow truck, so we'll leave as soon as it comes."

So the new guy was Mason. Kisa watched Felicia climb into a white Civic and drive away. Not the car their attacker had driven. It'd been too dark and everything had happened too fast for her to ID the vehicle, but she knew the car had been dark-colored and larger. Sort of like Mason's car. She narrowed her gaze on the newcomer.

Daniel stuck his hand out to Mason. "Daniel Night. I don't think we've met."

The man's smile was a slash of white in the moon's dim light, and his dark eyes gleamed with wicked humor that didn't dispel her impression that he'd make a deadly enemy. He shook Daniel's hand. "Mason Clark. I've been at the inn for about a week. I like paranormal stuff." He nodded at the wreck. "As soon as I saw the car, I stopped to see if I could help." His gaze slid past Daniel to Kisa, but he made no comment about her impromptu outfit.

Daniel's eyes were cold. "Haven't seen you in any of the discussion groups. Something in particular interest you?" Nothing in his expression indicated anything but idle curiosity, but Kisa suspected Daniel had a reason for his question.

"Vampires." Mason's smile was easy, relaxed, but Kisa sensed that was only surface charm. Something dark moved beneath his friendly smile. "I've always had a thing about them. And you?"

Daniel's smile widened, but his eyes got even colder, if possible. "Hey, me too. Vampires fascinate me. We'll have to get together and compare notes."

Kisa shivered. The tension rolling off the two men was as suffocating as the fog beginning to drift across the road and wind among the dark tree shadows.

She looked at Mason again—really looked this time. Up until now she'd been wrapped up in Daniel and what had happened in the woods.

In his own way, Mason was as spectacular as Daniel. He was dressed for comfort in jeans and a sleeveless T-shirt. The two were about the same height, and both were broad-shouldered and muscular. Both had dangerous auras about them. But where Daniel's dark hair and in-your-face masculinity suggested controlled violence, Mason's tangled shoulder-length blond hair and wickedly exotic brown eyes gave the impression of wild recklessness. She didn't think it would be smart to mess with either man.

As the tow truck hooked up to Alan's car, Kisa climbed in the backseat of Mason's vehicle with Daniel and Julie. Alan lowered himself gingerly into the passenger seat beside Mason. Evidently the groom-to-be was still feeling the effects of being squished by his car.

Daniel looked at her expectantly as Mason turned his car around and headed back toward the inn. Kisa sniffed. No hint of catnip. She shook her head at Daniel. Mason wasn't the culprit, because if he'd been guilty, some catnip residue would've remained in his car, and her enhanced sense of smell would've picked it up. Good thing, because one whiff of catnip and Mason would have had a five-hundred-pound problem in his backseat.

Daniel nodded and then put his arm across her shoulders. He pulled her against his side and she rested her head on his shoulder. Wearily, she closed her eyes. The change always took a lot out of her, and the catnip stalker worried her.

What kind of motive could her attacker have? If he just wanted a one-of-a-kind trophy, killing her while she was in her cat form wouldn't work. When werecats died in their animal form, they immediately reverted to human again. No saber-tooth head above anyone's mantel. So what, then? She'd put that question aside for later.

But beyond the stalker, she couldn't stop thinking about the wonder of what Daniel had given her. Even if he left tomorrow, she wouldn't regret tonight. She almost hoped Sparkle was right that hooking up was always about lust, because she had a sinking feeling that if she let it become anything else, Daniel would walk away with more than her virginity.

She sighed and let all the unanswered questions drift away.

When they finally reached the inn, Reinn felt a strange reluctance to move. Kisa had fallen asleep with her head on his shoulder, and he hated to admit it, but he enjoyed the unfamiliar feeling of closeness to another person. And somehow it was a little harder tonight to call up the mantra of his crappy job—to stay uninvolved.

Mason parked the car and climbed out. Julie opened her door, got out, and then helped Alan up. Reinn couldn't sit there forever. Exhaling deeply, he touched Kisa's face. "Time to wake up, princess."

She raised her head and blinked at him. He pushed a few strands of hair away from her face.

"I'm sorry; I didn't mean to fall asleep." She blinked tiredly as she allowed Reinn to help her from the car.

Reinn glanced at Mason. He was about to ask the other man to send Kisa and Julie's mom out with some clothes when the inn's door was flung open and Helen Evans rushed out with two robes draped over her arm.

She stopped in front of her daughters, her eyes wide with concern. "Felicia told us you had an accident. She said you'd need something to wear. I brought your robes. Put them on. We'll go in the back door and hope we don't meet anyone on the way to your rooms."

Helen glanced at Mason. Reinn knew she was dying to question her daughters but didn't want to say anything in front of a stranger.

Reinn looked at Mason. "Let's go inside and get a drink. I think we need it." Mason nodded and went inside ahead of him.

As Reinn started to follow him, Alan put a hand on his shoulder. "Hey, man, thanks for what you did tonight. I didn't make you as vampire at first, and I guess that's the way you wanted it. But I owe you for saving my butt and for keeping Kisa safe."

"No problem." Damn, he wished Alan would act like a jerk so he could feel a little better about that sword hidden in the woods.

Reinn was getting way too involved with this family, and to stay alive in his job he needed to be coldly dispassionate. He should be trying to talk Alan out of marriage, but right now, with Julie's response when she'd thought Alan might die fresh in his mind, he couldn't.

Alan glanced at the tow truck. "Look, I've gotta take care of the driver. If there's any way I can pay you back, just say it."

Don't marry Julie so I won't have to take your head. "You would've done the same thing in my place. You don't owe me anything." Reinn turned and went into the inn.

As he walked toward the parlor, he stored away a couple of random thoughts for future mulling. Felicia had charged into the forest after Kisa. Why? They weren't friends. What did she think would happen to Kisa in the woods? Mason, on the other hand, had stayed with Alan and Julie. He'd called for a tow truck but hadn't felt the need to find Kisa. Nothing particularly suspicious there. But Reinn had stayed alive for centuries because he was always suspicious.

He found Mason waiting for him in the parlor. Reinn dropped onto the chair across from him. The other man didn't even give Reinn a chance to get comfortable before he attacked.

"You're not human. What are you?" Mason studied him with unblinking intensity.

Even now, when he was dead serious, Reinn sensed a reckless humor lurking just below what Mason was saying. There was something about the man's eyes that triggered a long-ago memory, but Reinn couldn't place where or when. He leaned back in the chair. "You don't waste any time, do you? Since you're no more human than I am, I don't see where you get off asking questions."

Whatever Mason had planned to say went unsaid as Ganymede joined them. *"Had to get rid of the taste of those damn turnips with some chocolate cake. Be glad you guys don't eat food. Sparkle can't do much to mess with your drink of choice. She'll kill all of us before she's done."*

Reinn didn't know whether to grin or curse. "Anyone ever call you on your big mouth, cat? What if Mason didn't want me to know he was a vampire? You just blew his cover." *Mine too.*

Ganymede's amber eyes turned sly. *"What's the secret? I'm a cosmic troublemaker; you guys are vamps; we have were-everythings here, plus a real pissant of a harpy. We're all just one big happy dysfunctional family."* He stared at Reinn. *"Aren't we?"*

Reinn shrugged. "Whatever you say. So what do you want?" Ganymede always had an angle. He wasn't here for just a friendly chat.

Mason stared blankly at Ganymede. He didn't look like he was about to add to the conversation anytime soon.

"See those three vamps sitting over in the corner?" He

nodded his head in their direction. *"Something's not right with them. They've been here a week and haven't left the inn once. We don't stock blood, so where're they getting their nourishment, hmm? You guys are vamps. Bond with them. Find out what their game is. I could read their minds, but I've already done some of that trying to find out who's planting the catnip. Don't want to upset them by getting into their heads too often."*

"And I'll do this, why?" Reinn thought he knew, but he just wanted Ganymede to verify his suspicions.

Amusement glinted in Ganymede's cat eyes. *"Because we're best friends and know each other's secrets."*

"Got it." Blackmail. Why was he not surprised? If word got out that he was the Guardian, everything would blow up in his face.

"I'm *not* your best friend, so why should I talk to them?" Mason had found his voice.

Ganymede flicked a few cake crumbs from his whiskers with one gray paw. *"I don't have to be your friend to know your secrets. And you have a biggie, bloodsucker."*

"You don't know anything about me." Mason didn't sound as confident as his words suggested.

"Sure I do. Want to test your theory?" Ganymede sounded eager.

Mason subsided. Score one for Ganymede. If the cat was bluffing, he was doing a damn good job of it.

"Both of you have tons of power, so maybe you could sort of work together to make sure things run smoothly when I'm busy doing something else." He gazed past Reinn.

Yeah, like eating. "We'll talk to the vampires."

Ganymede stood and stretched. *"See, that wasn't so hard, was it? Oh, and I think Trouble is looking for you, Daniel."*

Resigned, Reinn followed Ganymede's gaze to see the dog trotting toward him. Trouble planted his behind beside Reinn's chair and greeted him with a happy woof. *Great. Just freakin' great.*

Chapter Seven

"Who the hell is he, and what was that all about?"
Mason didn't look amused now, and Reinn could
see the reckless anger pushing at him.

"Someone you don't want to cross." Reinn was
just ticked off enough at Ganymede to not give a
flip what he wanted Mason to know about him.
"Like Ganymede told you, he, Sparkle, and Trouble
are cosmic troublemakers. They spread chaos
throughout the universe in a lot of different ways.
Sparkle's specialty is interfering in people's sex lives.
Trouble is too young to have a specialty yet. And
Ganymede? He's older than dirt and has more
power than any one being should have. Don't let his
good-old-boy act fool you. He's dangerous."

Mason nodded, and the humor returned to his
eyes. "Guess we'd better introduce ourselves to
those vamps or else Ganymede will reveal all our
dark secrets." The humor faded for a moment.
"Does he really know things, or was he bluffing?"

Reinn stared down at Trouble, who was busy

scratching a flea. "Ganymede knows things he has no right knowing. Thrain, the husband of the woman who owns this inn, told me Ganymede can move through time and space. So I guess he can go back and check up on our pasts. For that matter, he can check our futures, too. Scary." He looked at Mason and grinned. "By the way, Trouble is Sparkle's snitch. So don't say anything you don't want carried back."

Trouble paused in his scratching to peer up at Reinn. *"What? Were you talking to me? Did you say something important? Will you say it again? Sparkle yells when I don't hear stuff."*

Mason laughed and Reinn joined in, for the moment forgetting his suspicions about the other vampire. He caught himself, though, when he remembered that Mason was hiding something. Secrets could kill. And Mason had to be pretty old if he was able to keep Reinn from making him. With vampires, old translated to powerful most of the time.

Together they walked over to where the three vampires were seated and joined them. The two men and one woman didn't seem too welcoming. Humans who thought all vampires had *beautiful* written into their genes hadn't gotten a look at these three. They all looked like they'd been whacked with an ugly stick. Still, Reinn knew better than to judge by a person's face. Quickly skimming their surface thoughts before they realized he was in their heads, he came up with *nada*. No hearts of gold. Too bad. They really needed something to compensate for those faces.

Mason showed them the easy smile that would've fooled most people. "Hey, we saw you guys sitting over here by yourselves and thought we'd introduce ourselves. I'm Mason Clark, and this is Daniel Night. Daniel and I are into vampires. Someone told us you had lots of secret vampire info."

The woman sniffed. "Humans." She said it with the same tone of voice she'd use for *snail slime*. "What do they know? We are dachnavars, and your tiny human minds could never comprehend what powers we wield."

Reinn blinked and tried to look dumb. "Wow, that sounds cool. What do, uh, dachshunds do?"

Beside him, Mason choked and covered it with a cough. Reinn fought back laughter. How many centuries had it been since he'd laughed with another man? Too many to count. He'd shared misery and death with the men who'd fought beside him in battles, but they hadn't done much laughing together. There wasn't ever much to laugh about.

"*Dachnavars*," one of the men hissed. "We're Armenian vampires."

Mason looked intrigued. "Never heard of Armenian vampires. When I get back to my office in Philly, I'll have to tell all the guys that I met . . ." He waited for them to supply names.

The other man complied grudgingly. "I'm Levon, she's Voskie, and he's Zaven."

Reinn's turn to play the dumb ass. "Have you sucked anyone's blood since you've been here?" He hoped his expression of avid curiosity was convincing. "I know this place is supposed to be like a sanctuary. No biting or sucking. But you guys have to keep your strength up, you being so powerful and all."

Levon—or was it Zaven?—mellowed a little. "We have not done so yet, but our need grows great. We will feed soon."

Voskie gave him a death glare and he shut up.

Reinn decided they'd gotten all they were going to get from the three. "Well, have to walk the dog. It was great meeting you. Wasn't it great, Mason?"

"Great." Mason was still fighting to keep a straight face.

Voskie's expression turned sly. "The werecat, Kisa, is your woman?"

Reinn stilled. "We're friends."

She smiled. "Many people are interested in her."

Okay, he needed to tread carefully here. "You mean her family?"

"No." Voskie glanced away.

"And?" Reinn wanted to shake her until her fangs fell out.

Voskie shrugged. "I do not wish to say anything else. Perhaps at another time I'll tell more." She offered him a meaningful stare. "Important information is worth much to those who desire it." Dramatic pause. "And also to those who wish it kept secret."

"Cut the crap. What do you know, and how much will it cost me?" Reinn hoped Voskie realized he was showing her his friendly side. Push him and she'd see how unfriendly he could get.

120

"I will say nothing more tonight." Voskie's gaze skittered to her friends. They quickly looked away. No support there. "Maybe I was only joking." Suddenly she seemed to remember who was vampire and who was human. "Bah! Humans understand nothing."

Reinn pushed at her mind. He didn't give a damn whether she realized what he was doing or not. Her startled expression told him she'd felt him. She immediately blocked his probe. He was strong enough to blast past her defenses, but she'd be too panicked now to have anything in her mind but fear. He'd have to wait until she was relaxed and unsuspecting.

Mason touched his shoulder. "The dog is getting restless. Better walk him now."

Reinn nodded and strode away from the three. He stood at the door with Mason and Trouble. "They'd be smart not to play games with me." He rolled his shoulders to relieve the tension.

"Think they're going to sell their info to the highest bidder?" Mason stared at Trouble, while Trouble tried to avoid meeting his gaze.

The dog looked guilty for things he hadn't even done yet. "Maybe. I'll keep an eye on them. They might just be trying to play up their own importance." Reinn glanced at Mason.

"You going to tell me what's going on with Kisa?" Mason continued to watch Trouble.

"That's not my place." Reinn belatedly remembered that he didn't know anything about this man. "Come on, Trouble; let's go for that walk."

He nodded at Mason and then walked into the night.

"There're some humans in the woods pretending to be werewolves. Can I chase them? Can I, can I?" Trouble's tongue lolled out in a happy doggy grin.

"Knock yourself out, pup." He was in the mood to scare the hell out of someone. And then afterward he'd go back to his room, get on his laptop, and find out more about the dachnavars.

Kisa lay in bed with her eyes closed and enjoyed the feeling of being rested and worry-free for the moment. She knew the worries would come crashing down on her soon enough, but in these few minutes right after waking, she was still in a drowsy state of not caring.

She smiled lazily. Kisa didn't remember any specific dreams, but she knew Daniel had left his footprints all over them.

Daniel. Her mom hadn't given her a chance to say good-night to him before hustling Julie and her off to their rooms. Once Helen had finished talking the catnip problem to death and left her alone, Kisa had fallen asleep and stayed dead to the world the rest of the night and into the afternoon. If she shifted more often, she'd build up some stamina. She had to work with Daniel on her control. Kisa thought about last night in the woods. *In all things.*

Because no matter how much she wanted to lose her virginity, she had to be more careful. Last night she'd let the lingering primal instincts of her cat along with her own desire for Daniel lead her down a dangerous path. The bottom line was that she'd been ready to make love to a vampire she knew nothing about with hardly a thought about protection, sexual or otherwise. Really smart. Too bad *smart* didn't have anything to do with her feelings for him.

Sudden pounding on her door dispelled her feeling of well-being. Maybe if she pulled the sheet over her head the person would go away.

"Kisa, this is Sparkle. Time to rise, shine, and get sexy." The pounding continued.

Kisa struggled out of bed and to the door, all the while fantasizing about changing into her saber-tooth form just as she opened it. Ha, that would teach Sparkle to mess with her morning. Okay, afternoon.

She opened the door and Sparkle swept past her wearing silky black pants, a silky black halter top, and metallic leather wedge sandals. Her red hair fell around her face in carefully arranged disarray, and her amber eyes had an unholy gleam.

"No bitching, Kisa. This is important stuff. And yes, coffee is on its way." Sparkle laid the clothes she'd been carrying on the bed and dropped the shoes to the floor. She set a small case she'd tucked under her arm on the bureau.

"Do we have to do this now?" Kisa already knew the answer, but she had to ask for form's sake.

Sparkle raised questioning brows. "If not now, when? As much as I'd love to think you came back to the inn last night wearing Daniel's shirt because he ripped your clothes from your body, sadly I know it was simply that you shifted without removing your clothes first."

"And how do you know that?" Curious in spite of herself, Kisa picked up Sparkle's outfit.

"I read minds like crazy. How else?" Obviously cosmic troublemakers had no code of ethics.

"These clothes are—"

"Too sexy for their threads, right?" Sparkle beamed. "I absolutely love the high back and low waist of these Juicy jeans. You're a booty girl, and these jeans hug your derriere without flattening it. Men love something they can hang on to during those passionate moments."

"I guess so, but—"

"Speaking of things men can hang on to, don't you just love this little pink bra? It looks so innocent. Men love the innocent-wanton look. You wear this white shirt over it."

Kisa was doubtful. "That bra's awfully little, and there's a lot of me. And the shirt doesn't even come close to my waist. It doesn't have any buttons, and it's too short to tie, so—"

Sparkle sighed. "You are so not tuned in to what your sexual self is trying to tell you. We want the bra to frame you, not gobble you up. If you have it, flaunt as much as is legally allowed. And the shirt is meant to hang open, sort of a flirty tease." She narrowed her eyes at Kisa. "And don't even think about wearing panties."

Kisa narrowed her eyes right back at Sparkle. "My bottom, my choice." She frowned at the four-inch heels on the sandals Sparkle had brought. *Ouch*. She might never walk again. "Why do all your shoes give me nosebleeds?"

"Because heels make a woman's legs look long, lean, and sexy." She spoke slowly, as though she were explaining the alphabet to a small child.

"But I don't need all this. Last night Daniel and I . . ." *Oops. Open mouth, insert foot.*

Sparkle went on point like a well-trained bird dog. Then she relaxed. "Hey, that was a great beginning, but you're still a virgin. We need to get you over that hump." Her smile turned wicked. "Literally. And I'm glad you found out that he's a vampire. One less secret to protect."

"Stay out of my mind. And I don't think—"

"How would I find out things if I stayed out of your mind? And you don't have to think. That's why you have me." Sparkle looked militant. "Sit down."

Surprised, Kisa obeyed. "Now what? Aren't the clothes enough? I'll be crowned Slut Queen of the Woo Woo Inn as soon as I go downstairs."

Sparkle smiled. "Sister, every woman in this place will be tugging her pants lower and unbuttoning her shirt trying to compete. Now stop whining. Your coffee's here."

A little mollified, Kisa waited until the maid had left before grabbing the mug. Holding it with both hands, she thanked the god of coffee beans for the gift of caffeine. After her first few sips she noticed what Sparkle was doing.

"I have a few accessories here." Sparkle rooted

around in the case she'd brought until she found some dangling silver earrings. "Let's give you a little more dramatic look for tonight." She pulled makeup from the case.

Kisa studied the earrings and makeup. "Gypsy isn't a good look for me." She should stop Sparkle, but she had to admit she'd gotten a rush from Daniel's response to Sparkle's last outfit.

"Be quiet and sit still." Sparkle considered her makeup choices.

Enough. Even Kisa's mother knew better than to use that tone of voice on her. "I don't think so. I think you need to put a lid on your box and go cook some turnips."

Sparkle looked startled. Evidently she wasn't used to her victims talking back. She sighed. "All right, what do you want in return for letting me make you beautiful?"

If that comment was meant to make Kisa feel guilty, it didn't. "I want you to let me cook dinner tonight."

"But you don't understand my sensual cooking techniques." Sparkle looked longingly at all her makeup.

"Take it or leave it. I cook dinner and you get to put makeup on me. Fair trade."

"Fine. Cook whatever you want. But don't blame me if it's a sensual disaster." Sparkle unscrewed the tops of tubes with vicious intent. She didn't accept defeat gracefully.

They were well into the makeup session, and

Kisa was watching, amazed, as a sexual temptress took shape in her mirror, when Sparkle spoke.

"You need to cut Daniel some slack when he goes all alpha on you. He's had a tough life." She picked up eye shadow. "Close your eyes."

"What?" Kisa closed her eyes. "Did I miss something? Were we talking about Daniel?" Fine, so she was *thinking* about him.

Sparkle ignored her sarcasm. "The sex will be a lot better if each of you understands where the other is coming from. He pretty much knows all about you, the cat and virginity issues. But what do you know about him? Zip."

Kisa opened her eyes. "Uh-huh. And you're dying to tell me, right?" *And I'm dying to know, right?*

"Of course." Sparkle's eyes glittered with the joy of a dedicated gossip. "He's very old, so he's had a lot of time for bad things to happen to him."

"Like?" Kisa knew she shouldn't be listening to Sparkle tell tales about Daniel's life that he might not want her to hear, but she couldn't help herself. She wanted to know everything about him, and he wasn't about to tell her. She closed her eyes again and waited to hear what Sparkle had to say.

"Daniel's at least a thousand years old, so his childhood village was beyond primitive. When he was about ten, a group of night feeders attacked his home."

Kisa relaxed into the brushstrokes across her closed lids. "Night feeders?"

"They're a loosely organized group of vampires

that travel in packs because they're not as powerful as other vampires. Anyway, they wiped out everyone in the village except Daniel."

"How horrible." Kisa opened her eyes. She'd led a comfortable life surrounded by a loving family. She couldn't imagine how a ten-year-old boy could've survived something so horrific.

Sparkle looked thoughtful. "Yeah. That sort of set him on his path for the rest of his life. He became a mercenary and fought for anyone who'd hire him."

"When did he become vampire?" If harshness and coldness were all he'd known, no wonder he wasn't a social person.

"I think I've told you as much as I should." Sparkle leaned back to study her work. "Seduce him, talk to him, understand him, and see where things take you." She smiled. "If this look doesn't take care of the seducing part, then I'll hand in my troublemaker certificate."

Suspicion touched Kisa. "How do you know all these things about him, and why do you want us to hook up so badly?"

"I'm very old, Kisa, and I know stuff about a lot of humans. I take a personal interest in a few of them. You and Daniel are two of the lucky ones." Sparkle was totally focused on Kisa's lip color now. "Why? Because you two are so wrong for each other, you're right. At least for my purpose. I take it as a personal challenge to bring together people who would never in a million years find each other." She took one last look at Kisa and then began putting her stuff back into her case. "Done. You're perfect."

"But I need to know more about—"

Sparkle smiled her sneaky smile and headed for the door. "Go get him, tiger." And then she was gone.

Well, hell. Now that she'd had a little taste of what made Daniel Night tick, she wanted more. She wanted him to trust her enough to open his heart to her as well as his body.

Heart? Had she thought that? She didn't want his heart. But if he was her ticket out of the state of virginity—and he was—then she wanted to know a little of what lived in his soul. Assuming he had a soul. She did a mental eye roll. Was that hokey or what?

After finishing her coffee, she got dressed. She had a few hours before sunset, so she'd see if her mom had anything for her to do and then plan dinner before Daniel rose.

Deep in thought about Daniel and dinner, Kisa almost ran into a guest. Mrs. Baker was hopping toward the registration desk on one bare foot. The woman was still in her robe, and her eyes were wide with alarm.

Sparkle was sitting at the desk reading *In Style* when Mrs. Baker tottered over to her. Kisa paused to see what the drama was all about.

"What kind of a place are you running, missy?" All of Mrs. Baker's chins wobbled their anger.

Sparkle raised one brow. "Missy?"

129

"A bug bit me while I was sleeping." Mrs. Baker glanced at Kisa to make sure she was a witness to the outrage. "Look at the marks it left." She held up one very large foot. And sure enough, there were two puncture marks on her big toe.

Sparkle put down her magazine to take a closer look. "Oh, gross. Did you put something on it?" She offered Kisa a finger wave.

"Put something on it? I need more than antiseptic and a Band-Aid. I need a tetanus shot. I want someone to drive me to the nearest doctor, and I'll expect the inn to pay. Then I'm checking out." She harrumphed. "And to think I came here to celebrate my divorce."

"Don't be such a baby, Mrs. Baker. It's just a little bug bite. We're in the middle of the woods, for crying out loud. Bugs everywhere. I'll take care of you as soon as I finish this article." Sparkle went back to her magazine.

Kisa smiled. Sparkle might know a lot about sex, but her people skills were nonexistent.

"Is that all you're going to say?" Mrs. Baker was puffing herself up like a frog. "What kind of horrible bug would bite like that? Maybe it's poisonous." She suddenly went pale. "In fact, I do feel a little weak." She collapsed into the nearest chair. "Once I get back to Trenton, you'll hear from my lawyer."

Uh-oh. This would not be a good thing for the inn's owners. "Uh, Sparkle, Mrs. Baker doesn't look well. You might want to drive her to the doctor yourself."

Okay, if Sparkle could read minds, then let her read this. *"Yoo-hoo, Sparkle."*

Sparkle blinked and glanced up at her.

Good, she had her attention. *"Your friends who own this inn are going to be pretty steamed when they come home to a lawsuit. Maybe you should show some concern here. And if you have a bug in this inn that can deliver that kind of bite, then you need an exterminator."*

Sparkle looked startled and then thoughtful. Finally she smiled sympathetically at Mrs. Baker, stood, and came around the desk to kneel beside her. "I'll call Dr. Simpson now, and then Kisa will drive you to her office. I'm so sorry this happened to ruin your stay. We have an exterminator come in every month, but living so close to the forest . . ." She shrugged to indicate that all kinds of mutant insects could crawl in through the cracks between visits.

"Whoa. What will Kisa do?" Maybe she'd heard wrong.

"It won't take you any time at all to drive poor Mrs. Baker to the doctor's office." Sparkle brightened. "And while you're waiting for Mrs. Baker to get her shot, you can pick up what you'll need for dinner. You might want to check the fridge and freezer to see what we have."

Before Kisa had a chance to open her mouth, Sparkle helped Mrs. Baker to her feet and guided her toward the back of the inn. "Aren't we lucky that Cindy had an elevator installed? We'll get you dressed and into the doctor's office in no time."

Kisa closed her gaping mouth. That manipulative witch. She took a couple of deep breaths to calm down. The trip into town wouldn't take her long, and she did need to buy a few things for dinner. Resignedly, she headed for the kitchen.

Chapter Eight

Reinn came downstairs to chaos.

He was already in a bad mood because he'd gotten an e-mail from the council wanting to know if he'd taken care of the Alan Mackenzie problem—their civilized way of asking if he'd whacked Alan yet. His return mail had been way less civilized: *Butt out unless you want to off him yourself. Have I told you lately how much I hate this crappy job?*

But he couldn't ignore the situation for long. It was Tuesday, and the wedding was Saturday. First he'd have to find out if Alan had his sword with him. If not, he'd have to get one for him. Then he'd have to lure him into the woods for the confrontation. Finally he'd have to kill him. That last part sucked big-time, so he wouldn't think about it now.

Reinn had planned his agenda for the night. He'd practice Kisa's cat-control skills with her, and then they'd put their heads together—and possibly other body parts—to see if they could come up with a reason for the catnip attacks.

But already his agenda was shot to hell. Sparkle was standing on the chair behind the registration desk waving wildly at him while a mob of guests shouted and gestured at her. He did *not* want to get involved in whatever this was.

"Daniel, help." Her waving grew more frantic. "I need you."

He thought about bolting, but figured she'd track him down later and make his life a misery. Muttering an expletive, he walked over to see what was up.

"Here he is. Here's the exterminator." Sparkle pointed at him, and everyone turned to stare.

What the . . . No way could she be telling the world that he was the Guardian of the Blood.

"These people have a problem, Daniel." For the first time since he'd met her, Sparkle didn't project *cool* and *in control.*

A skinny old man shook his finger at Reinn. "Look at my toe." He kicked off his shoe and held up his bare foot. There were two puncture marks on his big toe. "I lay in bed all day because I didn't have the energy to get up. It's because of this here bite. If you don't do something, me and the wife are leaving."

The rest of the mob echoed his complaint as they all held up their big toes for him to see. Just what he needed to start his night; a mob of big ugly toes with big ugly bites on them. *Escape.* "Uh, where's Ganymede? He's good at handling this kind of thing."

Sparkle pushed her hair from her face and glared.

"In town getting a Big Mac and a large order of fries. I hope he enjoys them, because that'll be his last meal."

"What about our toes?" The shout came from a small woman who looked like a retired school-teacher until you peered into her eyes. Pure evil.

Sparkle shrugged, smiled weakly, and threw Reinn to the lions. "Beats me. *He's* the exterminator."

Well, hell. Better say something fast. "Unbelievable. How did a bunch of people like you get so lucky?" As they stared at him blankly, he planted the suggestion in their minds that everything he said was true. And also that they were experiencing a wonderful and memorable moment at the Woo Woo Inn. "The world thinks the vampirus toesuckem is extinct, but it's alive and hiding somewhere in this inn. Catch one of those babies and a bug scientist will pay you thousands."

With a collective gasp, the mob fractured and raced in every direction, searching for the elusive vampirus toesuckem. It was sort of like an Easter egg hunt in which the eggs had legs.

Sparkle threw up her hands in disgust. "Great job, hot bod. Now they'll rip Cindy's inn apart looking for a stupid bug."

Reinn shrugged. "You asked for my help. I gave it. At least they're not running for phones to call their lawyers."

Sparkle looked thoughtful. "There's that."

"Vampirus toesuckem?" Kisa's amused voice behind him spun Reinn around.

135

He smiled. "Best I could do in a pinch." Amazing how Kisa could turn a really rotten evening around just by appearing.

Reinn slid his gaze the length of her body. "Wow. I go from a close-up of lots of ugly toes to a beautiful woman. You're so sexy, lady, you make me want to howl."

Her smile lit her up from inside. "Now, see, you just made up for Mrs. Baker."

"Mrs. Baker?" He felt a nudge against his leg, and looked down to see Trouble gazing up at him. *Damn.* When he'd left his room, the dog had still been sacked out at the foot of his bed. He'd hoped for a little more time alone.

Kisa sighed. "The vampirus toesuckem got her, too. She wanted a tetanus shot, so I drove her to the doctor." She looked around. "Could we go out on the porch? There's something I need to talk to you about."

"Sure."

Suddenly Trouble crowded against his leg. *"Uh-oh. Here comes Mason. I gotta go. I'll be under the porch if you want me."* Trouble tucked his tail between his legs and started backing away from the clearly furious vampire. *"Uh, tell him I didn't mean to do it. Sparkle told me to hide under his bed and tell her if he said anything interesting. And . . . well, his shoes were there. Nice soft new shoes. He was on the phone trying to find out about you. Boring. And those shoes were so soft, and shiny, and new, and . . ."* He whimpered as Mason bore down on them. *"Anyway, don't say anything important until I get back. Sparkle says I haven't given her shit.*" With that pronouncement he turned, squeezed past a man going out the door, and was lost in the night.

Mason stopped in front of them. "Where's that no-good excuse for a dog? He chewed up a brand-new pair of shoes. I know he was the one because I could smell him. Besides, he left brown hairs under my bed. I'll kill him." The vampire didn't look amused tonight.

Reinn shrugged. "He took off when he saw you. Get Sparkle to pay for your shoes."

"You smelled him?" Kisa looked puzzled.

"I have a great sense of smell." Mason's expression turned cautious. He glanced at Reinn. "Find out anything about our friends from last night?"

Reinn grinned. "Later." So many secrets. He didn't know what Mason's game was, Kisa didn't know that Mason was a vampire, Mason didn't know that Kisa shifted into a saber-toothed tiger, and neither of them knew he was the Guardian of the Blood. The whole thing would be funny if so much wasn't at stake.

Mason nodded his understanding and drew in a deep breath. "I don't usually lose it like that, but there's something about this place that puts me on edge. I'll go talk to Sparkle."

Reinn watched Mason walk away. So the vampire was trying to check up on him. Interesting. He wouldn't find anything, because Daniel Night didn't exist. But along with everything else, he'd have to keep his eye on Mason Clark.

Things were getting too complicated. If he were smart, he'd take care of Alan as quickly as possible and get out of here. Reinn turned to look at Kisa. She smiled and held the door open for him. He wasn't smart, though. He'd stick around a little longer.

She settled onto the porch swing, and he sat down beside her. "Something weird happened while I was in town."

He reached out to clasp her hand, and even as he did it, he realized this was the first time he'd ever held hands with a woman. He wasn't a hand-holder. He'd always thought it a big waste of touching. If you were going to put your hands on a woman, there were lots of better places to lay them. "Something weirder than Mrs. Baker?"

"Well, Mrs. Baker was weird in a funny kind of way. This was a scary sort of weird." She turned her face toward him, and her soft brown eyes seemed to have a direct link to his. . . .

He'd say *heart*, but that sounded stupid. Besides, it was impossible. He hadn't had a heart for a very long time. More likely the link was to a much more primitive and excitable organ.

"I'd just finished loading the stuff I'd bought at the supermarket into the car when I caught a faint whiff of catnip. It was coming from a car parked with its windows down about half a block away from me."

Reinn frowned. "You didn't . . ."

Kisa shook her head. "You would've been proud

138

of me. I could feel the change breathing down my neck, so I jumped into my car and put all the windows up. Then I sat and concentrated on staying in human form." She squeezed his hand. "It worked."

He felt a pride in her all out of proportion to what he *should* be feeling, which was nothing. "Way to go, tiger lady."

Her laughter was light and skimmed across his mind like a lover's fingers. His sexual self thought that was a great excuse to start pumping blood to appropriate organs. His sexual self didn't need much encouragement to party whenever Kisa was around.

"I began thinking. There must've been a lot of catnip in the car for the scent to carry so far. Loose catnip. It didn't make sense. Most people buy little sealed bags of the stuff for their pets. The car was a big old black Caddy." She leaned closer to him. "I took the license plate number and then waited a while to see if anyone would show up. I finally had to leave. It was time to pick up Mrs. Baker from the doctor's office, and I didn't want to keep her waiting."

"Give me the number." He pulled his cell phone from his pocket. "I know someone who can ID the owner for us. I'll call him tonight, but he won't have the info until tomorrow. I'll tell him to talk to you when he calls."

She nodded and then listened as he made his call. He watched her twirl a few strands of hair around her finger, a nervous gesture, and he got the impression she was trying to work up the courage to ask him something. Once he put his phone away, he sat back and waited.

She took a deep breath and then met his gaze. "Even in my human form, I have some cat characteristics. Curiosity might kill the cat, but satisfaction makes me purr really loud." Kisa smiled, trying to keep it light. "I'd like to know a little about the man who gave me an awesome orgasm. If you'd like to share, I'd like to listen. But if not"—she shrugged—"I'll understand."

Reinn watched her gaze grow uncertain and shift away from him when he didn't answer her right away. She thought he'd refuse her request. He should. Everything he told her could and would be used against him if he killed Alan. *Listen to yourself. When did the word* if *creep into your job description?*

Time for an honest assessment of the situation. He didn't want to take Alan's head. Alan was an okay guy. Reinn didn't see one damn reason why he shouldn't be able to marry Julie. Unlike the council, he didn't think the clan's blood needed to be kept so almighty pure.

He might not know what he was going to do about Alan, but at least he could make Kisa a little happier. And God help him, her happiness was actually starting to mean something to him.

"I'm over a thousand years old. I grew up during a time of primitive savagery. Back then, the clan was Viking. When I was ten, I came back from hunting one night to find my small village wiped out and almost my whole family dead. Most of the men had gone raiding, so those left behind didn't have a chance.

"They burned my family in our home." Members of the clan didn't become vampire until they were almost thirty, so his younger brothers and sisters had still been human. His mother, too, was still human. She'd been twenty-six when she died. "My father was with the men who'd gone raiding. He lived. Then there was Jorund. He was a member of our clan whom my parents had adopted when his own family died in an epidemic." He knew bitterness still lived in his eyes. "We'd sworn to protect Jor, but we didn't. Even though I never found his body, I knew he couldn't have survived. He was only six."

Not even a thousand years could wipe out the sights and emotions of that day. He'd cried, screamed, and cursed. And then he'd put his emotions away forever. Revenge was best served cold, and coldly he'd stalked the night feeders who'd slaughtered his family. He'd been twenty-nine and a vampire when he'd killed the last of them.

"How did you survive?" Her gaze was direct, there was nothing but sincere interest in her eyes.

Good. He didn't want sympathy for something so long past. "Hate kept me alive. Nothing more."

"That's a hard way to live your life." She didn't make it a condemnation, only an observation.

He shrugged. "Only the strongest survive." *Better*

skip the part about the clan settling in Scotland, building a castle, and calling themselves Mackenzies. "I learned how to fight and became a mercenary. I made myself valuable to the ones who hired me, because no one was better at planning and executing stealthy nighttime attacks. I fought, and I lived. Those who hired me are long since in their graves."

"And your father?" She'd moved even closer to him, and now snuggled against his side.

This was what it would be like if he allowed himself to care for a woman. Logic told him that he wasn't living in the same time as when his family died, but logic had nothing to do with his fear. *Fear*. He'd never acknowledged that feeling before.

He'd spent a lifetime fighting, and he knew how little it took to destroy life. If he didn't feel emotion for someone else, he couldn't be hurt when loved ones died or left him. That philosophy had worked for him, and kept him going when others had died of despair.

Like his father. "My father came home to find everyone dead but me. He never said a word, just turned and walked away. I got word years later that he'd died in Scotland." His father had purposely gorged himself on human blood, knowing what it would do to him.

A Mackenzie who took too much human blood became addicted. The blood turned him into a mindless, crazed killer, leaving only one option for the clan. Even insane, the instinct to return to the Mackenzie ancestral home ran strong in all clan members. When his father showed up at the clan castle in Scotland, the Mackenzie on duty fought him and took his head. His father had found peace in his own way.

A way that Reinn would never choose. He'd fight until he was torn and bloody. And even with his last bit of strength, he'd spit in the eye of fate. He glanced at Kisa and smiled. But tonight he wasn't torn or bloody, and life felt pretty good at this moment, with this woman.

Kisa watched his eyes in the darkness and saw the memories of things he hadn't told her. So many secrets. So much sorrow. He'd hate knowing she'd seen even that much of him. "Let's take a short walk before I have to fix dinner. Sparkle gave me permission to cook one meal. It'll be great to eat food that does absolutely nothing for my sex life." She stood, still clasping his hand, not giving him a chance to say no.

He nodded and led her around the inn and down the path to the cemetery. "Let's see what spirits we can scare up tonight."

"Hmm." Kisa thought about the convenient appearance of the first spirit she'd seen. She wondered . . . "You think we'll get lucky twice?"

Laughter lurked in his eyes. Did that happen a lot in his everyday life? Not often enough, she'd guess.

"Could be." He walked in silence for a few minutes. "I told you about *my* childhood. What about yours? Anything I should know?"

She nodded and grinned at him. "I always got my way."

He raised one expressive brow. "Because you were so kind and loving?"

143

"Because I was a little witch. Even though I didn't know exactly what form my cat would take, I did exhibit certain characteristics of that form. I was bossy and aggressive." She smiled sweetly. "I was a brat."

"No." He pretended shock.

"Oh, yes. Just ask my parents. As I matured I learned to control my need to dominate. I couldn't have any fun if no one wanted to play with me." Kisa shrugged. "So here I am now, a perfectly well-adjusted saber-toothed tiger."

His grin was a white flash in the darkness. "What happens when two dominant forces meet?" He stopped as they emerged from among the trees. The old headstones spread out before them.

"This?" She stood on tiptoe and kissed his chin. "If you'll work with me on this, I can get it right."

Smiling, he leaned forward, and she covered his mouth with hers. Wrapping her arms around his waist, she slipped her hands beneath his T-shirt to rub her palms up and down the smooth warmth of his back. He tasted of the night and barely contained desire. More than that, he tasted of unfinished business. Kisa wondered if he'd brought protection with him tonight. *She* certainly had. She wasn't dumb. Along with ground beef and fresh corn, she'd purchased some insurance against future passionate moments fizzling. Not that last night had fizzled exactly.

He deepened the kiss and she forgot about last night. When she explored his mouth with her tongue, he nipped it playfully, and then showed her how a true explorer worked. Wrapping his arms around her, he slid his hand beneath the back of her jeans and cupped her behind, pulling her tightly against his arousal.

An embarrassed woof interrupted their truly mind-blowing kiss. Kisa glanced down at Trouble, who stood, panting, with his tail wagging. She snarled. Trouble's eyes widened, and he edged behind Daniel.

Daniel exhaled sharply and raked his fingers through his hair. "Ran all the way, huh? Shouldn't you have stayed under the porch a little longer? Mason is really pissed."

Trouble stopped wagging his tail and glanced around fearfully. *"I think he's talking to Alan."* He looked at Kisa. *"Sparkle found me under the porch and told me to tell you not to forget about dinner."*

Daniel nodded. "In other words, Sparkle scares you more than Mason."

"You bet." Trouble didn't hesitate.

"Okay, now you've told us, so you can go back to the inn." Daniel was smiling, but Kisa hoped Trouble didn't interpret that as a happy expression.

Trouble cocked his head to stare at Daniel. *"Why should I do what you say?"*

"Because I have bigger teeth than you do." Daniel changed in the time it took for Kisa to take a deep breath. He lifted his lips away from his fangs in a snarl.

Trouble widened his eyes. *"Going right now."* He turned tail and raced back toward the inn.

Kisa would've laughed if his sudden change hadn't sucked all the breath from her lungs. "Wow, you're fast."

Once more in human form, he shrugged. "I'm old, and I practiced a lot." He stared at her.

Uh-oh. She knew what was coming. "I can't practice now. Show me a spirit, and then I have to cook dinner."

A smile lifted the corners of his mouth as a light breeze blew his hair away from his face. Even in just the moonlight, his eyes gleamed a spectacular blue. "Okay, you win this time."

She watched as he turned to face the graveyard. As before, a figure started to materialize. It didn't take long for Kisa to recognize the "ghost" as Sparkle Stardust. She was perched on a tombstone, legs crossed, short black dress riding high on her thighs, filing her nails.

Kisa put her hand over her mouth to keep from laughing.

The spirit glared at Kisa. "I'm amusing you— why? I have tons of things I could be doing— arranging my nail colors in ascending order from hot to spontaneous combustion, exercising to my favorite CD, *Getting It On So You Can Take It Off*, or peering through keyholes to see who's doing it and who isn't."

Kisa found herself answering the apparition. "Okay, so what do you want to tell us?"

"I can say it in two words: Have sex. Lots and lots of sex. Daniel, forget your job and lose that I-am-a-rock attitude. Life is short. Well, maybe not for you. And Kisa, make the most of your opportunities. When you got up from that porch swing, you could've just as easily said, 'Let's take a walk to my bedroom and test my nice soft bed.' I thought cats were supposed to be sly." She sighed dramatically. "So little time, so many dumb people."

"I think that was more than two words." He sounded calm and slightly amused, but Kisa sensed his surprise.

They watched as the apparition slowly faded away.

"Weren't you putting the words in her mouth?" Honestly, Kisa couldn't imagine Daniel coming up with those things for the Sparkle spirit to say. He didn't think in terms of nail color and spying on people's sex lives.

"No. I create the apparition and then I tap into the essence of the apparition's real-life counterpart. Those are words that Sparkle would say. You gotta love a ghost who doesn't pull her punches." He shook his head in admiration.

Kisa frowned, and then realized what she was doing. She was absolutely *not* jealous of a spirit. Then something occurred to her and she gulped. "You mean the first ghost, the one with the bloody hands, is a real woman? And those were things she'd really say?" Kisa wouldn't angle for an intro to *her*.

"Lily? She was real as of ten years ago. Great-looking vampire with a wicked temper. She's gone through hundreds of husbands over the centuries. Very few of them died of old age."

Sheesh, where did his power end? No, she didn't

want to know the answer to that. But she'd reached her weird-stuff limit for the night. She'd just go back to the inn and work out her sexual frustration over a hot stove.

"It's getting late, and I have to start dinner." She reached for his hand, but he put his arm across her shoulders instead and drew her to his side. They walked slowly back toward the inn. "Why was Trouble afraid of Mason?"

She could feel his smile. "Trouble sneaked into his room and chewed up a pair of new shoes."

"Ouch." They'd almost reached the inn. Kisa hated to see their walk end. There had been something both intimate and relaxed between them. "I bet Mason—"

Kisa got no farther. Shrieks, shouts, growls, and roars shattered the silence. The noise came from the pond area. She closed her eyes and took a deep breath. "Not again. You don't think . . . ?"

But he was already moving in the direction of the noise. As she hurried to catch up, she passed the spot where she'd followed him into the forest a few nights ago. She'd never discovered what the man had given him. Whatever it was, Daniel had hidden it before he met her at the pond to help rescue Bernie. She would come back tomorrow while he was sleeping to search. And she refused to recognize the twinge of her conscience. She'd feel guilty afterward.

They reached the pond together.

"Oh, my God." She met Daniel's startled gaze.

Ocypete was at it again. The harpy was flapping

her giant wings frantically as she tried to lift one of the werewolf wannabes into the air. Two lions on the ground wanted a piece of him too. Each lion had attached itself to one of the baggy, furry legs of the man's costume. The tug-of-war was on.

The man shrieked and flailed away with his arms while his fellow "pack" members shook their fists and shouted useless encouragement to him.

Ganymede sat watching the whole thing with a long-suffering expression on his furry face. When he spotted Daniel and Kisa, he padded over to them.

"You know, I should let the harpy have that dumb ass. I was just getting ready to chow down on the last piece of Katie's apple pie I'd hidden away, when one of those fake werewolves ran in screaming for help from Sparkle. She's still pissed at me because I wasn't there when the vampirus toesuckem mob cornered her, so she made me come out here to save his stupid butt. By the way, bloodsucker, I like the way you think on your feet."

"Uncle Ed! Aunt Lucy!" Kisa shouted at the lions. "Why are they attacking that man?" She turned wide, horrified eyes toward Ganymede.

The cat plunked his ample bottom on Daniel's shoe. *"Your aunt and uncle were doing it under a tree over there. The guy hanging in the air saw them and hid in the bushes to watch. He stayed too long and was enjoying it too much. If they hadn't stopped to shift, they would've gotten him before the harpy."*

Ocypete screamed her fury. "Let go of him. He's mine. I know he's the one I was supposed to snatch for Hades, because only someone who was ready to punch the great time clock in the sky would spy on lions while they were mating." She flapped her wings harder. "I *need* it to be him. Hades phoned to find out why I'm behind schedule. He'll dock my pay if I don't get moving."

Daniel glanced down at Ganymede. "You going to end it?"

"*Yeah, yeah.*" The cat didn't move, didn't even twitch a whisker, but suddenly the man disappeared.

The harpy squawked her rage at losing her prey, but the lions just looked confused.

Kisa stared wide-eyed at Ganymede. "Whoa, totally impressed with your power. What did you do with him?"

"*He's in his room just waking up from a weird nightmare.*" Ganymede looked up at Daniel. "*Why don't you take care of the memory-loss part?*"

Daniel nodded and then concentrated on the harpy, lions, and pack members. The harpy rose into the sky without another word, and the lions padded back into the forest. The pack members milled around and then trudged toward the inn. "They won't remember anything."

Ganymede fixed his amber-eyed gaze on Kisa. "*I'll walk back to the inn with you. So what're you cooking for dinner?*" He looked hopeful.

Kisa was still trying to come to terms with the demonstrations of power she'd seen tonight. Definitely overwhelming. "Dinner? Oh, tomato salad made with Jersey tomatoes, meat loaf, mashed potatoes, corn on the cob, biscuits, and ice cream for dessert. And I bought some nice salmon filets especially for Seth. I wanted to keep the meal simple."

Ganymede's eyes glazed over. *"You're a goddess. Anything you want is yours. Anything."*

Kisa smiled as Daniel held the door for her and the cat. "I'll remember that." She glanced at Daniel. "If I'm allowed."

Once inside, Daniel excused himself and disappeared for a while, but showed up just as she took the meat loaves from the oven. Even with the air-conditioning and her skimpy outfit, she'd done a lot of sweating. Finally she'd closed the kitchen door so no one would see her, and then had taken off the white shirt. It was a lot cooler working in just the pink bra.

He stood behind her, so close that she was pressed against his body. "You'll be sorry. We'll stick together," she said.

"And that's a bad thing?" His soft laughter touched her like a caress. "I like your bare-essentials look." He slid his fingers across her back and lingered a moment on her bra. "It would be so easy to slide this off. Then I'd have my own naked chef." Reinn ran his palms over her shoulders before reaching around her to cup her breasts. "Free these and see what kinds of recipes I can cook up."

"Not in my kitchen." But her voice lacked conviction. She turned her head to look up at him, and felt her heart do a *ka-thud* at the heat in those blue eyes. Between the oven and Daniel Night, everything in the kitchen would melt down to a sticky, sex-charged puddle.

"I just spent a few hours fighting the good fight and lost. I'm going to make love with you, Kisa. Tomorrow night. Your choice of setting. Your pleasure." Without another word, he turned and left the kitchen.

She stared after him with wide eyes, and then she grinned. *Well, what do you know?* She'd gotten her dessert early.

Chapter Nine

Reinn stood on the darkened porch, listening to the inn's guests heaping praise on Kisa for her dinner. Seth had practically cried when he saw the salmon. Reinn half expected the inn's carnivores to hoist her on their shoulders and carry her through the halls in triumph.

All he'd have to do was open the screen door and go inside to join her. But he'd bring a rotten mood to her triumphant moment.

Alan had sat with Julie at dinner even though he didn't eat. So Reinn took the opportunity to search his room to see if he'd brought his sword. He hadn't. For some reason, that made Reinn angrier than it should have. Didn't Alan know the power of the council could reach him in New Jersey? Did he think they'd ignore his marriage to a werecat? He tried to rub the tension out of the back of his neck. Hell, he didn't want to kill the man.

But it was his life or Alan's. If he refused to do his job, the council would eliminate him and choose a new Guardian of the Blood. That was why he'd just gotten off his laptop. He'd ordered another sword, and it would be delivered tomorrow by the same courier to the same spot.

He didn't like himself much right now. Tomorrow night he'd take a step closer to destroying Kisa's almost-brother-in-law and then make love with her. A better man would at least spare her that memory, but he wanted her too much. He'd never wanted a woman more. Who would've thought he was so self-indulgent?

"Well, you'd think a food critic would've at least cooked a gourmet meal. She didn't even serve wine."

Reinn started at the sound of Sparkle's voice right behind him. He'd been so involved in his own misery, he hadn't heard her come outside. A dangerous lapse for someone in his business. "It was the right meal for a country inn. And the werecreatures don't handle liquor too well. Would you want a werebear lumbering down the middle of the road, or maybe two lions dropping in on some campers?"

Sparkle made a rude noise.

"Where's Alan?" Maybe he should take a last shot at talking him out of the marriage.

"Inside with Mason." She moved up beside him. "Don't go there, hot bod. Something's happening between you and Kisa. Don't blow it. Take the great sex and then disappear."

Sparkle would normally be the last person he'd spill his guts to, but he needed to talk it out with someone. "You don't understand how the Mackenzie clan council works. Once they choose you as Guardian of the Blood, it's a till-death-do-us-part thing. If I don't do my job, they'll send hunters after me. I'll be dead within days."

She smiled at him, and for once there was nothing sexual in it. "Hey, you have friends in high places. I bet this council is a bunch of old farts. I'm not talking age here; I'm talking attitude. Ganymede could make them go away for you. Permanently."

Tempting, but he'd never let others fight his battles. It was an ego thing. "Thanks, but no thanks. I don't want to involve you guys in this."

She shrugged. "Friends are for using. That's what makes them friends. Okay, if you don't want Ganymede involved, why not get some other vampires on your side?

He thought about that. "You mean like try to make the council change its rules?"

"Something like that."

He shook his head. "They haven't changed any clan laws in five hundred years."

Sparkle sighed. "Then kill the council's asses. Simple."

Before Kisa, that would've been his solution, too. But now he found himself worrying about what would happen to her if war broke out at the Woo Woo Inn. He exhaled deeply. He'd never cared about collateral damage before, but suddenly it was all he could think about.

Reinn nodded. "Thanks for listening to me and offering help. I appreciate it." He couldn't believe he was thanking Sparkle. The person he'd been when he'd arrived at the inn didn't thank people for anything. He was turning soft and spongy even as he stood here.

She went back inside and left Reinn alone in the dark. An eager woof hinted he wasn't as alone as he'd like to be. "What's up, Trouble?"

"I got to chase a rabbit today, and Kisa gave me some meat loaf, and I pooped a big pile right next to the back door." He wagged his tail at the joy the day had brought.

"Thanks for warning me, kid." He didn't want to talk to the dog, but it wasn't Trouble's fault that Reinn's whole freakin' life had gone south. "Is Mason still talking to Alan?" He'd have to fill the vampire in on what he'd found out about the dachnavars.

"Yeah. He must like Alan, because he's always near him. I wish you liked Alan." Trouble's tail stopped wagging at the thought that Reinn didn't like Alan.

"Alan's a great guy." *But I can't let him live.* "Look, a rabbit just ran across the lawn." That was low, but he really wasn't in the mood for a doggy conversation.

"Where, where?" Trouble bounced up and down a few times trying to see. *"There it goes! Bye."* And he was off and running. Reinn hoped the rabbit wasn't one of the inn's guests.

He stared into the night for a moment and then went back inside to search for Mason. Reinn found him where Trouble had said he'd be, talking to Alan.

Suspicion touched him. Trouble was right: looking back over the last few days, he realized Mason had always been somewhere near Alan. Not always talking to him, but just standing near him. Reinn remembered the accident. Mason had just happened to be driving toward town at the same time they had. Coincidence? Felicia had run into the woods after Kisa, but Mason had remained standing next to Alan.

Mason? The Protector? Possible. Reinn had survived so many centuries because he didn't dismiss possibilities. After all, the Protector didn't have to be a werecat. Although he couldn't for the life of him figure out why a vampire would want to set himself up to fight against his own kind.

Raising his shields so Mason couldn't get anything from his thoughts, Reinn walked over to the two men. "What's happening?"

Alan shrugged. "Nothing new. While Julie's family plans the wedding, Julie and I've been talking about things we want to do to finish our house. We're thinking of ditching the honeymoon and putting the money into a screened-in porch. We can take a honeymoon once the house is finished."

No, you can't. Guilt weighed Reinn down. He'd killed thousands of men on battlefields around the world and never felt his conscience doing a job on him like this. *They were anonymous faces. You didn't know their families or their dreams for the future. It wasn't personal.*

Alan glanced past Reinn and his eyes lit up, eyes the same shade of blue as his. Didn't Alan notice the eye color? All Mackenzies had the same blue eyes. Didn't he suspect even a little?

"Hey, gotta go. Julie's waving at me." He strode across the room to his fiancée.

Illogically, Reinn was furious at the man he'd have to kill. Not only was love blind, but it made you so stupid you didn't see the danger right under your nose.

"Let's sit in the library. It's usually empty," Mason suggested, interrupting Reinn's inner rant against Alan.

Once seated, Reinn studied the other vampire. That sense of familiarity still poked at him. Brown eyes, so he wasn't a Mackenzie. Where had he met Mason before? Because he was becoming more and more certain they'd crossed paths somewhere.

"So what did you find out about the dachnavars?" Mason leaned back in his recliner, relaxed.

He wouldn't be so relaxed if he knew who and what Reinn was, especially if Mason was the Protector. "Did you notice how everyone was hobbling around tonight?"

Mason grinned, and the wild, reckless nature Reinn sensed in him shone through. Mason would smile as he killed you. "Yeah. The attack of the vampirus toesuckems." His grin widened. "Don't tell me."

Reinn nodded. "The dachnavars. Toes are their thing." He held up a hand to keep Mason from interrupting. "Don't ask; I don't get it either. I'm a neck man myself. Guess they went on a feeding frenzy last night."

Mason laughed and shook his head. "Weird. You have leverage now, though." He paused and Reinn knew what was coming. "Tell me about Kisa. I could back you up if I knew what was happening."

"Maybe I'm the one you should ask about that." Kisa stepped into the room. "And yes, I was listening from the hallway. I can't read minds, but I have great hearing."

Reinn did a mental recap of what they'd said since entering the library. He relaxed. Nothing that would give Mason away. If he wanted Kisa to know he was vampire, then he could tell her.

Mason's smile slipped back into place. "So why don't you tell me what's going on, Kisa? I know these attacks on you have Daniel worried. You might need someone else's help, and I can keep my mouth shut."

Kisa glanced at Reinn, and he nodded. Whether Mason was the Protector or not, he was a source of power they could use in an emergency. Other than Ganymede, Reinn didn't sense any other powerful entity in the inn.

"Do you believe in shape-shifters, Mason?" She speared him with a hard stare.

"Yes." No hesitation, no smile. "I also believe in vampires." He looked at Reinn.

She studied his expression and then seemed to come to a decision. "I'm a werecat. But I'm unusual in the werecat world." Her smile was easy, but worry shadowed her eyes. "Catnip doesn't just make me act silly; it makes me shift. In the last few days, I've been the object of a catnip attack three times."

"Catnip attack?" Mason's smile widened. "Okay, I understand that it's annoying, but I don't see that it's any big deal. Sounds like a prankster to me."

Kisa returned his smile, but it didn't reach her eyes. "I told you I was unusual in the werecat world. Would you think it was a big deal if I said I changed into a saber-toothed tiger and that I can't control my cat? Would you think it was a big deal if you were in the room with me when I shifted?"

Mason's eyes grew wide. "You're kidding, right?"

"Afraid not." She glanced at Reinn. "You're sure these dachnavars are responsible for the toe attacks?"

He nodded. "They're Armenian vampires. I did some research on my laptop. They suck blood from the toes of their victims. Can't see Hollywood making any movies about them anytime soon, though. Not many people would go to see *Night of the Living Toe Suckers.*"

No matter how upset she was, he could still make her laugh. Kisa appreciated that in a man. "Why do you need leverage against them?"

Daniel stood. "The woman, Voskie, hinted that she knew something about the person who's after you. She also hinted that her info might be for sale. I offered to pay her, but she wasn't ready to talk. Now we try good honest blackmail."

"How? There's no way to prove they're responsible for those bites." Kisa noted that Mason still looked dazed.

"I'm not threatening her with the law. I'm threatening her with every nonhuman entity in this inn. This place is a sanctuary. Cindy doesn't allow any action that could expose the true natures of her nonhuman guests. Say this story about the toe bites gets to the media. Reporters take an interest and show up to poke around. Pretty soon all the nonhumans would have to look for another place to play."

Kisa looked in Mason's direction. How much did he know about the woo-woo elements at the inn? A lot if Daniel was talking this freely in front of him.

Mason intercepted her glance. "I know Daniel's a vampire. I also know that humans aren't the only guests here."

"Do you have any idea where the dachnavars are now?" Daniel walked to the door and waited for Kisa to join him.

"They spend their nights sitting in the parlor. I guess if toes are your prey, you don't need to run around in the woods." She frowned. "When do they get to feed if the humans are sleeping at the same time they are?"

Daniel stopped to look around the parlor. "Probably right before dawn. Most of the humans are sleeping by then."

"A saber-toothed tiger. Damn." Mason was still with them.

Kisa pointed to where the three vampires sat in a corner. Daniel didn't ask for permission to join them. He simply sat, so she and Mason did the same.

"Lots of sore toes tonight." Daniel's smile was friendly. His gaze wasn't.

Levon and Zaven looked nervous.

Voskie shrugged. "There will be more tomorrow."

Kisa had to sort of admire Voskie's attitude. If you were going to suck toes, you might as well be arrogant about it.

"Wouldn't count on that." Mason's smile was so

beautiful it could cause global warming on a massive scale. Until you looked into his eyes. Instant ice age.

"Who's going to stop us? Two puny humans?" Voskie put just the right amount of contempt in her voice. "Even if you told the other humans, they wouldn't believe you." She shrugged. "And if they did, we'd just leave. We're only staying two more nights anyway."

Obviously they didn't know that Daniel was a vampire, too. But they knew who *she* was. "You're right. You don't have to worry about the humans. But you'd better worry about every nonhuman entity in this inn, because we *will* stop you. This place is our sanctuary, and you've broken the rules. When we're through with you, there won't be enough left to stake."

Voskie's gaze skittered to Levon and Zaven, but they didn't offer any encouragement.

Kisa allowed the silence to drag on just long enough for Voskie to realize she was in real trouble.

"*If* I tell them, that is." Kisa crossed her legs and wished she'd changed out of Sparkle's outfit. It was hard to be intimidating dressed like a sex kitten. The dachnavars sure didn't have to worry about her hiding any weapons.

"What are you suggesting?" Voskie narrowed her gaze.

"Tell us what you know about the attacks on me, and I won't say anything." Would that be enough of an incentive?

"And my offer to pay you is still good." Daniel

looked relaxed, as if he bargained with sleazebags every day. Maybe he did.

Voskie didn't have a chance to answer, because just then Kisa's mom, along with her sisters and Felicia Carter, descended upon them. They laughed and chattered as they surrounded her. How could they be so happy when her world was spiraling out of control? Of course, they didn't live in her skin, so they didn't know how much she feared her uncontrolled cat.

Helen Evans leaned down to kiss her daughter's cheek. "Don't look so glum, Kisa. Felicia's planned a bachelorette party for Thursday. We're all going to the Bare Truth to watch hot men shake their booties. Julie wants you to be there." She patted Kisa's back. "We'll take precautions. The girls will do a catnip check before you go in." She glanced at the dachnavars and Mason. "We'll talk more about it later." Then they were gone.

Voskie had evidently used the break to come to a decision. "Meet me at the old Hart mansion in an hour. Bring cash, and I'll tell you what I know." She seemed agitated before turning away, effectively dismissing them.

Kisa stood and left the parlor. A few seconds later Daniel followed her. Mason stayed to join Alan in a discussion group.

She ran her fingers through her hair. "I'm going to my room to change out of this outfit. I'll meet you on the porch in a half hour."

For a moment she thought he'd ask to join her.

He didn't. She was glad, in a disappointed kind of way. Did that make sense? No.

Kisa really did need a few minutes of downtime away from the stresses pounding at her from all sides. Like her growing feelings for a certain vampire, her sense of being hunted by an anonymous someone for an as-yet-unknown reason, and her increasingly urgent need to control her cat.

Once in her room, she breathed a huge sigh of relief, kicked off Sparkle's four inch instruments of torture, and flung herself onto the bed. Ah, the bliss of being alone.

She'd just closed her eyes for a few seconds when a pounding on her door jerked her to a sitting position. *Damn, damn, damn.*

"Open your door, Kisa. Or not. Because I can unlock it from my side. But I thought you'd feel more empowered if *you* opened it. I have important stuff to discuss with you." Sparkle Stardust.

And even as Kisa covered her eyes and groaned, the pounding began again. "What important stuff?" She might not be able to keep Sparkle out, but she didn't have to give her okay for the forced entry.

"The setting for your big love scene." The pounding stopped for a moment and blessed silence reigned.

Kisa had her mouth already open to tell Sparkle to go away. She shut it. Setting? What was that all about? Curiosity, the weakness of all werecats, whispered that this might be worth investigating. Reluctantly, she got up and opened the door.

Sparkle swept in, this time without clothes

draped over her arm. "Well, it took you long enough. My time is valuable, sister."

"What love scene and what setting?" Kisa walked over to her sitting area and dropped onto a chair.

Sparkle remained standing. "You're going to have sex with Daniel tomorrow night; everything has to be perfect."

"How do you know about tomorrow night?" Why bother asking? Kisa wondered why Sparkle didn't have rotating ears so she wouldn't have to turn her head to pick up every whisper that might have sexual implications.

Sparkle widened her eyes to indicate her innocence of all wrongdoing. "I came to the kitchen to ask about your menu for the night and I heard you guys talking."

"Uh-huh. And you just happened to have your ear pressed to the door when you heard all this." Kisa couldn't even work up a good mad, because she didn't think Sparkle had ever met a closed door she didn't take as a personal challenge. Put her in the middle of the desert with nothing for hundreds of miles in any direction except for a closed door—no building, just the door—and she'd feel compelled to press her ear to it.

"I tripped and fell against the door, so yes, my ear was next to it." Sparkle glanced around the room. "You need some sensually exciting stuff in here. I could loan you a few erotic paintings."

Kisa would *not* be sidetracked. "You were spying on us."

"And that's wrong because . . . ?" She wandered

over to the closet and looked inside. "Where do you keep your scented candles, the ones guaranteed to rev up a man's lust level? I don't see any sex toys in here either. Tell me you at least have something for those moments alone when you feel the need for a satisfying climax."

Patience. It would not be a good thing if she kicked Sparkle's behind out of her room. "What do you want to tell me?"

"Many, many things, but I'll restrain myself and just discuss where you'll be losing your virginity tomorrow night." She sat in the chair across from Kisa.

"My bed?" Kisa had a feeling that wasn't the right answer.

Sparkle sighed dramatically but refrained from flinging her hand across her forehead. "Why do virgins have so little imagination?" She glanced at Kisa. "No, don't answer that. Do you have any idea how powerful Daniel is?"

"No." She'd wanted to ask him, but the right moment had never come up.

"He can make real any fantasy you want. Think of some completely outrageous place to make love." Sparkle's eyes gleamed with all the erotic choices. "Maybe on the beach of a tropical island or in a hot tub filled with rose petals."

"Mars."

"What?" Sparkle blinked. "I thought I heard you say Mars. I was wrong, right?"

"Other planets fascinate me, so yes, I'd like to make love on Mars." The possibilities for having

sex where no one had had sex before were as limit-
less as the universe.

Sparkle didn't try to hide her horror. "Mars isn't
sensual. Wasn't Mars the god of war? What's sexy
about that? And aren't those rover things still there
peering around with their big camera eyes? NASA
would never recover from the shock."

Kisa grinned. "Bet they'd move up their manned
mission plans fast, though." *Put on your brakes and
park your imagination at the curb*. This would be a
fantasy, as in not real.

"It absolutely can't be Mars. Think of someplace
else." Sparkle looked determined. "Daniel also has
preternatural speed. He could whisk you away to
anyplace on earth."

Losing patience here. "Then maybe he could take
me to his home." What kind of place would a man
like Daniel call home?

"No chance." Sparkle sounded sure of that. "He
protects his privacy with the ferocity of a grizzly. I
don't know of anyone who's gotten an invite to his
home."

"How do you know so much about him?" Daniel
had said he knew Sparkle from his visit to the inn
last year, but he'd never said they were close friends.

Sparkle wore her secretive smile, the one that
promised she was so much more than Kisa could
ever understand. "I know all there is to know about
Daniel and you. I know how your mom cried when
she found out your cat was a saber-toothed tiger. I
know how careful you are when you visit human

friends who have cats for fear they might have catnip in their homes. I know your hopes, your fears,
and that you really like Daniel Night."

Kisa pressed her back against the chair in an attempt to keep in touch with reality. "And how do
you do that, Sparkle?"

Sparkle grinned and then stood. "My secret. If
you can't think of anyplace special to make love, I'll
get a list to you tomorrow of hot spots that sizzle."
She swayed to the door on her Manolo Blahnik
stilettos. "I'll also bring you a sexy little something
to wear for the big event. Remember, presentation
is everything." She was humming when she left.

Kisa spent the rest of the hour trying to relax,
but thoughts of tomorrow night, along with fears
of when the next catnip attack would occur, did a
frenetic dance behind her closed lids. She was almost relieved when it was time to meet Daniel and
Mason. Putting on comfortable shoes, she headed
downstairs.

Once together, they walked through the woods to
the old Hart mansion. The forest reminded her that
tomorrow afternoon she should hunt for the package Reinn had hidden here somewhere—not a
search she looked forward to. The night sky was
overcast, so the darkness was almost complete.
Daniel and she had enhanced vision, though, so
they didn't need flashlights. Mason followed in their
footsteps.

The old mansion was a perfect complement to
the Woo Woo Inn. Vines, brush, and trees en-
croached on the ruins. Windows with no glass were

the empty black eye sockets of the building's skeleton. If ghosts were for real, they wouldn't hang around the cemetery; they'd be here. This was way scarier.

Daniel turned to Kisa and Mason. "Stay here while I take a look around." And then he faded into the darkness.

Kisa shivered in the warm night air. "This place is seriously chill-worthy." She glanced at Mason. "A lot of my nightmares when I was a kid took place in buildings like this. There was always a monster hiding under the stairwell or in a closet. I'd end up with the monster chasing me through the house, and I could never find the exit. What about your night frights?"

The eyes he turned toward her were flat, without any gleam of humor in them. "I lived my childhood nightmare, so there wasn't anything in my dreams that could scare me."

Whoa. Major touchy subject. "I'm sorry." She didn't have to think of anything else to say, because Daniel appeared out of the darkness.

His expression was hard. "I found her, but someone else found her first. She's dead."

Kisa felt as though someone had punched her in the stomach. All the air left her lungs in a whoosh. "Dead?"

Mason touched her shoulder. "We'd better take a look."

She wanted to say, "No. You take a look. I'll stay right here and wait for you." She'd never witnessed violent death. Even though her whole family turned into cats in one form or another, they were civilized cats. In a fit of feline exuberance they might bring down a rabbit, but that was the extent of their rampant killing sprees.

Kisa *really* didn't want to see this. Daniel and Mason waited for her response. She nodded.

It was both not as bad as and worse than she'd expected. Voskie had almost completely disintegrated already, leaving only clothes and the wooden stake used to kill her. Not as bad to look at as Kisa had expected.

But Voskie had died because of Kisa, because of something she knew that the killer didn't want her to pass on. The attack of conscience Kisa felt was worse than she had expected.

Mason stared down at what was left of the dead vampire. "Too bad she had a heart."

Puzzled, Kisa looked at him. "What do you mean?"

"There're physical differences among vampire groups. For example, when members of the Mackenzie clan become vampires, their body systems change. They don't have a heart as we know it, so staking them wouldn't do any good. The night feeders have hearts but heal quickly, so if you want a permanent solution, you'd better separate the heart from the body." He looked down at Voskie. "She must've had a heart, but there won't be any regenerating taking place here."

"You know a lot about vampires." Kisa had to say something, anything, to take her mind off Voskie's death.

"I've done a lot of research." Mason didn't seem about to expand on that.

"But you didn't know who the dachnavars were." Daniel sounded like he was simply making a statement of fact.

"I didn't do *that* much research. Come on, how many people know about them? They're pretty obscure." Mason's tone was casual.

Then why did she sense something defensive in his voice?

Daniel shrugged. "I guess so." He raked his fingers through his hair. "Police won't do any good here. We need to tell Sparkle what happened and then talk to the other two dachnavars." He looked at Kisa. "Whoever is behind the attacks on you is playing for keeps. I guess I couldn't convince you to stay in the inn with family members around you at all times."

"I won't hide behind my family. But I won't be stupid either. I'll make sure someone is with me whenever I go out." She knelt down to take a closer look at the clothes that were all that was left of Voskie. "Look at her clothes. They look like someone slashed them."

Mason peered closer. "A knife?"

"Werecat's claws?" Daniel's voice was soft, but that didn't make it any less dangerous.

"Why would—" She didn't get any farther.

There was the sound of flapping wings above them, followed by breaking branches, loud curses, and a solid thud as the harpy hit the ground.

"Landing at night in the forest is a real bitch."

She picked herself up and scuttled on vulture's legs over to the pile of clothes. "Hell, I'm too late. If I hadn't taken the time to change from human form, I could've snatched her right up and been on my way to Tartarus. This is turning into a real stinker of an assignment." Making a disgusted sound, she flapped her wings, rose into the air, and was gone.

"Let's go." Daniel grabbed Kisa's hand as they hurried back to the inn. Mason stayed right behind them.

Once inside, Mason went in search of Levon and Zaven while Kisa led Daniel to where Sparkle sat in the kitchen with Ganymede. For once Ganymede wasn't eating. Kisa hoped he was feeling okay.

"One of your guests is dead." Daniel didn't waste time on small talk. "Someone killed Voskie out by the Hart mansion."

Sparkle paused in the act of turning a page of her *Cosmo*. "Why would someone do that?" She looked at Ganymede. "Cindy and Thrain will blame us." Then she seemed to think about how that sounded. "Not that our first thoughts aren't for the poor victim."

"Do you know where her two friends are?" Kisa had a bad feeling about this.

"They checked out just a little while ago." Sparkle pushed her magazine aside, a testament to how upset she was. "Just came downstairs with their bags, paid their bill, and drove away."

Ganymede was sitting on the table and so far hadn't said anything. He spoke now. *"This have anything to do with Kisa's catnip stalker?"*

Kisa closed her eyes against her growing horror.

"Yes. Voskie said she had information about the person who was doing this to me. She agreed to meet us out by the Hart mansion. When we got there, she was dead."

Ganymede summed things up for everyone. *"This catnip thing didn't seem too serious at first, but now someone's willing to murder to keep their secrets. Hell, this is going to interfere with my meals. I can tell already."*

"Are all the werecreatures out in the woods tonight?" Kisa didn't have much hope that this question would lead anywhere.

"All except Julie and Bernie. She stayed here with Alan, and Bernie's been afraid to go outside since the harpy almost got him."

Ganymede narrowed his amber eyes to angry slits. *"I think I'm pissed off now. I'm the only one here who's supposed to cause trouble. Someone's poaching on my territory."*

Sparkle slid her fingers over his head and down his back. "Calm down, sweetie. We'll find out who's responsible and then—"—slow, evil smile—"we'll take care of the problem."

Ganymede looked grumpy. "Can't destroy anyone. The Big Boss won't let me." He glanced at Daniel. "You can, though."

Daniel didn't deny it.

In a perfect world, they'd find the killer, then turn him or her over to the police. But you couldn't report a murder with no body, especially when the victim was a vampire. So it became an internal affair.

Kisa rubbed her forehead. She'd had enough for

the night. "I'm going up to my room, guys. Did Voskie leave any information that could help you find her next of kin?"

Sparkle and Ganymede shook their heads and then went back to their own conversation about how to punish the guilty without bringing the Big Boss's wrath down on Ganymede. When Kisa left the room and closed the door behind her, Daniel came with her. He remained strangely quiet.

Even though she hadn't done much tonight, she felt exhausted. "Thanks for all your help." She met his gaze directly. No I'm-making-love-with-him-tomorrow jitters. "I'll ask Julie to check my room for catnip. Guess I'll see you tomorrow."

"No."

She blinked. "No?"

"No, you won't ask Julie to check your room. I'm going up to your room with you, and I won't be leaving it tonight." His gaze was just as direct.

She shut her gaping mouth with an audible click. "Run that past me again, because I think I missed the part where you explained why you'll be staying in my room."

His smile was such a sensual power punch that she almost forgot about tonight's horror. Almost.

"Don't worry; tomorrow night is still on. But there's no way you should be alone until someone catches this creep. I know you could ask one of your sisters to stay with you, but I want to do it. You'll be safer with me." His smile almost liquefied the spine she'd been trying to stiffen. "And saying no won't do any good, because you're not the only one who always gets their way."

She'd make love with him right now without even blinking if she knew what was in the package he'd hidden in the woods. Something about his secrecy made her uneasy. And she wouldn't let any doubts take away from her enjoyment of making love with him.

Besides, tomorrow night was better. Tonight Voskie's death was in her head. It would leach some of the pleasure from the moment.

"Well, get set for a big disappointment, Night."

Chapter Ten

Kisa would make everything clear to Daniel while he waited for her to unlock her door. "I don't need you to sleep in my room. I have a lock on my door, plenty of family up and down the hallway, and enough sense not to open the door to a stranger." *Maybe the bad guy isn't a stranger.* A possibility. She'd make sure to cover her nose before opening the door to anyone. "And no offense, but you sleep like the dead. How much help will you be if an attack comes after dawn?"

Daniel took the key from her hand. "At least let me check the room before you go inside. And I don't 'sleep like the dead.' My rest is close to a human's deep sleep. It wouldn't take much to wake me. I can also stay awake a little after dawn and rise a little before sunset. A few of the perks of being a very old vampire."

He went into her room while she waited in the hallway, readying more verbal ammunition for when he continued the argument. And he would. It was in his genes. The gene even had a name. It was the alpha I'm-always-right gene.

Daniel came out of her room and handed her the key. "All clear." He took a step down the hallway before turning to look back at her. He grinned. "Sweet dreams are boring, so I'll wish you wicked dreams instead." And then he left.

Well, damn. She'd been looking forward to a fight. She had all these clever, zingy, sarcastic comments lined up to verbally blow him out of the water. Who would've guessed he'd give up? Now she was depressed. He didn't care enough about her to even make it a good brawl so she could get a rush from winning. *Rats.*

Kisa slammed the door behind her, locked it, and then got ready for bed. Finally tucked in, she closed her eyes. She was exhausted, so she wouldn't have any trouble falling asleep.

A half hour later she was rethinking her reasoning. She couldn't stop thinking about Voskie and the faceless person who'd killed her. And once she drove them from her mind, Daniel stepped into the void.

She'd just turned over for the fiftieth time when she heard the noise. It was only a small scraping sound, but it was coming from right outside her door. She held her breath. There it was again.

A brave person would fling open the door and confront whoever was on the other side. But a smart person would call Sparkle Stardust to check it out. Blessing her cat vision, she pressed the number for the desk without turning on the light. She didn't want to scare whoever it was away before Sparkle got a good look.

"Need help, Kisa? I'm getting ready to hand the desk over to Hal, the day guy. But if this is a sensual emergency, like you need some erotic props or a few inventive sex-play ideas, I'll hurry on up." Sparkle never took her eye off the goal.

"There's someone outside my room. Can you or Ganymede take a look for me? I don't want to open my door to a faceful of catnip." She listened but didn't hear any more noises. Had the person left?

"Will do." And the line went dead.

Kisa waited what seemed like forever to hear Sparkle or Ganymede at her door. Nothing. Maybe she should've tried to call Daniel. She didn't know his cell number, so Sparkle still would've had to put the call through. Besides, how smug would he be if she yelled for help after saying she didn't need him?

Just when she'd slid out of bed and grabbed a lamp, ready to open the door and do serious damage to the head of anyone there, the phone rang. Relieved, she snatched it up. "Yes?"

"No problem." Sparkle yawned. "Check for yourself."

"But—" Before Kisa had a chance to get an explanation, Sparkle hung up.

Kisa looked at the phone. *Check for yourself?* You bet she would. Fat lot of help Sparkle was. Okay, she needed something to cover her nose and mouth. Looking around the room, she saw nothing she could use except . . . She sighed. Not her first choice, but this was an extraordinary situation.

Once her makeshift mask was in place, she gripped the lamp, tiptoed to the door, flung it open, and . . . stared openmouthed as Daniel almost fell through the doorway.

He'd been sitting on the floor with his back braced against her door. He'd draped a blanket over his head and body. When she opened the door, he cursed as he caught himself.

Glaring up at her, he straightened the laptop he had open on his lap. "Give some warning, will you?" But his glare faded to a grin once he took a good look at her mask. "A thong?"

He laughed, and for once the humor reached his eyes.

Now it was her turn to glare. "I needed something I could tie on to protect me from catnip and still leave my hands free to whack someone over the head. I thought it was pretty clever."

"Hey, great creative thinking, sweetheart." He continued to chuckle.

"What're you doing sitting outside my door with a blanket over you? And what's with the laptop?" She should've felt relieved, but her scared tension of a few minutes ago had changed to another kind of tension altogether.

"It's almost dawn. The blanket keeps out any light. And Sparkle gave me a list of all the guests staying here. I'm doing a background search on each one. We might get lucky." He peered at the screen. "We have a couple of zoologists and one cryptozoologist here, but nothing in their backgrounds hints at an obsession with saber-toothed tigers. No criminal records either. Did you know that Seth, our big friendly werebear, has a CIA background?"

She narrowed her gaze. "How did you find out that stuff?"

His smile warmed, became more intimate, and that stupid melting sensation began again. Her body was *not* in sync with her mind.

"I know how to get what I want." He wasn't smiling now. "In all things."

A door opened down the hallway, and Felicia walked toward them. Her startled expression made Kisa realize she was standing in her short nightshirt with tangled hair and bare feet. But it was too late to slam the door shut. "Hi, Felicia. Still up?"

The wedding planner nodded at her, but Felicia's gaze was fixed on Daniel. Kisa didn't blame her. In a room filled with hundreds of men, most women would choose to stare at him. It wasn't just his height, muscular body, and breathtaking face that would always draw women. It was more primal than that. He would always be the dominant male in any group. And no matter how much lip service women paid to wanting a softer, gentler man, they'd always stare at Daniel because he called to the primitive in them. He was all things deliciously sinful and forbidden.

"I needed some ice." Felicia's smile said she knew what was going on, but that Kisa didn't have to embarrass herself by explaining. She walked past them and disappeared down the stairs.

Daniel stared after her. "She didn't have a container to carry the ice in."

Kisa shrugged. "Sparkle has plastic cups in the kitchen, so if Felicia just wants ice for a drink, she can use a cup to hold it." She studied Daniel. "You're going to park yourself in front of my door until I get up?" How could he manage to make her feel all safe and treasured at the same time he aggravated her to death?

"Yep." He drew the blanket over his head far enough so that it shadowed his face without covering it. The rest of him was protected except for the laptop.

Another door opened and Seth lumbered down the hallway. The big werebear grinned as he passed them. "Going down to see if there's any of that meat loaf still in the fridge."

Kisa watched Seth until he reached the stairs, and then she turned her attention back to Daniel. "What happens if someone comes along during the day and pulls off your blanket?"

"I rip his or her throat out." He laughed at her expression, and something of the boy he never was shone in his smile. "I won't burst into flame if dim sunlight touches me. I'll feel pain, but that's it. Prolonged exposure to full sunlight would eventually kill me, but only because of the unbearable pain."

Another door opened. Her sister Wendy's room. Enough. By afternoon everyone in her family would know that a man was sitting in front of her door. "Come inside. Now."

He slipped into her room, and she shut the door just as Wendy stepped into the hallway. She leaned against the closed door while she watched him spread his blanket over the couch and then sit. He'd shut down his laptop, so he was evidently finished for the night. He yawned.

"That couch is too short for you." She made it just a statement. No inflection, no emotion.

"Your bed isn't." He made it just a statement. No inflection, no emotion.

She bit her lip in indecision. What was the big deal? She'd be making love with him tomorrow night anyway. But beyond his secret package and tonight's horror was her dislike of being backed into a corner. He knew she wouldn't leave him sitting in the hallway, and he hoped she wouldn't let him sleep all scrunched up on the couch.

"Okay, you can sleep in the damn bed." She walked away from him, flopped onto the mattress, and pulled the sheet up to her neck.

"No woman has ever invited me into her bed with such . . ." He offered her a fake frown. "The word escapes me."

"Bitchiness?" She sighed. "I don't like being manipulated, Daniel."

"We're still making love *tomorrow*, and I didn't manipulate you." He got up from the couch, made sure the drapes were tightly closed, and then walked to the bed.

She turned her back to him and listened while he took off his clothes. The slide of material over smooth male flesh was so sensual, so tempting, that it almost felt as though she'd watched him strip. Kisa didn't know why she refused to watch, other than the fact that he wanted her to.

"Once dawn arrives, sleep is an irresistible force. I'll be out as soon as my head hits the pillow, so this wasn't a ploy to crawl into your bed for sex." She felt the mattress give beneath his weight. His soft laughter was much too close. "It occurred to me, though. And I was outside your door because you need protection whether you think so or not. Someone killed tonight, so that someone has raised the stakes. I don't know what they want from you, but I guarantee it's all bad."

She'd started to turn over to face him when the phone rang. *Yes, Mom.* Her mother had an uncanny instinct for calling at the wrong time, so this had to be her.

"Kisa, is Daniel with you?" Helen didn't sound upset. Surprising. Wasn't she afraid her daughter would mate with an unworthy?

"Yes." Might as well tell the truth, because her mom had a knack for recognizing a lie no matter how skilled the liar.

"Tell him not to worry about Alan. Mason told Alan he knew about the Guardian of the Blood, and he'd keep an eye out for the bastard."

Kisa smiled. The word *bastard* coming from her mother's lips just didn't flow. Her mom saved curses for special occasions. She didn't practice the words enough to feel at ease with them.

"I'll tell him." She let the silence grow. Helen would say what she wanted in her own time.

"I'm glad Daniel's with you, Kisa." Long pause. "You need someone to protect you now, and he's a powerful man. Sleep tight—I love you." She hung up.

Kisa stared at the phone as though it'd bitten her. Her mom *approved* of Daniel for her? Incredible. She smiled at the phone. Then again, maybe not so incredible. At least no one could accuse her of being with a man less powerful than she.

Replacing the receiver, she turned over. "That was . . ."

He was asleep. And she immediately forgot what she'd been going to say. *Holy cow, would you look at that?* No matter what popular culture said, he didn't look like any dead guy to her. Of course, what did she know about vampires? Mason had pointed out just a few differences between them, and Daniel had never mentioned dying.

He lay on his back, but unlike her, he'd only pulled the sheet to his waist. Sure, she'd seen his chest before, but like any great work of art, that wonderful expanse of smooth skin over hard muscle revealed new and tempting details with each viewing.

Relaxed in sleep, he couldn't distract her with those amazing eyes that said so much but revealed so little. She could concentrate on the complete masculinity of his face, which contrasted perfectly with his thick fringe of dark lashes and full, sensual mouth. Oh, yes, Mr. Night was a study in yummy contrasts.

Kisa slid her gaze over his chest and stomach, stopping only when she reached the edge of the sheet. What had he kept on? Did she care that much? Sure, she did. Crawling out of bed, she padded around to the other side, where he'd dropped his clothes on the floor. She did a quick inventory. T-shirt, jeans, and briefs. *Yes.* Life was good. Smiling all the way, she returned to her side of the bed.

She might not get a chance to see him when he woke, but just knowing he was naked beneath that sheet fueled her imagination. Every sheep she counted in a desperate attempt to relax had Daniel's face on it. She fell asleep with a smile on her lips.

Kisa woke with a frown on her face. Eyes closed and still groggy from sleep, she knew there was something she had to do that wasn't going to be a whole lot of fun.

And as she lay there trying to remember what it was, she felt the press of another body next to hers. She opened her eyes so quickly, she was surprised she didn't hear a popping noise.

Daniel. How could she have forgotten? He was naked beside her. It took every ounce of her self-control to stop from tearing off her nightshirt so she could enjoy the total skin-to-skin experience. Turning her head, she realized she must've slid toward the center of the bed sometime during the night. He lay sprawled in the same position as when he'd fallen asleep. No slippage in the sheet area. *Too bad.*

She was trying to decide whether to take a peek beneath the sheet before her morning coffee when she remembered why she'd awakened with a frown on her face.

She'd planned to search for whatever he'd hidden in the woods. *Forget about it. You don't need to know.* The temptation to abandon the search was there, but if she didn't look, she'd imagine all the wrong things about him. It would color their lovemaking, and she didn't want anything to spoil that.

Sighing, she glanced at her clock. Late afternoon. Reluctantly she abandoned his luscious body and got ready to go downstairs.

Once showered and dressed in shorts, a halter top, and flat sandals—oh, the joy of choosing her own outfit—she once again walked to Daniel's side of the bed to look at his clothes. She needed to borrow one thing for about an hour. That would give her plenty of time to return it before he woke up. Only one thing was small enough to hide under her top. She picked up his briefs.

He didn't budge as she tiptoed from the room and closed the door quietly behind her. She'd just reached the bottom of the stairs when Sparkle waved her over. "Call for you. I was getting ready to put it through to your room when I saw you." She handed Kisa the receiver.

"Kisa Evans?"

"Yes." She didn't recognize the man's voice.

"I'm supposed to give you info on a license-plate number. The owner of the car is a Harry Lynch, thirty-two, lives at—"

"Wait while I get something to write on." Kisa

grabbed paper and a pencil from the desk. "Okay, go ahead."

Once he'd given his information, Kisa waited for the man to identify himself. He didn't. He simply hung up.

Was he a secret informant or something? But to be fair to the man, he wouldn't want a stranger to know his name, especially if he was giving out confidential info. That would be a fast track to the unemployment office.

Sticking the paper in her pocket, she went in search of Wendy. She found her sister listening to more of their mom's last-minute ideas for the wedding. Wendy looked like she needed rescuing.

Kisa was just trying to figure out how she could pry Wendy away from Helen without having to face her mother's inquisition about Daniel when salvation arrived in the form of Julie. While Helen turned her attention to the bride-to-be, Kisa beckoned to Wendy.

Wendy hurried over, and they escaped outside to the porch. No sun today. There was a thick cloud cover, and a light rain was falling.

"I need a favor, sis." Kisa considered how much to tell Wendy. "I like Daniel. A lot. But the other night he did something strange. He came downstairs right after dark, didn't speak to anyone, and went into the forest. Correction—*sneaked* into the forest. His body language definitely said, 'I don't want anyone to see me.'"

"Another woman?" Wendy looked intrigued.

Kisa didn't blame her. After a week of hearing nothing but wedding plans, they'd all welcome a diversion. "Maybe. Anyway, I don't want to make a fool of myself over him if he's meeting someone else. I'd like to know where he went." She lifted her top and pulled out the briefs. "Would you shift and try to find his trail? I know the scent's a little old, but it hasn't rained enough yet to wipe it all out. If he was meeting a woman, you might pick up her scent, too."

Wendy's smile was a gotcha grin that promised she'd hold this over Kisa for eternity. "His briefs? Won't he miss them? No, don't tell me. I don't want to know." Her sly expression promised that she already knew.

Kisa drew in a deep breath of patience. "Will you do it?"

"Let me see. Choices: go inside and listen to more wedding plans or follow the trail of a sexy guy. Uh, I guess I'll trail the sexy guy."

"Thanks." Relieved, Kisa led Wendy to the spot where Daniel had entered the woods. Kisa's sense of smell was awesome by human standards, but only in her cat form would it be good enough to track someone.

With the smoothness of long practice, Wendy shifted into bobcat form. Within minutes she had the scent and was leading Kisa through the trees. After about five minutes of walking, Wendy stopped. They were outside an old ruined church. Like the Hart mansion, it was falling down and slowly being reclaimed by the forest. But someone had been here recently, because the vines and weeds had been cleared from the doorway. Guests from the inn? Possibly.

Tentatively, Kisa pushed at the door. It made the prerequisite creepy creak, but opened. She stepped inside to darkness. The glass in the windows was long gone, and only pale light from the overcast day cast narrow beams into the church.

Wendy sniffed around the small area before shifting back to human form. "I didn't pick up any recent female visits. In fact, Daniel's the only one who's been in here for a while." She smiled. "Satisfied?"

Now for the hard part. "Look, now that I'm here I want to explore a little. I won't keep you, sis. You must have stuff to do back at the inn."

Wendy shook her head. "Nothing except listen to Mom angst over a wedding that's been planned to death. I'll help you explore. Besides, after those catnip attacks, Mom and Dad would pitch a fit if I went off and left you by yourself."

Damn and double damn. "Yeah. Thanks." Kisa began searching. She'd have to find the package first and then think of an excuse to keep Wendy from seeing it.

After about fifteen minutes, she was almost ready to give up. Wendy wiped sweat from her eyes. "Jeez, it's hot in here. I'm done playing explorer. I need some fresh air. I'll meet you outside."

Kisa nodded absently as she continued poking around the old altar. She'd give it another five minutes and then call it a wash. Maybe he'd hidden it somewhere else entirely.

As she walked behind the altar, she stepped on a loose board. Hey, she'd seen enough movies to know that people hid things beneath loose floorboards. Bending over, she gripped the board and yanked. It came up easier than she'd expected, and she fell backward into the altar. And through it. The back must have been only propped up, because it now lay on the floor. She didn't have to look under the floorboard, because the long package lay inside the altar.

She reached for the package at the same time that she wondered about the strangeness of a vampire hiding something on consecrated ground.

It was a long zippered case. No paper to rip off. No way that Daniel would know she'd peeked inside. No way that Daniel would even know she'd been here if she propped the back of the altar up again. Temptation said that it was okay to look inside the case, because she had a right to know about him before tonight. Her conscience reminded her that she never got away with stuff like this.

Temptation won. She unzipped the case and then stared wide-eyed at what was inside.

A sword. Big. Real. Deadly. *Oh, my God!* The Guardian of the Blood? Why else would he hide it out here?

"Because Ganymede has mine locked up until I leave, and I don't feel comfortable without a sword handy. So I e-mailed a friend and had him bring me a new one. I hid it out here because I didn't want to take the chance of leaving it on my bike, where someone might lift it." Daniel stood by the door, a tall figure in a cowl that left his face in complete shadow.

He looked like the ghost of a long-dead monk who'd be right at home haunting this old church. His voice was deep, threatening, and echoed eerily in the silence. Okay, she was officially weirded out.

"If I were the Guardian, I'd have two choices: Allow Alan to burn along with his car and then leave the inn with no one ever realizing I was the Guardian." He moved forward, as soundless as the phantom she imagined. "Or wait, and not only have to kill Alan, but everyone else at the inn who could ID me. At least, that's what everyone says the Guardian always does."

He moved even closer, silent and oh so dangerous. "So what would the Guardian's choice be? Let Alan's car do the job for him or put his own life on the line by trying to take out an inn full of shifters and other nonhuman entities?"

Her mouth, always a loose cannon, spoke without her permission. "You can erase memories, so you wouldn't have to kill everyone." They could carve on her tombstone, SHE DUG HER GRAVE WITH HER MOUTH.

Daniel reached her, moved into her personal space big-time, and did some heavy-duty looming. He bent over her, and he was so close that she had to lean back to keep from touching his nose, or maybe his mouth. Even in this extreme situation, the thought of touching his mouth was a momentary blip of excitement on her personal pleasure monitor.

"But why would I want to erase memories when I enjoy killing so much?" His voice was a low rumble of menace.

Faster than she could absorb the horror of his words, he became vampire. His eyes glowed in the semidarkness of the church, and he lifted his lips to expose his fangs. A sudden wind whipped his cloak away from his body and swirled the dust of years into the air. Then the whole building shuddered as though a giant hand were following the directions on a carton: *Shake well before opening*.

His smile was wicked and showed lots of fang. "Are you afraid, Kisa?"

She gave the question considerable thought and then . . . she laughed. Maybe not the best response, and maybe future visitors to the cemetery would talk about seeing the ghost of the laughing corpse, but she couldn't help herself.

"That was so gothic I felt like I should be wearing a long, flowing white nightgown. Loved the wind and shaking, though." What if he wasn't playing a part? He could kill her before she had a chance to shift. But somewhere deep inside where truth made its home, unaffected by surface distractions, she knew he wouldn't hurt her. "You're right, though. You could've let Alan die in the car wreck. Why did Ganymede take your sword from you? In fact, why carry a sword at all? A gun can do the same amount of damage."

He frowned. "I thought I was pretty scary." Then he shrugged. "Ganymede doesn't want any weapons inside the inn. And a lot of the really old vampires carry their swords everywhere. It's the weapon we're most comfortable with. Call it our medieval security blanket."

Kisa nodded. It all made sense, and she was so relieved she felt like sitting down and crying. Which she wouldn't do because he'd think she was crazy.

She watched him return the sword to its hiding place and then replace the back of the altar. "Uh, I thought vampires couldn't enter holy places."

He looked at her, but she couldn't see his expression because of the hood. "Holy objects and places don't affect me. Besides, no place is completely holy. Even consecrated ground sees evil in its time."

They walked to the door together. He opened it for her and she stepped into the fading light of day. "Where did Wendy go?"

"I told her I'd make sure you got back to the inn safely, so she left." His smile was a flash of white within the shadow of his hood. "I think she thought that's what you'd want her to do. Was it?"

"Yes." Kisa thought of something. "Oh, and you read my mind when you first came into the church. Stop it." Did she look stern enough? It was tough to twist her lips into a frown when they kept wanting to turn up in a silly grin.

His soft laughter was so sexy it made her teeth hurt. "Sweetheart, I've been in your mind since you woke up this afternoon." He held up his hand as she opened her mouth to let him have it. "As of this moment, I promise not to touch your thoughts again unless you invite me in."

"Ha, you'll take root and sprout before that happens." Beyond her outrage, she was horrified to remember what some of those thoughts had been.

"You disappointed me. I was waiting for you to lift that sheet and see how ready I was for you." The light touched his eyes, and she saw the gleam of laughter there. "It's your fault I'm standing here without briefs. Where are they?"

The mental image derailed her train of thought. "What? Oh, your briefs. I left them in the church. Somewhere." She blinked. "Give me a minute to think about it." Oh, yes, yes, yes, she was certainly thinking about it. "I'll go back in and search."

"Leave them. I'll pick them up later." There was no teasing in his voice now. "I want you, Kisa. And making love tonight isn't going to stop the wanting."

She stared at him, not knowing what to say. *Ditto? Me too?* Should she reach for him? Physical contact was always good. Kisa wasn't sure, because she'd never been in this situation before. What would he expect? She thought too much. Why couldn't she just react without thinking? It was a moot point now. The silence had dragged on too long.

Daniel solved the problem for her as he opened his cloak and enveloped both of them inside it. He'd thrown on only his jeans before coming after her. She wrapped her arms around his waist and sank into all that warm, muscular strength.

With her face pressed to his bare chest and his thighs parted so she could feel proof of his wanting, she found the natural response that had eluded her a minute ago.

She kissed the smooth skin over his heart, and if

he didn't have a heart, that didn't matter. It was the symbolism that counted. "Tonight can't come soon enough." How trite was that? She hoped he heard the emotion behind the comment.

He released her. "I think we'd better get back to the inn before I convince myself that making love on the ground under this cloak would be unique and memorable."

Clasping his hand, she walked beside him toward the inn. "How did you manage to not only wake up but follow me when it was still light out?"

"I was a mercenary for centuries. Even though I did my work at night, there were times when things would've been easier if I could've faced a little daylight. With age came the power to wake before darkness and to tolerate an overcast day as long as I covered up. I'm lethargic when I rise early or stay awake past sunrise, but I can function."

They'd reached the inn, but since Kisa didn't want to run a gauntlet of her relatives, they opted for going in the back door. They were passing the kitchen when Sparkle hailed them.

She stood in the kitchen doorway wearing her favorite color, black: black shorts, black top, black stilettos, and a black scowl. "That's it. I'm finished. I just got a death threat. It was from a freakin' group of low-life jerks. The cowards didn't even sign their names. They threatened to steal all my sexy black outfits and replace them with pale pink. *Pale pink!*"

Daniel looked as if he wanted to laugh, so Kisa cast him a warning glance before turning to Sparkle. "Uh, that's awful, but it doesn't sound like a death threat." She backed away from the vicious gleam in Sparkle's eyes.

"It *is* for them. Threaten my clothes, threaten me. I'll hunt them down like the dogs—or cats, or wolves, or bears—they are. I'll leave them bleeding all over their polyester pants and plaid walking shorts."

"Why the threat?" Daniel wasn't doing a terrific job of looking serious.

Ganymede appeared in the doorway beside Sparkle. *"They want her to stop cooking. Said they didn't give a flip if they were sensual or not."* Ganymede's shifty-eyed glance suggested he might've been one of the cowards who'd contributed to the note.

"I'm turning in my whisk and blender. Let them wallow in what they laughingly call their sex lives. See if I care." She crossed her arms over her breasts. Really great breasts. Daniel and Ganymede both noticed.

Kisa narrowed her eyes on Daniel before she realized what she was doing. So what if he wanted to look at Sparkle's boobs? She didn't own him. Then why was she still mad?

"Would you cook dinner again tonight, Kisa? I promise it's the last time you'll have to do it. I'll have a cook in here by the end of the week if it kills me. Until then, I'll improvise."

"It can't kill you, honey bunny. You're immortal." Ganymede didn't look too crushed that Sparkle's cooking career was over.

Kisa sighed. "Okay, one more time. You have steaks in the freezer, so we'll go with them tonight."

She'd make this a quick and easy meal, because she had a hot vampire to make love with tonight.

Sparkle frowned. "You know, I expected a food critic to go for more exotic stuff."

"Gourmet doesn't always translate into good." Kisa did *not* want to get into a food discussion with Sparkle.

But Sparkle was still fixated on food. "If I don't have a cook by tomorrow I could have the nearest Chinese restaurant deliver. But what about Friday? Guests won't want takeout two days in a row."

"You have a wonderful porch and a beautiful lawn. It cools down at night, and you can put stuff out to keep away the mosquitoes. Why not take dinner outside? Bet your guests would love barbecue."

Sparkle's eyes lit with the same excitement she usually reserved for a new pair of sexy shoes. "You're a genius. Yes, I can do this." She looked down at Ganymede. "Remember Billy Bob and Bubba's Badass Texas Barbecue in Houston?"

Clapping her hands, she smiled at Kisa. "This will be so great. I'll call them right now and get them on a plane tomorrow morning. The brisket takes a long time. They'll have to start cooking tomorrow so the barbecue will be ready Friday night. It'll be wonderful."

Ganymede looked pained. *"They do great barbecue, but they're hard to take, even for an easygoing guy like me."*

Daniel tried logic. "Why not bring in someone from around here?"

Sparkle looked puzzled by Daniel's suggestion.

"Then it wouldn't be real Texas barbecue. I mean, if I want Jimmy Choo sandals, would I go to a discount shoe store? I think not."

Kisa smiled weakly. "Good luck with your barbecue plans."

Daniel leaned close to Kisa. "I think this idea might come back to bite you." To demonstrate, he scraped his teeth lightly along the side of her neck. "But we have our own plans to make. Let's get out of here."

Relieved, Kisa abandoned Sparkle to her phone call and Ganymede to his doubts about Billy Bob and Bubba.

Gazing at the heated desire in Daniel's eyes, she smiled. "I think *our* brand of fire and sizzle will be more fun."

Chapter Eleven

Spontaneous was better. Spontaneous didn't give you time to think about *things*. Worry about *things*. Rack your brain for *things* to say once he got there. Kick her if she ever planned ahead for another one of these.

The knock on her door drew a startled squeak from Kisa. He was early. Was she dressed right? Maybe she should've met him wearing only a smile. Maybe she should've met him dressed in a sexy nightgown. But that wasn't her. Besides, she hadn't brought any sexy nightwear with her. So she'd meet him at the door in shorts and a sexy red top. Her feet were bare and her hair was loose. That had to count for something.

Taking a deep breath, she opened the door.

Sparkle smiled at her. "See, I knew you needed me. The biggest night of your life and you're dressed like Daisy Duke." She edged past Kisa into the room. "I've brought a sexy little something for you to wear tonight, along with a list of hot places to make love." Sparkle put the "little something" on Kisa's bed and drew the list from her shorts pocket.

Kisa walked over to take a look at what Sparkle expected her to wear. She held it up. Not bad. A cream silk beaded camisole with . . . She frowned. "Sparkle, I guarantee I won't be keeping on any thong that has a string of beads between my—"

"Once Daniel sees you in that outfit, he'll have it off in two minutes. You can even recycle the beads. Use them creatively during sex. Can we say erotic turn-on? Dip them in chocolate, put them in unexpected places—navels are always good—and suggest he remove them with his tongue. Anything involving tongues is a winner. Trust me on this."

Sparkle handed the list to Kisa. "Notice that none of the places say 'here.' " Her expression turned thoughtful. She glanced at her watch. "He should be along any minute now. If you guys leave right away, you can be back in time to cook dinner. Five or six hours should be plenty of time to make long, leisurely love." Not waiting for Kisa to reply, she stepped into the hallway. "I would've brought along a few sensual toys for you to experiment with, but you're not ready for them yet. Maybe next time." And then she was gone.

Kisa closed the door and leaned against it. Daisy Duke? She'd wear Sparkle's sexy camisole and thong, but forget the list. What was wrong with making love on her bed?

This time when the knock came, she reminded herself of how much she wanted to make love with

Daniel, pushed aside all the things making her nervous, and opened the door.

He'd dressed casually, too. Jeans and a white T-shirt. She relaxed a little. "Hey." She stepped aside so he could enter.

"Hey, yourself." He wrapped his arms around her and covered her mouth with his.

It was a long, drugging kiss that heated her blood and turned her heartbeat into a drumroll of sexual excitement. He was good. Very good.

Daniel finally lifted his head, and she expected him to lead her to the bed. He led her to the window.

Kisa knew she looked puzzled. "Um, it's sort of foggy and rainy out there. Not much to see."

He didn't say anything as he unlatched the old-fashioned floor-to-ceiling window and pulled it open. The damp night air blew in.

Okay, this was weird. "So you like lots of fresh air when you make love?"

He smiled at her. "We're not making love here, Kisa." Even as he held out his hand for her, he became vampire. "I'm not taking a chance of anyone interrupting us. We'll go someplace else."

"And that would be where?" Now she was getting nervous again. But she trusted him enough to take his hand. "What're you going to do?"

"I have preternatural speed. It'll come in handy tonight." He squeezed her fingers.

If that was supposed to give her courage, it wasn't working.

"You can close your eyes for the trip or keep

them open. But even if you watch, you'll only see a blur. We'll be moving too fast for sightseeing." He looked around the room. "Want to take anything with you?"

Kisa knew her eyes were probably taking up half her face by now. "Yes." He dropped her hand. She walked to the bed and picked up the camisole. During the short walk, a thousand thoughts pushed and shoved at her consciousness. Did she want to do this? Did she trust him to take her safely wherever they were going? Did she have the strength to walk back across the room to him?

He smiled that totally sensual smile, but beneath it she sensed uncertainty. Daniel thought she might refuse to go with him.

She walked back to him on slightly rubbery legs. "Ready." Kisa clutched the camisole as she took his hand. "Let's do it."

He pulled her to him, wrapped his arms tightly around her, and then they were gone. Kisa saw nothing but a dark blur around her, wasn't even aware of motion. But suddenly they were standing somewhere else.

"I'd throw up, but I left my stomach back at the inn." She spoke in short gasps as she tried to catch her breath. "Where are we?"

Daniel reached out, turned on a light, and she gasped. "A log home! What a gorgeous great room." She forgot everything as she slowly turned to admire the massive rock fireplace, the high ceiling with exposed beams, and the wall of windows. Kisa barely controlled her urge to jump up and down and clap. "I love log homes. I want to own one someday."

He smiled, his eyes warm with happiness that she liked the place he'd chosen. "We're in the Colorado Rockies. I hope this place is special for you."

"Oh, it is." She ended on a sigh of pleasure. "Is this a resort or what?" Maybe he'd show her the rest of the place. "I wish it weren't dark so I could see the view."

"This is my home."

Shock stilled her while Sparkle's comment replayed in her mind: *He protects his privacy with the ferocity of a grizzly. I don't know of anyone who's gotten an invite to his home.*

She had. He'd chosen to make love to her here. The pure joy of knowing this filled her with so much emotion that it overflowed. Kisa hugged him and stood on tiptoe to whisper in his ear, "Thank you, Daniel, for inviting me into your home." She emphasized her thank-you by nipping his earlobe.

Laughing, he scooped her up and lowered her to the comfortable couch facing the fireplace. Suddenly the lights went out. But before Kisa could comment, there was a loud poof, and a blazing fire appeared in the fireplace. Instant ambience.

Kisa didn't hide her awe. "You did all that with your mind, right?"

He nodded, never moving his gaze from her face. "Once I became vampire, it didn't take me long to realize that mental power trumped physical power in every way. My body could do only so many things." Daniel shrugged. "I've spent centuries developing my mental strength." His smile promised that she'd like what he could do with his mind.

She waited for him to rise and lead her to his bed. She'd bet he had a master suite to die for.

"What's your favorite season, Kisa?" He rose and pulled her up with him, but instead of heading for a bedroom, he went toward the front door.

Huh? "I love every season, but winter is special. Snow brings out the kid in me." What was this all about?

He flung open the door. She could see the dark silhouettes of mountains and trees. Summer nights were cooler in the mountains than in Jersey. She shivered. Kisa didn't understand.

"Look at me, Kisa." His voice was seductive persuasion.

When he sounded like that, who could resist? She looked at him.

"Allow me into your mind. I can give you winter and the joy of making love in the snow without the cold. I can control the seasons." He touched her forehead. "In here."

Why not? Kisa wanted this to be the most memorable night of her life, so why not indulge her fantasy? She nodded.

He didn't stare deeply into her eyes. She didn't feel him poking around in her brain. Daniel simply took her hand and led her into the night.

"Holy wow! How many ways can I say spectacular?" A full moon shone on a glistening blanket of new-fallen snow. Snow lay heavy on pine boughs, and the snow-covered mountains were things of beauty in the moonlight. "How can you . . ." She stopped. Kisa didn't want to know how; she wanted to live the fantasy.

She let the essence of the crystal-clear mountain air touch her, but felt no biting cold. Kisa drew in a deep, invigorating breath and reveled in feeling totally *alive*. Reaching down, she scooped up a handful of snow and flung it at him. Then she turned and ran.

His laughter trailed her as she tried to escape through the deep snow. Not exactly a graceful gazelle escape. She felt him behind her a second before he grabbed her around her waist and lifted her into the air.

She screeched and laughed as she tangled her fingers in his thick hair. When he dropped her into a snowdrift, she kept her fingers clamped in his hair and brought him down with her. They rolled around in the snow until Kisa was breathless.

As suddenly as the play began, it ended. She lay in the snow with him leaning over her, and his gaze was hot enough to melt all the snow on the mountains. Sometime during their wrestling he'd returned to human form.

Not knowing what to say in the face of his naked desire, she asked a stupid question: "Ever seen Bigfoot around here?"

Daniel looked blank for a moment and then smiled. "No, but I've seen big . . ." He took her hand and placed it over his arousal. "Bigfoot, big whatever, any body part gone wild can be dangerous."

"Hmm." Kisa tried to look serious. "Is it ferocious?" She massaged his arousal through his jeans.

He groaned. "You bet. And hungry." Daniel slid his tongue across her bottom lip. "And impatient."

Kisa grinned as she tugged at his T-shirt. "I've seen about all I want to of this. Take it off." She wanted him naked, a powerful animal on his own hunting grounds. The whole back-to-nature thing Daniel had going here brought out the stalking cat in her.

Sitting back on his heels, he pulled off the shirt. His hard-muscled chest gleamed in the pale light of the moon. "Your turn now. I've waited as long as humanly—no, inhumanly possible to touch your breasts."

Always cooperative, Kisa sat up and raised her arms so that he could slip her top over her head. She hadn't worn a bra, and his gaze alone sent a sizzle of need along every nerve ending. All that sizzle eventually found a home low in her stomach, where it happily curled up and purred.

He started to reach for her, but she shielded her breasts with her hands. "Uh-uh. Not until I see you naked in the snow." She smiled at her whimsy. "*Naked in the Snow.* Sounds like a best-seller title. The story of two visitors to a nudist colony lost in a blizzard."

Unbuttoning his jeans, he stood long enough to get rid of them and his shoes, and then knelt in the snow again. He wasn't wearing briefs. Great minds thought alike, because she wasn't wearing panties. He'd find that out in a few minutes.

"So what happens to them?" He deftly unbuttoned her shorts, and she couldn't help wondering how much unbuttoning practice he got on a regular basis. Not a jolly thought.

"Our naked hero and heroine realize they're in deep doo-doo. So they find a cave, gather dry wood, and make love until the heat from all that sex ignites the wood. Think the public would buy it?" She lifted her hips as he slid her shorts off. "No, I guess they wouldn't believe the nudist colony part."

He slid his gaze the length of her body, and the sizzle purring low in her belly stretched and unsheathed its claws. Her nipples pebbled, and it had nothing to do with the cool air. She arched her back, an instinctive offering of her body.

Daniel surprised her when he slipped his hands beneath her bottom and lifted her. He kissed her gently, low on her stomach, and liquid heat pooled where his lips had touched.

"I'll never again be able to look out over this meadow without seeing you lying here, your body tempting and perfect in the moonlight." And then he laughed. "I can't believe I said that. I never say stuff like that. It's all your fault."

She felt ridiculously happy about that. "Lie beside me. I want to touch every inch of your body, know it so well that fifty years from now you could blindfold me and I'd recognize it."

"Blindfolded? I'm impressed." He lay down on his side beside her and supported himself on one elbow. "Touch away."

Kisa didn't need a second invitation. She ran her hands over his shoulders and chest, enjoying the flex of his muscles beneath her exploring fingers. She touched the tip of her tongue to each hard male nipple and was rewarded with a groan.

She slid her hands down his back, memorizing the smooth flow of warm flesh ending at the base of his spine. Warm flesh? Was he really warm or was that another illusion he was creating? She'd have to ask him later.

"Good lord, woman, you've been at it for three hours already. I'm suffering here." His voice was husky with need.

She shook her head. "Exaggeration, exaggeration. I'm going as fast as I can." Kisa slowed down. She had a sadistic streak. *How delicious.*

As she kneaded his excellent ass, she closed her eyes and controlled her urge to make kitty-cat noises of pleasure. "You smell of pine, snow, and wild places. Yummy." She opened her eyes to his soft chuckle.

"I'm more basic. You smell of pleasure, and there's nothing else I can compare it to." He brushed a few strands of her hair away from her face. "I love your long hair. Never cut it."

She'd let it grow until it dragged on the ground, if that was what he wanted.

Moving down his body, she explored the backs of his hard thighs and strong calves. Then she reached for what she'd wanted to touch all along. He put his hand over hers.

"Not a good idea. Touch me and you'll be look-ing back at your virginity in the rearview mirror, wondering when the hell you lost it."

He rolled her nipple between his thumb and index finger. How could something so small deliver such a surge of sensation? As he paid equal attention to her other nipple, she mentally urged him to put his mouth on her. Why wasn't he doing his mind-reading thing when it would do some good?

Daniel took his hands completely off her. "Kisa, I want to make what happens between us tonight a defining moment for you. In your future, whenever you experience pleasure, I want you to compare it to this. Do you trust me to make tonight that special?"

Defining moment? "Are all vampires cryptic?" She understood he was asking for permission to do something without being specific. But her body wanted to get on with it, so she didn't probe. What could be wrong with more pleasure? "Bring on the defining moment." She pushed him onto his back and then rolled on top of him.

"I can't stand it. I have to feel every inch of you all at once." She pressed herself flat against him and then did some wiggling to enhance the experience. "Mmm. And you have so many inches to feel."

He lifted his hips, pushing his arousal tightly between her spread thighs. "Just in case you needed to measure again."

She felt a little breathless. It must be the thin mountain air. Kisa pushed off his body and knelt beside him. With the tip of her finger, she circled his heavy sac and then traced a spiral up the length of his erection. "I'll need to do a visual on this."

"The hell with visuals. I need some tactile sensations." Reaching up, he drew her down to him.

As his sexy mouth came within tongue distance,

she traced the sensual shape of his lips. He buried his fingers in her hair and pulled her close, his tongue tangling with hers. He tasted of her, him, *them*. She couldn't separate the impressions.

He kissed a path to her breasts as she raked his back with her nails. *Uh-oh*. Her feline nature was showing. Closing his lips over her nipple, he drew a deep sound of pleasure from her. In one of the few working cells left in her brain, she marveled at how tongue, teeth, and the mouth's power to create suction could actually curl her toes. Amazing.

Her moans grew frantic a few minutes later when he spread her legs and slid his tongue across that deliciously sensitive nub of flesh. She bucked and pleaded. When he slipped his tongue inside her, she was already wet and ready for him.

As he knelt between her legs, all logical thought gave way to primal sexual hunger. She wanted him inside her now. Kisa's last fleeting thought was the worry that when he entered her, the physical and emotional surge might trigger her change.

"Come with me, Kisa. I'll bury myself deep inside you, and all you'll feel is pleasure. So much pleasure. What I feel will be yours as well. The sensations will be doubled."

Daniel's shaft nudged between her legs, and she held her breath, as if by not breathing she could hold on to this moment, this memory. He slid slowly inside her, stretching her, filling her. She knew when he reached the barrier, but she was too aroused to worry about pain.

"Do it now." She felt as fierce as she sounded.

Waves of desire, need, and hunger flowed over her, and if she was aware that some of the sensations weren't hers, she didn't give a damn.

With a sudden push he was past it. She was too aroused to wonder at the absence of pain. Raking her fingers down his back, she dug them into his butt and pulled him to her, forcing him deeper inside her.

She made little whimpering noises as he slowly drew out and then slid back into her. Each time, the sense of being stretched and filled pushed her toward a release she knew was just ahead.

Daniel's body grew slick with sweat even in the mountain air. He murmured words she couldn't hear, couldn't understand past the roaring, foaming river of sexual hunger carrying her toward that moment. Her sense of rightness accepted without question that his feelings were joined with hers, his rising surge toward orgasm enhancing hers.

She drove her body upward to meet his as he plunged into her again and again and again.

Almost . . . almost . . . almost . . . "Yessss!" Kisa hung high on that incredible moment when time itself seemed suspended. She held her breath, her body rigid, as spasm after spasm shook her. While waves of pleasure washed over her, she felt his explosive release as well.

And for just a moment, she felt her cat stir. It stretched and then unsheathed its claws. Kisa closed her eyes, willing it back into the darkness.

Slowly she relaxed into the lethargy of the afterglow. She was still breathing hard, and her heart hadn't stopped beating triple-time yet, but she'd engaged her brain and was thinking again.

Daniel had lowered himself to the ground beside her. He didn't look too steady either. *Good*. She would've hated to think he got off at the station before hers on this trip. She focused her gaze on the part of his body that she admired beyond all other body parts.

"You're wearing protection." Okay, she didn't remember that happening. Wouldn't she have remembered a pause in the proceedings?

"I hid the memory with a little mental static. It wouldn't have added to your pleasure." He seemed unconcerned that he'd manipulated her mind.

She couldn't complain, though, because she'd given him permission to mess with her thoughts. "Sharing your pleasure as well as my own could spoil me for . . ." Kisa had been going to say *for other men*, but realized at the last second that right now she couldn't imagine doing this with another man. Maybe once her stay at the inn was over and she was back home, she'd feel differently. She sure hoped so, because wanting Daniel Night on a permanent basis would be a mistake. Wouldn't it?

His scowl told her he knew what she'd been about to say and didn't like it. That scowl perked her right up. "Look, we were so hot we melted the snow."

He looked around him and then smiled. "Who needs a snowblower?" There was bare ground in a large circle around them. That was pretty symbolic of what she'd done to him. She'd cleared away his

I-don't-need-any-woman attitude, and he didn't know if he'd ever get it back.

This hadn't gone down as he'd planned. Reinn had wanted to make her first time wonderful while remaining emotionally uninvolved himself. He'd thought if he didn't heighten his own sexual enjoyment by bringing his fangs into play at the moment of orgasm, then he wouldn't feel so intensely. Yeah, that had worked well. He'd barely stopped himself from spouting the old, reliable, "How was it for you? It was great for me." Not that the word *great* described anything.

So he said nothing. No words about how making love to her had rated the top score on his long list of sexual encounters. No explaining what this had done to him emotionally. No hint of how touching her body, her mind, was undermining his determination to complete his assignment.

Kisa looked puzzled. She was about to start asking questions. He didn't want to answer any right now.

"How about changing to your cat form and taking a run in the forest?" That should get her attention.

Her eyes lit with joy for a moment before she remembered why she couldn't do something like that. "I'm still not completely in control."

He shrugged. "Doesn't matter. I can keep an eye on you. Besides, there're no humans around here. You can't hurt anyone." Reinn added the clincher: "I have the power to take the same form as yours. I can run with you. This'll be your only chance ever to play with another saber-toothed tiger. Don't turn it down."

"You can do that?"

She gave him a wide-eyed look of awe that he wasn't sure he liked. Yeah, he was guy enough to want his woman . . . No, not *his* woman. Definitely not his woman. But he did get a rush from knowing she thought he was special in a few ways. On the other hand, he didn't want to scare her. And he knew from centuries of watching people's reactions to his power that almost everyone eventually decided he was a scary guy.

You're going to kill her brother-in-law. Couldn't get much scarier than that. He purposely blocked that line of thought. He'd live in the moment.

"I can be whatever I want to be." *Except free of my crappy job.*

"Thank you." Her smile made it all worthwhile. "For once in my life I want my cat to run free."

He'd always remember her like this—her expression open and trusting, her long, dark hair a tangled glory around her face, and her body beautiful beneath the full moon. The memory was all he'd ever have of her.

Reinn smiled. No more depressing thoughts. Tonight was for living and loving. Visualizing Kisa's cat, he shifted.

After shrieking and jumping away from him, she steadied and then gave herself over to her own change.

Unlike Kisa, he was all himself within the sabertooth's body, so he didn't have to deal with any primitive impulses. He led her into the forest. They raced the wind, and somewhere along the way he lost himself to the joy of the chase. And by the time they returned to his house, winded yet exhilarated, he'd made a decision.

He wasn't going to kill Alan. He'd try one last time to convince him to abandon the marriage, and then he'd play his ace. He'd tell Alan who he was and explain a basic fact of life: if Reinn didn't kill him, the council would simply send someone else to do the job. And that someone *wouldn't* let emotion get in his way or care if Alan's new wife died with him.

Then Reinn would make plans for the hunters that the council would send after their former Guardian. He was the oldest and most powerful of the Mackenzies. He'd make anyone who came after him pay. In fact, maybe he'd take the fight to the council. They'd be sitting back thinking they were safe in their homes. How many centuries had it been since someone hunted *them?* The thought made him smile. Not a nice smile.

Reinn watched Kisa shift back to human form. "You're doing better," he noted. "You were in control the whole time." He picked up their clothes from the ground.

She stood naked with her long, dark hair flowing across her shoulders. A light breeze blew a few strands away from her face as Kisa took a deep breath and lifted her gaze to the night sky.

The breath focused his attention on those perfect breasts that filled his palms so well. His hunger for her stirred again. And when she looked at him, he saw the same desire reflected in her eyes.

Uh-uh. Wasn't going to happen. He put his hunger for her to bed for the night. She'd be sore tomorrow, and more lovemaking would just pile on the hurt. Besides, when she found out who he was, she'd be sore in a whole new way. The word "sore" had no positives.

He was doing the right thing. Fat lot of comfort that thought gave him. "Let's go inside."

Reinn led her into his master suite by way of the French doors off his covered porch. And while she was busy looking into every corner, he went into the great room to get her . . . He didn't know exactly what to call it, but it was small, sexy, and she was going to wear it to bed. Or not. The beads on that thong weren't made for sweet dreams.

As he walked back into his bedroom, she spun to grin at him. "How can you ever leave this place? If I had this kind of bedroom, I'd make sure I slept in it every single night—or in your case, day—of my life."

He turned to look at it through her eyes. Yeah, it was spectacular. It felt good to have someone remind him of that. "You can shower first." Reinn opened his closet door and pulled out one of his robes. "This is too big for you, but it's the best I can do."

Her eyes shifted to the sexy little night outfit with the killer beads.

"Lady, you couldn't be sexier than you were tonight, so you don't have to torture yourself with that to turn me on. Save it for another night." Another night? Probably wouldn't happen, because he'd have to talk to Alan tomorrow night.

He'd stay to keep the bridegroom alive until after the wedding, but he didn't think Kisa would be in the mood to make love once she found out who he was. And right after the wedding he'd be on his way to Scotland to take on the freakin' council.

She didn't argue, but accepted his robe and hurried into his bathroom. He could hear her oohing and ahhing over that, too. Reinn slipped into another robe and waited for her to come out. He wiped all thoughts from his mind, because thinking wouldn't make things better.

When she finally came out all warm from his shower and smelling of his soap, he had to beat down his hunger once more. He hurried into the bathroom before temptation reared its persistent head again.

Reinn opted for a cold shower. Cold showers were overrated. No matter that he was freezing his butt off; his sexual interest was hot and ready to party. Lucky for him, when he walked into the bedroom, the object of all his hot interest was asleep on his bed. How could he feel relieved and disappointed at the same time? *Go figure.*

Reinn glanced at the graying sky. Dawn was near. He pulled the heavy drapes across the windows he loved. Which was just crazy. Windows obsessed him—the more the better. And yet he couldn't look out them on a sunny day. But it wasn't all bad. With his enhanced vision, things were always visible.

On an overcast or stormy day, he could even rise early to enjoy the view. Nights when the moon was full, he'd turn off all the lights and sit in the darkness gazing out at the mountains and forests. Maybe in a few years when his power had grown even greater, he'd be able to look out the windows on a sunny day for a short time without the pain.

But for tonight, he wouldn't worry about the view outside his windows, because he had everything he wanted to look at curled up in his bed. The robe he'd loaned her lay beside the bed. *Good.* Even though the familiar lethargy that came with every dawn pulled at him, he'd make sure to stay awake for a while to enjoy the feel of her bare body against his. He'd better make the most of it while he could.

Dropping his robe, he slid the covers over her and climbed into bed beside her. Reinn pulled her tightly against him. He smiled into her hair. She'd forgotten all about cooking dinner for Sparkle.

Chapter Twelve

"I wanted her to have fun, but not this much fun." Sparkle tapped a perfectly shaped nail with its fresh coat of Dark Desire nail color on the kitchen table. "She's been gone since last night. I had to deal with dinner myself, for crying out loud." She tapped the toe of her Prada sandal along with her nail to add emphasis to her annoyance. "Are you listening to me, Mede?"

"*Yeah, yeah. You made Bernie cook dinner. So what's the big deal?*" Mede liked to eat his cake first and icing last. He was at the icing stage.

Sparkle glared at him. "It was still stressful. And if you keep stuffing your furry face with cake, you'll have to hit the gym when you return to human form."

Ganymede didn't even pause to look up at her from where he crouched on the floor over his huge blob of icing. "*I have a great human form, and I don't like being away from it. So I eat cake to make me feel better. It's my comfort food, okay?*"

Sparkle sighed. How many millennia would it

take before she learned just to let him eat? Nagging and sarcasm didn't work on Ganymede. Besides, he was right. He had a hunkalicious body in his human form. "Fine. Eat yourself into a stupor."

Maybe she was being too negative. There were plenty of positives here. "Things are really working out between them." A little backpatting was in order, but she'd have to do it herself. The universe would implode before Ganymede admitted she'd done a good job. "I think this could be my crowning achievement. I hooked the Guardian of the Blood up with a werecat who changes into a saber-toothed tiger. No cosmic troublemaker has ever done that before."

"Who'd want to?" His comment was a mental mumble.

"What?" She narrowed her eyes to angry slits. "At least *my* plan is working. Yours isn't rolling along too well, is it, hotshot?"

Ganymede finally lifted his head from the empty plate. He had chocolate icing all over his face. She couldn't help it; she grinned.

Now it was his turn to narrow his eyes. *"What's so funny?"*

She laughed out loud. "I'm sorry, but there you crouch, the biggest badass in the universe, with icing all over your face."

"Hmmph." He sat up and started cleaning his face with one furry paw. *"Your little scheme could still go bad. What happens when Kisa finds out that Reinn is her worst nightmare? Won't be much left of the Woo Woo Inn if a saber-toothed tiger and one of the most powerful vampires in existence duke it out here. Don't think*

Cindy and Thrain would invite us back." He paused in the cleaning process. *"But I guess it'd be tough for them to invite us back to a pile of toothpicks."*

Sparkle felt a shimmer of excitement behind his scowl. Ganymede got off on things falling down, or blowing away, or sinking beneath the sea, or—

"My setup is a little trickier than yours. You could work on the sex angle to bring Kisa and Reinn together. I have to go with pure talent to make my plans for Reinn and Mason work. It took pure brilliance just to get them in the same building." Finished cleaning his face, he leaped into Sparkle's lap.

This thing between Reinn and Mason made her nervous. "One of them could die, Mede."

Surprisingly, he didn't deny it. *"Yeah, but I'm on top of things. I'll step in if I have to. But I had to go with it, babe. The payoff was too big for me to resist. Think of the big moment when they both realize that—"*

Sparkle's cell phone rang and spoiled the moment. God, she hoped it was a cook dying to do his, her, or its thing at the Woo Woo Inn. She'd called the Chinese restaurant last night, so tonight's dinner was covered. "Hello. The Woo Woo Inn."

"Hi, sensual food lady. Katie, your ex-cook, here. I've given you a few days to try out your style of cooking. How's it working for you?" Evil chuckle.

If Sparkle could have crawled through the phone line, she would have gleefully whacked the old witch upside her head with her own broom. She took a deep breath. The bottom line? She wanted out of the kitchen and Katie back in it. Time to toss aside pride and bargain with the biddy.

"It's not working. I'm dealing with a bunch of sensual zeroes here. Come back and you can cook whatever you want." That was about as self-abasing as Sparkle got.

"You won't set foot in my kitchen?"

"Not even one stylish toe."

"Maybe you'll suggest that I get a raise when Cindy and Thrain come home?"

"You're pushing it, Katie. But okay, I'll mention it to them."

"How about if—"

"Bargaining done. Deal?" Sparkle made ugly-eyes at Ganymede, who was laughing in her head.

"Deal." Katie sounded a little too triumphant. "I have dinner covered for tonight and tomorrow night, but I'll need you for the other meals."

"I'll be there." Katie paused. "My broom still doesn't like you."

"You can tell your broom I've seen better-looking straw butts sweeping barns." Sparkle might have to make nice with Katie, but the broom was a different matter altogether. The broom didn't make mashed potatoes or apple pie.

"Tsk, tsk." Katie needed an attitude adjustment. "You've hurt Broom's feelings. He'll remember that."

"Yeah, like I care. Gotta go now." Sparkle hung up.

"*Katie's coming back?*" Ganymede sounded way too happy. He could at least pretend he'd liked her cooking.

"I wish just once you'd be supportive. I'm sort of tired of listening to you go on about your freakin' power and glory when you're always acting like what I do has no value." She sniffed. "I wouldn't expect any cuddling for the foreseeable future if I were you." *Jerk.* She blinked rapidly. And she was *not* getting all emotional over his constant trivializing of her calling in life.

"*Yo, babe, I didn't mean—*"

"Stuff it, Mede." Turning her back to him, she walked from the kitchen, the *click-click* of her stilettos punctuating her anger.

She'd just slammed the kitchen door with a satisfying bang when Hal met her.

"Those barbecue guys, Billy Bob and Bubba, just got here." Hal's expression said he didn't quite know what to do with them.

Sparkle drew in a deep breath and controlled her urge to scream. *Just freakin' great.*

Reinn sat relaxed in one of the chairs in Kisa's sitting area, watching her root around for the piece of paper that had the information about the catnip car's owner.

When he'd risen this evening, he'd found her sitting in his great room staring out at the panoramic view of the mountains fading into dusk. Reinn had prepared himself for dozens of questions, maybe some accusations. At the very least she'd expect to discuss their "relationship" and whether they'd make love again. She'd ignored the expected in favor of something more immediate.

"You don't have coffee. You don't have *anything* in your kitchen. What happens if you have visitors?"

She looked outraged. "I'm cranky all day without coffee."

"I don't have visitors, so I don't need stuff in my kitchen." He'd memorized how she looked sitting there with the mountains as a backdrop. Good memories. He hadn't had a lot of them in his life. But he wasn't complaining. Kisa made up for the bad ones.

She'd sighed. "I guess it's time to go back."

Still no mention of last night. "Yeah." He'd smiled. "You didn't get a chance to wear your sexy outfit."

Kisa had returned his smile. "Maybe next time."

"Definitely." A thousand years of practice had made him a good liar.

She still hadn't complained about being sore. He wasn't in her mind to take the pain away now, so she had to be hurting. No questions about his powers. No questions about anything.

They'd watched in silence as darkness swallowed the mountains, and then, wrapping his arms around her, he'd returned them to her room at the Woo Woo Inn.

She handed him the paper. "The guy's name is Harry Lynch. His address is there, too. Can you dig anything up on him?"

"Shouldn't be a problem." Reinn stood. He thought about walking out the door without touching her. Because as soon as he finished checking on Lynch, he'd be dealing with Alan. That wouldn't be pretty. And she'd probably regret it if he kissed her now.

Oh, what the hell. He walked to her and then pulled her into his arms. When he covered her mouth with his, she met him with the same eagerness as last night. Sliding his palms down to her bottom, he cupped her cheeks and pulled her tightly against him. At least she wouldn't have to ask if he still wanted her.

He absorbed the texture and taste of her mouth. If this was it for them, he'd make it good.

When they finally separated, he was ready to drag her into bed and stay there for the rest of the night. From the glazed look in her eyes, she wouldn't say no.

Alan. He stood between them and would remain there until Reinn settled things. The problem was, once Alan was out of the way, Reinn's life expectancy would shorten considerably. If he could survive the council . . . No, he wouldn't look past tonight.

He forced a smile to his face as he left. "Don't forget, you're going to the Bare Truth tonight." Reinn pretended to glare. "Just remember to keep your eyes closed."

"You bet." Her smile seemed a little strained, too.

Reinn wished he could stay and straighten things out between them, but he couldn't. Not now. Maybe not ever. He closed the door quietly behind him and went to his room.

Once inside, he checked his e-mail. The first message brought home how thoroughly Kisa was driving everything from his mind. He'd missed the delivery of the extra sword he'd ordered for Alan.

The courier wanted instructions. Reinn typed in two words: *Cancel delivery*.

Then he went on to do a search on Harry Lynch. A half hour later he sat back to digest what he'd learned. Interesting. He'd pass what he'd discovered on to Kisa, and then he'd look for Mr. Lynch.

No way would he find the guy before Kisa's trip into town tonight, though. So Reinn would have to be there to keep her safe. If they weren't on speaking terms after his talk with Alan, he'd cloak his presence and tag along anyway. He'd be there for her one way or another tonight.

He showered and changed into a clean pair of jeans and a T-shirt. He should be glad Sparkle didn't focus her talents on male fashion, because he was just a jeans-and-T-shirt kind of guy. He'd drive her crazy. Or maybe the other way around.

Time to put his plan in motion. First he'd take care of Mason. If the vampire *was* the Protector, he'd be glued to Alan. Downstairs, he found Mason and Alan talking in the parlor while everyone was eating breakfast.

He walked over and stood in front of them. "Hey, Mason. Can I talk to you for a sec?" Reinn cast an apologetic glance at Alan.

Alan smiled. "No problem. I have to hunt down Julie anyway." He glanced at Mason. "Talk to you later."

Mason didn't look happy about leaving Alan. "So what's up?"

Reinn glanced around the room. "Can we go to your room? I want this private."

Reluctantly, Mason led Reinn to his room. "Okay, we're alone."

Reinn strode to Mason's closet, flung open the door, grabbed all of Mason's clothes and tossed them on the floor, and then pointed to a far corner of the closet. "Take a look."

Frowning, Mason peered inside. "I don't see—"

Instantly Reinn became vampire so he'd be at his strongest, and then he gathered his power. He visualized a giant hand shoving Mason. With a startled grunt, Mason fell into the closet. Before the other vampire could recover, Reinn slammed shut the door and erected his strongest mental shields around the closet walls as well as the ceiling and floor.

Reinn smiled grimly. Mason's shouts wouldn't be heard, and if he had his cell phone in there with him, it'd be useless. Even his mental shouts would go unnoticed. Mason was stuck in there for a while. He might be powerful, but not as powerful as Reinn. Given time, Mason would probably gather enough power to batter his way out, but by that time Reinn would have had his talk with Alan.

He walked from the room and calmly shut the door behind him. Now for Alan.

Reinn went to a small clearing in a deep part of the forest and sat on a fallen log. He hadn't practiced his compulsion skills for a long time. Since his days as a mercenary, he hadn't needed them. He'd use them now.

Closing his eyes, he called. Then he waited. About ten minutes later, a bewildered Alan stumbled out of the forest.

"What the hell am I doing here?" He rubbed a hand across his eyes. "One minute I'm talking to Julie, and the next I feel like I have to get out of there and go for a walk by myself. Now I'm here." His gaze sharpened. "And you're here. Why?"

Reinn smiled. *Good.* He was suspicious. It showed he wasn't completely clueless. "Sit down, Alan. We need to talk."

Alan never took his gaze from Reinn as he chose a log on the other side of the clearing to sit on. "Okay, talk."

"Guess it won't change your mind about marrying Julie if I tell you she'll want to share the remote, or that she'll drag you to see relationship movies where nothing gets blown up."

Alan just stared at him.

"Didn't think so." Reinn speared him with a hard stare. "I'm the Guardian of the Blood, Alan, and the council isn't too happy with your wedding plans." He kept his voice soft, knowing that quiet was a lot scarier than shouting could ever be.

Alan stiffened, but he didn't jump up and try to run. "Why didn't you let me burn in the car?"

Reinn sensed his fear. It was evident in the harshness of his voice and the slight tremor of his hands. Too bad. He would've liked having Alan for a friend. Before Kisa, he hadn't wanted friends. He'd better recapture his old I-don't-need-anyone attitude fast.

"You know the rules of the game. A Mackenzie has to be given the chance to defend himself with his sword. You wouldn't get that chance if you'd died in the accident." He shook his head. "You didn't bring your sword with you. I checked. Not too smart, Alan."

Alan's expression turned bitter. "Why bother? I don't know how to use a freakin' sword. So let's get this over with. The only thing I ask is that Julie never finds out what happened. Let her think I got cold feet and ran. I don't want her or her family coming after you and getting themselves killed." He glanced around the clearing. "Where's your sword?"

"So you're not going to fight? You'd just let me kill you?" Reinn was curious. If he were in Alan's shoes, he'd fight for the right to stay with Julie.

Alan glared at him. "Oh, I'll fight. But I'm not stupid. The Guardian is always the oldest and most powerful. The outcome won't be in much doubt."

"Now, see, there you're wrong." Reinn knew his smile showed no happiness. Because in sparing Alan, he was probably condemning himself. "I'm not going to kill you."

Alan stared at him in stunned disbelief. "Why not?"

Reinn shrugged. "I don't like the council's rules. Night feeders whacked the old Guardian last year. I was next in line. You don't say no to the council. Anyway, this is my first job, and I've decided that killing you just because you love Julie is a serious waste. So I won't do it."

"Oh, my God." Alan slumped like a puppet whose strings had been cut. "Thanks. Anything you ever want from me, you got it."

Reinn didn't know if Alan had the power to cry. He hoped not. "Don't thank me too soon. You're not safe yet."

Alan straightened, but the hope was back in his eyes, along with a determination to live. *Good for him.*

"The council will send someone else, won't they?"

Reinn nodded. "As soon as they find out I didn't kill you, they'll appoint a new Guardian of the Blood. The next one won't let emotion get in his way, and he damn well won't care if he kills Julie along with you. Like I said before, you might want to reconsider this marriage."

Alan looked frantic. "There has to be something we can do. Hell, you're the most powerful Mackenzie of all. With you on our side, we can kick some council butt."

Whoa. When had this become a *we* thing? "I'll try to take the council down, but I work alone."

"Why? You'll have a lot better shot at it if you get all the werecats behind you." He thought for a moment. "If we can get a message to the Protector, I bet he'll help."

Reinn thought of Mason locked in his closet. "Wouldn't count on that."

"We need to talk strategy." Alan was adamant.

Talking wouldn't hurt anything. Reinn would humor the kid.

"What's your real name? It isn't Daniel Night." Alan was sounding surer of himself.

Reinn smiled. A real one this time. "I'm Reinn Mackenzie."

* * *

Kisa couldn't find Daniel, Alan, or Mason. She'd already searched downstairs, and now she was hitting each of their rooms. What were the chances of their all being gone at once? Maybe they'd found a lead on her attacker and were following up on it. Without her. Typical male behavior. It never occurred to them that someone who could change into a saber-toothed tiger might be good to have along when they were chasing bad guys. Besides, who had the biggest stake in this whole thing?

She took a deep breath as she stood outside the last door. Mason's room. *Calm down.* She was rushing to conclusions. But then, she'd been running on nerves and emotion ever since last night. She knocked at his door. Nothing.

Kisa was just about to turn away when she thought she heard a faint shout. So faint that if she'd been a normal human she wouldn't have caught it. She listened more carefully. It was as though someone was calling from a long distance, but it sounded like the voice was coming from Mason's room.

She wasn't sure what to do, but then decided to take the chance of looking foolish by calling Sparkle.

When Sparkle and Ganymede joined her, Trouble was with them. Kisa put her finger over her lips. "Listen."

Ganymede nodded. *"Something's going on in there. Open the door, sweetie."*

"Sweetie" refused to look at him as she unlocked

231

the door. All was not peace and harmony in the cosmic troublemaker world. They all trooped into the room.

Ganymede padded over to the closet door. *"The shouts are coming from in here."* He stared at the closet for a moment. *"Uh-oh. Someone's trapped Mason in here. And there's only one person staying at the inn powerful enough to put up that strong a mental shield."*

Sparkle looked really scared, which in turn terrified Kisa. Something had to be seriously wrong to put that look on Sparkle's face.

"Where's Reinn? I thought you said you were on top of things? Where's Alan?" A panicked note crept into Sparkle's voice. She looked down at Trouble. "You were supposed to be keeping an eye on him. What the hell have you been doing?"

Trouble dropped to the floor and put his front paws over his ears. *"You're not supposed to curse in front of me. I have young and impressionable ears. And I was chasing rabbits, big fat bunnies with fluffy white tails. I can't help it that there're so many bunnies in the woods."*

Sparkle narrowed her eyes to amber slits. "You are so not going to ever see your second birthday."

Trouble scrambled to the door, ears flattened and tail tucked. Kisa could hear his panicked yelps all the way down the hall.

"Who's Reinn, and what mental shield are you talking about?" Fine, so she was officially confused as well as frightened.

Ganymede glanced at Sparkle. *"You explain it to her while I get Mason out of here."*

Sparkle bit her lip. She obviously didn't want to tell Kisa anything. Finally she took a deep breath and met Kisa's gaze. "Daniel Night isn't Daniel Night. He's really Reinn Mackenzie, Guardian of the Blood. He's here to make sure Alan doesn't marry Julie. We knew that, but Mede warned him off, so we thought everything was cool." She glared at Ganymede's back. "Mr. I'm-on-top-of-things underestimated Reinn. Now we've got a situation."

Kisa closed her eyes and swallowed hard. Poor Alan, poor Julie, poor *her*. She'd made love last night with the Guardian of the Blood, and even as he'd entered her, he'd known he was going to kill Alan. He knew what that would do to her whole family, to *her*. The scope of his betrayal squeezed her heart into a hard little kernel of . . . hate? She didn't know; the hurt was too immediate to sort out feelings.

Her beast roared to life, beating at her consciousness, clawing at her insides. She shoved it away for the moment. But when the time came . . .

She didn't get a chance to think about what she'd do when the time came, because at that moment Ganymede brought down the shields holding Mason captive in the closet.

"That son of a bitch!" Mason burst from the closet.

Ganymede was still just a gray cat, but the air around him shimmered with power. *"Calm down. Going all crazy won't help us. We've got to find Reinn and Alan right now."*

"Reinn?" For just a moment, Mason looked like

someone had sucker punched him, leaving him gasping for air. Then he recovered. "Let me guess: his last name is Mackenzie, and he's the friggin' Guardian of the Blood." Mason oozed barely contained fury as he punched the air in frustration.

Strange. Kisa got the feeling all that anger was directed inward, not toward Reinn Mackenzie. Which didn't make sense. But then, nothing had made sense for the last few minutes. She was probably imagining Mason's reaction.

Ganymede glanced at each of them in turn. *"Any idea where he'd go?"* His gaze paused on Kisa.

"I know where he hid his sword." The nightmare just got worse and worse. Should she tell the other werecats? No, a horde of werecats charging through the woods would warn Dan . . . Reinn long before they got there.

Sparkle looked puzzled. "Mede took his sword away and hid it."

"He ordered another. It's hidden in the old church." How could her heart be pounding in anger and breaking at the same time? A mystery of nature.

Mason threw his hands into the air. "You knew he had a sword and didn't tell anyone?"

Good. Someone she could yell at. "Back off. How was I supposed to know he was the Guardian? He didn't kill Alan when he had the chance. Besides, the explanation he gave for the sword made sense."

"He couldn't kill Alan then. The Mackenzie council has decreed that a condemned clan member has to have a chance to defend himself with a sword." Mason couldn't contain himself. He paced the room with angry strides. "This is all my fault. I was suspicious, but I couldn't come up with any real evidence."

"Okay, I'm confused. What do you have to do with all this?" She glanced at the others. "And we have to get moving."

"I'm the Protector, and I've just blown a save." He spoke through gritted teeth. "We'll find the church and go from there."

A *human* was the Protector? How could a human stop a vampire? And the Protector had been around a lot longer than a human life span. Maybe it was a family thing, passed from father to son. Something to ask about when they weren't in the middle of a "situation."

"I might be able to find him in my cat form, but it would be a long shot. I don't know where he entered the forest or if he even did. He could've taken Alan somewhere else."

"Don't change." Everyone spoke at once.

Kisa nodded. They were right. In her present state of mind, her cat would run wild. "Let's hit the church first. If they're not there, we can bring in the other werecats to help us hunt."

Ganymede looked steamed. *"We won't need the other werecats. We'll hit the church first, but if Reinn isn't there, I'll find him."* His amber eyes glowed with something that made Kisa shiver. *"Never doubt it."*

Even though she was furious with Reinn and terrified for Alan, the part of her that didn't recognize logic was afraid for the man who'd made love with her. But she'd have to keep reminding herself that

Daniel Night didn't exist except in the fantasy world he'd created.

As she led the others into the woods, Kisa moved gingerly. She was sore today, but it was a good sore, sort of like a woo-hoo-goooood-bye-virginity sore. Or it had been until she'd found out the truth. At least the pain wasn't a fantasy.

They hurried along the forest path, Sparkle trying to keep up as she ran on the toes of her stilettos. But when they reached the church, Reinn wasn't there.

Kisa looked behind the altar and pulled out the sword. "He didn't take his sword." She needed two hands to hold it up for the rest to see. "What does that mean?"

Mason seemed to relax a little. "I don't know what game he's playing, but he's not planning to kill Alan right now if he doesn't have his sword with him."

Sparkle leaned against a crumbling wall. "Jeez, my feet are killing me. I hope he's not too far away."

Everyone watched Ganymede as he grew still. He radiated so much focused power that Kisa had to step back from it. *Remind me never to make Ganymede mad.*

Ganymede didn't waste time in explanation. *"Follow me."*

A few minutes later, their search ended in a small clearing. Reinn sat on a log while a very-much-alive Alan relaxed on another.

Reinn glanced at them as they charged out of the forest. His gaze touched her for a moment and then went on to Mason. "I know you didn't get out of that closet by yourself, so I guess Ganymede helped you."

Mason took an angry step forward.

"Let's all relax and cool off." Ganymede padded over to the log Reinn sat on, jumped up beside him, and sat down.

It was pretty obvious to Kisa that he was positioning himself near the one he considered the most dangerous.

Sparkle wasted no time in dropping down next to Alan. She slipped off her shoes. "The best part of wearing man-killer shoes is taking them off. But that's okay, because I'm willing to suffer for style. Too bad more people don't appreciate what I do on a day-to-day basis." She sent Ganymede a hard stare.

Kisa would have liked to remain standing, but she didn't want Reinn to think he was making her nervous, so she sat next to Sparkle.

Mason refused to sit. He leaned against a tree trunk and crossed his arms over his chest. "We know you're the Guardian of the Blood, Mackenzie, so why is Alan still alive?"

Mason stared intently at Reinn while some strong emotion Kisa couldn't identify moved in his gaze. She knew one thing: whatever he felt for Reinn, it wasn't hatred.

Reinn looked relaxed, but Kisa had no doubt he could destroy all of them except maybe Ganymede within seconds if he chose to. A scary thought.

Did she think he'd kill her? No. Her reason? She just knew. How was that for logic?

Reinn glanced around the small group and then shrugged. "I quit my crappy job."

Chapter Thirteen

"You can't quit. Guardian of the Blood is a lifetime job." Mason seemed outraged that Reinn would dare change the rules of the game. "And if you weren't going to kill Alan, why'd you lock me in that damn closet?"

Reinn smiled but stayed alert. Ganymede was the most dangerous one in the group, but he was calm, less volatile than Mason. He wouldn't attack without a good reason. Mason's emotions were closer to the surface, and Reinn would have to watch him. "You stayed close to Alan all the time, so I figured you were the Protector. I needed to talk to Alan alone."

"Get over your mad, Mason." Sparkle wiggled her toes, probably trying to bend them back to their original shape after wearing those shoes. "Everything worked out fine. Alan's okay, so we can go back to the inn." She sighed. "I'd go back barefoot, but I might chip my toenail color."

"Alan's still not safe." Ganymede understood how the council worked.

"Ganymede's right." Reinn forced himself not to look at Kisa. She hadn't spoken yet, but he'd bet once they were alone she'd have a lot to say. Which wasn't all bad. Better than her *never* talking to him again. "Once the council finds out that Alan's still alive, they'll appoint another Guardian of the Blood to take him out. And the next one might not care about collateral damage so long as Alan's dead."

"I'll be ready for him." Some of the anger had faded from Mason's voice.

"Like you were for me?" Mason was powerful, but he wasn't vicious. The next Guardian would kill Mason, not just stick him in a closet.

"I won't go near any closets next time." Unexpectedly, Mason smiled. "And all the werecats will be on high alert for him."

Reinn was surprised at Mason's attitude. If another vampire locked *him* in a closet, he'd still want to kill the bastard. Reinn found himself studying Mason again. There was something about his smile that once more nudged Reinn's memory, as though he'd known this man in another time.

"Did we ever meet?" He couldn't quite touch the memory, and it was driving him nuts.

Mason shifted his gaze away from Reinn. "Maybe. I've lived a long time, and I've met a lot of people."

Alan stood up. "If you're all finished talking about my chances of surviving my marriage, I'd like to go back to Julie." He looked at Reinn. "I'd still like you to stick around. We could use your support. But whatever you decide, thanks for giving me a second chance at life."

Reinn nodded, and then watched him disappear into the night. Ganymede and Sparkle followed close behind. Kisa announced her intention to stay by not moving from her log. Mason seemed uncertain what to do.

Reinn studied the other vampire. "Sorry about the closet, but I had to get you out of the way."

Mason nodded, but he seemed preoccupied with other thoughts.

Kisa still didn't know that Mason was a vampire, so Reinn opted for mental questioning. *"The Protector. Kind of a strange job for a vampire, isn't it? Do you belong to a clan or group? I know you're not a Mackenzie with those brown eyes."*

Even though Reinn was purposely not looking at Kisa, he could feel her gaze on him. He was tempted to slip into her mind, but he'd made her a promise not to. He could keep that promise, at least.

"I belong to myself. I don't need anyone at my back." Mason moved toward the forest. *"And I work for the werecats because I owe them, will always owe them."* Then he, too, left the clearing.

Alone. Reinn looked at Kisa and waited. Once again she surprised him.

"Now tell me the true story of your life." Her expression unreadable, she stretched her legs out in front of her.

He shrugged. "Everything I told you was true. I

just left out the part where the clan moved to Scotland and became Mackenzies."

"How do you become vampire?" She was putting off the tough questions.

Reinn didn't blame her. "We simply change. Usually it happens somewhere around thirty. We're still alive, but we have a different physiology."

She nodded and then hit him with the big question. "Why'd you make love to me, knowing how I'd feel when I found out who you were?" Now that she'd worked up the courage to ask, her gaze never wavered from his face.

"Pure—or maybe you'd call it impure—selfishness." He wouldn't back away from taking responsibility for what he'd done. Truth was, he didn't feel a whole lot of guilt anymore. If the council's hunters took him down, he'd go out with one great memory. "I wanted you so badly, I could almost taste you. Your scent was with me all the time, and I won't even talk about how much I wanted to run my fingers over your body." He returned her stare. "I still want you."

She didn't comment on the wanting. "When did you decide to let Alan live?"

"When we were running through the forest last night." He didn't elaborate. Reinn could see her trying to resist her need to know.

She gave in. "Why *then*?"

"Because I decided it was wrong to kill a man for loving a woman the council didn't like." *Especially when I think I might be doing the same thing.*

She nodded.

"And because of you."

"Me?" Her tone was neutral.

It didn't give him hope, but it didn't squash him like a bug, either. "I didn't want you looking at me like I had 'scum-sucking bastard' tattooed across my forehead."

That earned him a faint smile, the first he'd seen since she'd rushed out of the forest. "I like brevity. I would've left it at 'bastard.'"

"So where do we go from here?" He braced himself for a you-can-go-to-hell retort.

"Back to the inn, because I have to change. Tonight's Julie's party at the Bare Truth." She stood and started walking toward the trees.

He caught up with her. "I'm going with you tonight."

She looked at him and then nodded. "I'd like to make a grand exit by saying I don't need a scum-sucking bastard for a bodyguard, but that would be stupid. I don't know where the next attack will come from."

Reinn felt like a one-ton Clydesdale had just stepped off his chest. "By the way, I got some interesting information on Harry Lynch, your catnip-car owner. He's a biochemist. I called the apartment complex where he used to live, and the woman in the office said he moved out of his apartment a few weeks ago. Didn't leave a forwarding address. He told her he was moving in with his girlfriend."

Kisa frowned. "Not much help. Did she give a description?"

"Yeah. About five feet, ten inches, short brown hair, and a good body."

"That would describe a lot of men." She headed across the lawn at the back of the inn. "Looks like the barbecue team is settling in for the long haul. Good barbecue takes a long time to get right."

Reinn stayed by her side as she walked over to the two men standing in front of the big commercial barbecue pit.

"Hey, guys, how's it going?" She smiled that open, friendly smile Reinn would kill to have directed at him again.

Both men were walking stereotypes—cowboy hats, checked shirts, worn jeans, and scuffed boots.

"Well, hi, there, little lady. I'm Billy Bob and this here's Bubba." Billy Bob grinned at Kisa and then acknowledged Reinn with a nod. His gaze immediately returned to Kisa.

Reinn knew when he'd been relegated to afterthought status. Good old Billy Bob probably thought he should get lost, but Reinn wasn't leaving Kisa alone with anyone until he'd caught her attacker.

Bubba slapped Kisa on the back, and Reinn grabbed her before she went facedown from all his enthusiasm. "Y'all are in for a treat tomorrow night. Billy Bob and me make the meanest barbecue in the entire U.S. of A. We're the Badass Texas Barbecue team from Houston."

Reinn eyed the long table filled with things he guessed were part of barbecuing. Besides the table, there were two lawn chairs and a cot set up under a large canopy. "Looks like you take your barbecuing seriously."

"You betcha." Billy Bob's grin widened. "You ain't tasted nothin' till you've tasted our brisket and ribs. We've got our own secret blend of herbs and spices. And we do a marinade with Cajun seasoning that'll make you get all weepy. We'll start smoking the meat in a few hours, and then watch this baby"—he nodded toward the barbecue pit—"work her magic all day tomorrow. We stay on duty the whole time. One of us sleeps while the other one takes care of things. Got lots of snacks to keep us going."

Reinn couldn't resist. He slipped into Billy Bob's mind. When he slipped out again, he was grinning. "Okay, what're your real names, and what do you sound like when you're not barbecuing?"

Bubba looked insulted. "We're one hundred percent Texas proud. We always talk this way."

Kisa backed Reinn up. "Don't mess with Reinn, boys. He's a mind reader. He's probably already been inside both your heads. You can't keep secrets from him." She glanced at Reinn, her expression reminding him that secrets got people in trouble.

Message received. No more secrets.

Billy Bob glanced around to make sure no one was nearby. "I'm Clarence and this is Eugene. We moved down from New York about ten years ago and opened a furniture store. The store did great, but we both like to cook, so we do this on the side. Perception is everything in any business. People don't want their barbecue team to be two furniture-store owners from New York." He shrugged. "So we give them what they expect."

Reinn laughed, and that surprised him. He hadn't thought he'd find very much funny after Kisa learned that he was the Guardian of the Blood. But he had a small ray of hope now, because she hadn't left him sitting alone in the woods, and she'd accepted his offer of protection. Even knowing the council's hunters would be descending on him soon couldn't dent his small core of returning happiness.

"I'll be looking forward to some great barbecue tomorrow night." Kisa smiled and waved as she continued toward the inn.

Once inside, Reinn stopped. "I think I'll get on the phone and call some of the places still open in town to see if anyone recognizes Lynch's name. It's a long shot. He's probably using an alias."

She nodded. "Felicia's going to drive us to the Bare Truth in the Woo Woo Inn's van. There won't be room for you, so you'll have to follow on your bike."

He wanted to pull her into his arms and cover her mouth with his. But it was too soon, so he just nodded and went into the parlor where Alan and Mason sat. He joined them.

"I'm going to the Bare Truth with Kisa and the other women. We don't know when the wacko who's tossing catnip at her will strike again." He looked at Alan. "The council expected you to be dead by now. I haven't reported in, so they know something's wrong. They don't take chances. Another Guardian might already be on his way. I think you should ride with me tonight."

Alan nodded. "Makes sense. We can take my car."

"I'm coming, too." Mason looked at Reinn. "Will you recognize the new Guardian?"

"Maybe not personally, but all I have to see are his eyes. Mackenzies all have eyes the same shade of blue. Reinn glanced at Alan. "That's why I expected you to make me right away." He stood. "I have work to do in my room. I'll meet you here in an hour."

"Wait, wait, I want to go with you." Trouble bounded up to them, tail wagging and eyes pleading. *"Sparkle won't be mad at me anymore if I go with you. And I can smell all kinds of stuff far away. Please, please, please."*

Mason and Alan groaned.

Reinn weighed the pros and cons. Lots of cons. "They won't let you inside the club, but you can wait outside and give a mental shout if you smell catnip on anyone going in. Do you know what catnip smells like?"

Trouble nodded eagerly. *"I smelled the parlor after someone put catnip in the air-conditioning vent."*

"You're on. We're meeting here in an hour." Reinn ignored Mason's and Alan's pained expressions as he walked away.

Kisa looked in the mirror. Sexy outfit. A metallic silk camisole, silk-chiffon ruffled skirt, and ankle-strap sandals. Accessories—gold bangles, dangly earrings, sequined flower pin, and metallic leather handbag. Pink and all-out girlie. The best part? Sparkle had left the outfit in her room with just a note: *I gagged on the pink, but Reinn needs to see the softer you to balance your big, bad kitty persona.*

She glanced at her watch. It was time to take her girlie self downstairs. Which brought her thoughts back to Reinn, not that they'd been far from him to begin with.

Had she forgiven him? Almost. She understood why he'd decided to keep quiet. If he'd admitted he was the Guardian of the Blood, she wouldn't have waited around to hear his explanation. Besides, she hadn't exactly shouted from the rooftops that she turned into a saber-toothed tiger. Kisa even understood why he'd made love to her, knowing how mad she'd be when she found out. The last few days had taught her a lot about lust.

She might understand why he'd made love to her while keeping quiet about his job, but understanding didn't cancel out the hurt. And yes, she was honest enough to admit he'd hurt her. Now for the hard part. He had the power to hurt her because she'd started to care a little too much. She wasn't quite sure what to do with that knowledge.

She thought about Reinn all the way downstairs. When she reached the foyer, Julie and the others were waiting for her. Reinn, Alan, Mason, and Trouble were standing to the side. Trouble?

Felicia frowned at the men. "Why are they coming? This is Julie's bachelorette party."

Kisa looked at her sister. She knew Alan had probably told Julie everything, so her sister understood the importance of having Reinn and Mason with Alan. She'd also know that Reinn had to stick close to Kisa.

Julie aimed her brightest smile at the wedding planner. "I want them with us, Felicia. Indulge me. Strange things have been happening lately, and I'll feel safer with them close by."

Brilliant. Julie was just telling the truth. What could Felicia say?

She didn't say anything. Felicia simply climbed into the driver's seat and waited for everyone to pile in. Everyone didn't quite fit, so they rode to the club all stuffed together. Kisa thought longingly of Alan's nice, roomy car. Then she remembered Trouble. He was in the car, too. Doggy breath, doggy hair, and nonstop doggy exuberance. Maybe the van wasn't so bad.

Once at the club they all tumbled out, a giggling mob of women with nothing on their minds except seeing hot, almost-naked men dance. Subtract two from the carefree crew. Kisa and Julie had plenty on their minds.

Kisa looked back as they went inside. The men were right behind them. They must've left Trouble outside. She had no doubt they'd get into the club. Reinn could twist the minds of the club's employees into pretzels if he wanted to.

Okay, time to settle down and enjoy the show. She was aware of Reinn standing in the back watching everyone around her. Alan was keeping track of anyone coming into the club, while Mason stood to the side of the stage keeping an eye on the dancers.

It didn't take her long to notice that the women in the audience were a little distracted. All the hot men weren't onstage. Reinn and Mason made a spectacular pair. She'd bet a lot of the women thought they performed here. Kisa could almost feel her eyes turning more catlike with every second as she watched the women watching Reinn. *Mine.*

Whoa! Mine? No, definitely *not* hers. Where had all that jealousy come from? She had no hold on him. *But you want to.* Kisa avoided facing that truth by concentrating on the rest of the show.

No big surprises. A few medium surprises, and even one small surprise, if she could judge size through the dancers' G-strings. There was the usual policeman, who did a lot of hip thrusts to show off his hidden weapon. Looked like a small-caliber. And a cowboy who wiggled his butt to prove that only his horse had saddle sores. The undercover agent didn't have much to uncover, but he did it with lots of rhythm and enthusiasm.

Kisa tried to be honest and admit that the dancers would have impressed her a lot more if she weren't comparing them all to Reinn.

She was relieved when the finale arrived. All the men came out onstage together. So many bare male bodies boggled the mind and worked the female audience into a frenzy of screaming. The men reached into their G-strings and scooped out gold dust that they flung into the crowd. Who would have thought they could stuff so much dust into an already overcrowded space?

250

Wait. She focused on the dancer directly in front of her. He hadn't performed tonight, so why was he out here now? *Five feet, ten inches, with short brown hair and a good body.*

Uh-oh.

Her *uh-oh* was followed closely by Trouble's shouted warning in her head: *"I smell catnip, but it's not from anyone near the front door."*

Just as Mason reached the same conclusion she had, the man scooped a handful of catnip from his G-string and flung it in her direction.

Oh, hell. That was her last coherent thought as she felt the change washing over her. She had a muddled impression of Mason taking vampire form and then clutching his eyes. Mason a vampire? There were screams beating at her sensitive cat ears. But she focused her attention on one person.

As the audience shrieked and fought to get out of her way, she leaped onto the stage. She could see that Reinn was already in vampire form as he effort-lessly cleared a path leading to her. Too late.

Inside her saber-tooth, Kisa struggled for con-trol, but her cat was focused on the man who'd forced her to change. Not as desirable as a woolly mammoth, but okay for a practice run.

The man's eyes widened as he realized he was about to become a saber-tooth's midnight snack. Even as he raced toward the back entrance, he shifted into a small leopard. A werecat.

Kisa roared her fury at the realization that one of her own kind had betrayed her. Knocking tables, chairs, and anything else that got in her way aside, she charged after the leopard, gaining on him with every leap.

She wasn't sure what she'd do when she caught him. Her cat held on to a single thought: *Kill*. Kisa still fought for control and had a less bloodthirsty goal: *Capture*. The man's fate rested on who was on top—cat or human—when Kisa caught him.

Then she heard Reinn in her head.

"Calm your cat, and then shift back to human form, Kisa. You don't have to catch him. Your sisters have changed. They'll get him."

Her cat shook its massive head and roared its unhappiness at the thought of abandoning the hunt. Out of the corner of her eye, Kisa thought she saw Felicia. But her cat didn't care about the woman; it wanted only the man. Kisa brought all her concentration to bear on her human self, pushing her cat nature away, sending it back to the hidden place in her mind.

"Do you want me to add my strength to yours?" Reinn remained calm, steadying her for the change to come.

"No." She could manage only the one word.

Gathering her power into one tremendous act of willpower, she returned to human form.

Reinn stood beside her, a tablecloth in his hand. He too had returned to human form. "You need to buy clothes with lots of Velcro so that when you shift back you can just stick your clothes together again."

Kisa allowed Reinn to wrap the tablecloth around

her. She was still a little disoriented from the change. "Thanks for having enough confidence in me to let me shift by myself." Glancing around, she realized the club was empty. "Where is everyone?"

"Running away as fast as they can, I'd guess." Reinn retraced her path of destruction and found the spot where she'd become a cat. He picked up her scraps of clothing along with her purse and handed them to her. "Your sisters are chasing down our catnip stalker, and Alan is following them to make sure they don't tear the guy apart. I don't know what happened to Mason. He—"

"Mason's a vampire." Kisa remembered now. He'd changed as soon as he realized she was in danger, but he'd done it too late to stop anything. "Why didn't I sense that he was a vampire? I couldn't sense it in you either. Does that mean he's as powerful as you are?"

"He's powerful, but I'm more cold-blooded. Cold-blooded wins every time." He didn't ask her permission to pull her into his arms. "And no, I didn't tell you he was a vampire. Mason didn't want anyone to know, so I figured he had a right to keep it a secret if he wanted to."

Kisa didn't even consider moving out of his arms. Right now she needed the comfort he offered. "I thought I saw Felicia a few minutes ago. Did you see her anywhere around when I shifted back to human form?"

He frowned. "No. Every other human ran away. Smart people. Why would she stick around?"

Kisa shook her head. "I probably imagined it."

As much as she wanted to stay right here in his arms, she had to know what was going on outside. "It must be chaos out there. I started it when I shifted, so I'd better see if I can do any damage control."

"I think we need to—" He stopped. "Do you hear that?"

She listened. "Back in the bar area. Someone isn't too happy. I've never heard some of those words used in the same sentence."

Reinn strode toward the voice. Kisa went with him. They found Mason on his hands and knees poking under the bar. He'd returned to human form.

"Have a problem there?" Reinn stopped beside him.

"Yeah. I lost something." He didn't look up at Reinn.

"What did you lose?" Kisa joined Reinn. "Whatever it is, you can come back later to get it. We need to go outside."

Mason stopped rooting around underneath the bar. He sat back on his heels, but kept his eyes focused on the floor. "When I changed, I forgot I was wearing contacts. They popped out." His voice was low, somehow weary.

"Contacts?" Reinn sounded puzzled. "What the hell would a vampire need contacts for? We have perfect everything."

Mason stood and slowly raised his head so he could meet Reinn's gaze. "To change my eye color."

Kisa gasped. Mason had eyes the same brilliant shade of blue as Reinn's.

Reinn seemed stunned. "You're a Mackenzie." As he stared at Mason, he grew still. "Your face. You remind me of . . ." He scrubbed a hand across his eyes. "No. That was so long ago. He was only six. It couldn't be." But even as he denied his thoughts, his gaze never left Mason's face. "Jor?"

Mason looked away. "Yeah. I felt the same way when I heard your name."

Kisa would never know what the men would have said to each other, because Alan rushed into the club at that moment.

"We've gotta do something. The people who ran out of the club are telling other people. Pretty soon the cops will be here. And I lost Julie and the others in the woods." Alan looked panicked. "The media storm from this will ruin the Woo Woo Inn for us. No more sanctuary."

Reinn tore his gaze from Mason and looked at Kisa. "I'm calling in Ganymede." He glanced back at Mason. "Go with Alan and see if you can find Kisa's sisters. I'm staying with Kisa in case Lynch wasn't working alone."

The two men left while Kisa found her purse and pulled out her cell phone.

Reinn came up behind her and put his hand over her phone. He still looked shocked by Mason's— no, Jor's—admission. "I don't need a phone to talk to him."

She dropped onto the nearest chair. "Of course

you don't." And here she'd always thought that turning into a saber-toothed tiger was the most bizarre thing in her life. That was before she decided to visit the Woo Woo Inn.

Chapter Fourteen

Jorund was alive. The reality of that pounded at Reinn as he tried to focus on reaching Ganymede. His feelings for Kisa? They'd blindsided him, and he was still reeling. He tried to push everything aside for a moment as he touched Ganymede's thoughts.

"Whatcha want, bloodsucker? I'm in the middle of one of Katie's orgasmic brownies right now. It's so chocolaty and moist it brings tears to my eyes. This had better be important."

Reinn held on to his temper. Barely. *"The catnip creep struck again. Kisa shifted. He shifted. All Kisa's sisters shifted. Mason and I took vampire form. And there're a bunch of panicked humans running around who think they saw werecats and vampires. They'll spread the tale. Fast. Get your ass here now, or the Woo Woo Inn is history."*

He'd barely concluded his thoughts when Ganymede padded into the club.

"I left Sparkle at home. Okay, so I didn't tell her I was

leaving. Call me a real meanie, but it gives me a chuckle to know how pissed she'll be when she finds out where I've gone. She'd never miss a chance to see a bunch of almost-naked men. Since she's already ticked at me, a few more dirty looks won't matter. Besides, the only naked man I want her looking at is me." Ganymede leaped onto the bar and sniffed around. *"I could use a shot of something."*

"Forget it. A drunken cat won't do us much good." Kisa quickly filled Ganymede in on the details.

Just as she finished, Kisa's sisters burst through the door, dragging a groggy Harry Lynch behind them. They were all naked.

"We caught the sorry son of a bitch. I wish he'd put up more of a fight." Wendy's eyes were narrowed slits of anger.

Reinn reached them in one stride. While the sisters grabbed tablecloths to wrap around themselves, he shoved Harry into a chair and then dropped a tablecloth into his lap. "Talk, and talk fast. I haven't fed tonight, and I get a real shot of energy from bastard blood."

Harry's eyes widened to saucer size. "It wasn't my idea. This person e-mailed me and offered a fortune if I could develop something that would keep werecats in their animal forms permanently. I finally came up with a formula I thought would work, but I didn't get a chance to field-test it. The person wanted it right away. For the kind of money I was getting, I didn't ask questions. I left the formula where I was told to leave it."

"Didn't you worry about developing something

258

that could be used against you?" Reinn thought Harry might be a smart biochemist, but he was a dumb werecat.

"I'm not in danger. Whoever this is, they want Kisa because she's unique. There's only one of her. Lots of werecats change into leopards." He seemed smug about that.

Reinn really didn't like this guy. "So you've tried to trigger the change four times."

"I only made her shift twice—that time on the road and tonight. My partner was supposed to be close by to inject her with the formula." His gaze skittered to Kisa and then away. "I didn't do the things that they"—quick fearful glance at Wendy and the girls—"said happened inside the inn, though. Someone would've noticed me there."

"If I were in your partner's shoes, I'd inject that formula into *you* once you'd served your purpose. Good way to make sure you never talked to the wrong person." Reinn got lots of satisfaction from the shocked look on Lynch's face. The dumb ass hadn't thought of that.

"What about Voskie?" Kisa's expression hovered somewhere between furious and horrified.

Harry avoided Kisa's stare. "I was told to get rid of her. If I didn't do it, and she gave you information, I'd go down, too."

Reinn controlled his need to end Lynch's miserable life. "A name."

Harry cringed away from the menace Reinn knew he was projecting. "I never got one. I couldn't trace the e-mail messages, and whoever it is drops my money at different places."

"We can't go to the police with this." Kisa spoke for everyone.

The werecats looked at one another. Killing one of their own in the heat of battle was one thing, but this would be different. No one wanted to kill Harry, but something had to be done about him. Like vampires, they didn't have a legal system to handle someone like Harry, so punishments were usually permanent.

"What'll we do with him?" Julie's tone said she'd go along with everyone else's decision.

Reinn didn't offer to make the problem go away. Harry was a werecat. Their problem, their solution. But if he felt Lynch was still a danger to Kisa, he'd do what needed doing to keep her safe.

Ganymede had plunked his wide bottom on the bar, and if a cat could look amused, he looked amused. He yawned and then glanced at Harry. Harry disappeared.

A chorus of gasps greeted this feat.

"Where is he?" Reinn knew Ganymede's power, so he bypassed the gasp-of-awe step.

Ganymede stuck his nose into a half-filled glass of Kahlua and cream that a terrified customer had left behind when she'd fled the club. *"I sent Harry to a jungle in a time where humans aren't the dominant species. He'll be too busy trying to keep his butt alive to bother anyone again. I would've sent him to the big litter box in the sky, but the Big Boss doesn't let me whack people anymore."* He slurped down the remainder of the drink and then licked his mouth. *"Now we need to take care of all those nice customers who saw what happened tonight."*

Ganymede leaped from the bar and padded out the door. Everyone trailed after him. Once outside, he looked up at Reinn. *"Pick me up. We'll need to merge powers for this. I've already sent out a mental SOS to Mason. He can help. Trouble's chasing rabbits in the woods behind the club. He's too young to do much anyway."*

Jor came around the side of the building and joined the group. "What's up?"

He met Reinn's gaze and then smiled. Reinn remembered that smile now that all the pieces were in place. Even at six years old, Jor's smile had made people want to smile back.

"Reinn's going to pick me up, aren't you, bloodsucker?" Ganymede looked at Reinn out of amber eyes gleaming with wicked enjoyment. *"Then we'll join powers to make every person who was at the club tonight believe they just came from a great show with amazing special effects. Nothing more."*

"Why do I have to pick you up? You weigh a ton." Reinn recognized the sulky kid in his voice.

"Because you don't want to, and I love making you. It's a power thing. Since the all-righteous party pooper formerly known as the Big Boss started telling me I couldn't do this and I'd better not do that, I get my power fixes where I can. Now pick me up."

Kisa held her tablecloth in place with one hand while she wrapped her other arm around Reinn's waist. She smiled up at him. "Humor him. Pick him

261

up so we can get this over with. The longer we mess around, the farther away some of the audience will be." She glanced down at Ganymede. "Some of those people burned rubber leaving the parking lot."

Mumbling his opinion of all cosmic troublemakers on power trips, Reinn hauled Ganymede into his arms. He made a big deal of doing a lot of grunting as he lifted the cat.

Ganymede settled into a comfortable position and then looked at Jor. *"We need physical contact, so touch my head, Mason. Make sure you scratch behind my ears as we merge powers."*

Jor laughed out loud. "I bet Sparkle would set your ass straight if you tried this on her. And Mason isn't my real name. I'm Jorund Mackenzie."

There were more gasps all around.

Reinn watched Ganymede's eyes. *He* wasn't surprised.

"Whatta you know, you changed your name along with your eyes. For your info, Sparkle worships the ground I walk on, or lie on, or sit on, or—"

"Looked more like she wanted to bury you in that ground. From the stares she sent your way tonight, she'd be whistling while she worked." Jor grinned at Ganymede.

Ganymede glared at him. *"Let's get this done."*

Jor laid his hand on Ganymede's head as Reinn closed his eyes. Kisa still had her arm around his waist, and the realness of her touch grounded him.

Reinn visualized white light spreading out from the three of them, and within the light was the message that everyone had enjoyed a great show with unbelievable special effects.

Jor's power spun through Reinn, and the white light in his mind grew brighter, more intense. But when Ganymede merged his power with theirs, it was like being slammed with a boulder. Reinn staggered under the force of it. The white light shimmered with pulsing bursts of color, and the message he was projecting almost caused a mental sonic boom.

The whole thing ended just in time. Reinn had been close to dropping the fat cat with the impossible power. After setting Ganymede down, he looked at Jor to see his reaction.

Jor shook his head. "Never, absolutely never, have I felt that kind of power." He studied Ganymede. "And all packed into such an unassuming body, too."

Ganymede narrowed his eyes. *"This is a terrific body."* He thought for a moment. *"Yeah, so it's not as terrific as my human body, but it's still excellent. It's all part of my charismatic self."*

Jor seemed to make a real effort not to comment on Ganymede's "charismatic self." He turned to Reinn. "Felicia got so scared, she jumped in the van and took off. I tried to stop her, but no luck."

"I'll have Sparkle send a car to take everyone back to the inn." Ganymede glanced at Kisa. *"Since you seem permanently attached to the bloodsucker here, I guess you'll ride back in Alan's car with the men."*

Kisa nodded. "I have a question before you leave, though. If you can just poof yourself places, why'd you stay with us when we were looking for Reinn and Alan?"

Ganymede looked bored. *"Poofing takes energy. I'm lazy. Ask Sparkle; she'll tell you. So if walking is easier, I walk."* He did the equivalent of a cat shrug. *"This was an emergency."*

Ganymede cast Reinn and Jor a strangely satisfied look, and then was gone.

While the others headed for Alan's car, Reinn took Kisa's tablecloth in hand. When he'd finished wrapping, tucking, and tying it, Kisa was wearing a makeshift toga.

She sighed as she looked at the remains of Sparkle's girlie outfit, which she still held. "Sparkle's going to give me grief over this."

Reinn cupped her jaw gently and leaned toward her. "You survived. Nothing else is important."

Her gaze softened. "Thanks." Then she turned away, effectively hiding any other emotions she might be feeling.

The only one talking on the drive back to the inn was Trouble. *"I don't think it's fair that those bunnies can run so fast. How do they do it? I have long, long legs and they have short, short ones. So why can't I catch them, huh?"*

"You have to think like your prey if you want to catch them." Reinn cast Kisa a long-suffering glance as he put his arm across her shoulders and pulled her tightly against his side. Alan was driving, and Jor sat in the passenger seat next to him. That meant Kisa and he had to share the backseat with Trouble.

"Think like them?" Trouble sounded like that concept was way too complicated.

Jor looked over his shoulder at Reinn. "We have to talk."

Reinn nodded. A thousand years to catch up on. So many questions about the day that changed their lives. But there were good memories too, of the few years before the slaughter. How much of those early years did Jor remember?

"Do you know who was helping that bad man do mean things to Kisa?" Trouble seemed really worried about Kisa, which immediately made him more lovable to Reinn. *"Why did he do those things to her?"*

"I don't know." Reinn squeezed Kisa's shoulders. "But we'll find out."

Kisa rested her head on his shoulder. "The person has to be staying at the inn. Did you have a chance to do a background check on everyone?"

He shook his head. "I've concentrated on the guests who aren't family or friends. So far nothing." Reinn thought for a moment. "I've pretty much eliminated any of the staff. They've been with Cindy since the place opened. And I bet she did a background check before she hired them. I'll finish looking up information on all the others when I rise tonight."

As soon as they climbed from the car, the smell of wood smoke hit them. Kisa sniffed. "Billy Bob and Bubba have started smoking the meat." She took his hand. "Let's go in the back way. I'd like to see how they're doing."

Trouble trotted along beside them, but not even his doggy talk could dent Reinn's growing happiness. Kisa had forgiven him sufficiently to let him touch her again. That was enough for now.

Howls, roars, and other assorted predator noises came from just beyond the tree line around the back lawn. Trouble bounced over to the barbecue pit and sniffed. *"Do Billy Bob and Bubba ever barbecue bunnies?"*

"No." Kisa didn't elaborate.

Some of the human guests were sitting around talking and drinking beer with the two men.

Reinn listened to the sounds of hungry werecreatures. Humans would smell only the wood smoke at this early stage, but the carnivores out there smelled meat. "Let's hope no one eats them before they finish the brisket and ribs."

Billy Bob waved to them and then stared at Kisa. "What happened to those pretty pink duds you had on?" He peered closer. "Looks like you're wearing a tablecloth. You're still right pretty, though, except for that mustard stain on your hem."

He forgot about Kisa's clothes, though, as he stared into the darkness. "Don't reckon I expected to hear them noises here in little old New Jersey. Now, down in big old Texas, we'd be beatin' off the wolves and panthers with one hand while we slapped that marinade on the brisket with the other. You need to multitask in Texas."

Kisa smiled. "Really? I spent a few weeks in Houston. I don't remember meeting up with any wolves or panthers. Of course, I did a lot of shopping at the Galleria. Maybe they only roam the discount stores."

Twin roars rose above the other animal sounds. Bubba looked nervous. "Sounds sort of like two lions, doesn't it, Billy Bob?"

Billy Bob threw him a disgusted look. "Down in Texas the crickets sound fiercer than those puny meows. Hand me a beer, Bubba."

Bubba took a beer from their cooler but almost dropped it when Seth growled. "Sounds like a bear to me. A big bear."

Billy Bob yanked the beer out of his hand. "Don't have big bears in New Jersey. Maybe a few of those little black bears. Now down in Texas we have bears that'd tear the head off a T. rex."

The sounds got a little closer, and the humans not named Billy Bob or Bubba called it a night. Reinn could see the whites of Bubba's eyes. Billy Bob tore open a bag of chips and then sat down. He stared at the forest.

"Understand the Jersey Devil wanders around in these here woods. Any truth to that?" Billy Bob paused with his hand in the chip bag as the werewolves began serenading the night.

Don't say it. Oh, what the hell. Reinn tried to look thoughtful. "They had some trouble with the Devil last year, but he hasn't come around lately. He's still out there, though. And he likes to hunt on warm summer nights. Huge sucker. Swoops down on people stupid enough to be out late at night. The only warning they get is the flapping of those monster wings, and then—"

"Time to go in." Kisa dragged Reinn toward the inn.

Bubba definitely looked worried. "Don't think we have any of those down in Texas."

Billy Bob looked fierce in defense of his adopted state. "We have bigger and badder things than that. Hell, our mosquitoes have twenty-foot wingspans." He slapped at a New Jersey mosquito. "These mosquitoes here are itty-bitty things, but they got themselves a nasty bite."

Reinn was laughing as he went into the inn.

Kisa smacked him on the arm. "That was so mean. I'm telling Sparkle that she'd better get her behind out there to protect her barbecue team—along with their brisket—from all those carnivores."

Reinn's laughter faded to a chuckle. "Couldn't help it. They've played the part so long, I think they believe it." He grew serious. "I still have to stay in your room, you know. Until we know who's behind the attacks, you're in danger." Would she let him into her room?

Kisa nodded. "I'll be up as soon as I tell Sparkle her barbecue team's about to bolt." She pulled her key from her purse and handed it to him. "In case you get tired of waiting. I might be a while. Sparkle will have something to say about the outfit I'm no longer wearing." She tugged at the tablecloth before walking away.

He watched her go and then looked down at the key.

"Looks like you got lucky." Jor stopped next

to him. "Want to sit in the parlor for a few minutes?"

Reinn nodded. Dropping the key into his pocket, he followed Jor. They found two recliners in a corner. Reinn dropped into one. God, it felt good to relax. Then he looked at Jor.

Without warning, all the emotion he'd locked away for centuries rolled over him. "I hated thinking I'd failed you, Jor. You were the youngest, and part of my responsibility as the oldest was to protect you. When I came back from hunting and found everyone dead, I thought you were lying somewhere butchered, too. You were only six, and I couldn't see how you could've survived."

Even though Reinn no longer had to breathe once he became vampire, he'd never lost his reflex actions. He drew in a deep, calming breath. "I searched for your body. After a while I figured the animals had gotten to it."

Jor nodded. "I don't remember much of that night. It wasn't until years later that I knew night feeders had attacked us. It was dark out, and then suddenly they came out of the forest. They hit me and tossed me aside. They didn't bother feeding from me because they had bigger prey. I crawled away and hid in the trees. Later I saw the fire. . . ." He looked away, and silence filled the space between them.

Finally Jor looked back at Reinn. "I would've died, but a hunting werecat found me. She shifted to human form and then carried me back to her family. The werecats adopted me, raised me as one of them. That's why I do the Protector thing. It's the only way I know to repay them for saving my life."

Reinn felt the dark hole in his soul begin to fill and heal. "Dad was the only family I had left. When he came home and found out what had happened, he just walked away. I never saw him again." He shrugged as though it hadn't mattered that his father walked away from his living son as well as his dead family.

"It mattered." Jor hadn't been in Reinn's mind, but Jor and he had always understood the things neither would say out loud.

If the night feeders had never changed their lives, they would've been friends for as long as they lived. But it wasn't too late.

Reinn thought it was pretty amazing that a little less than a week ago he'd come here a whole other person. He'd wanted no friends, and he'd certainly not wanted . . . What *was* Kisa to him? He'd find out soon.

He looked over and saw that Kisa was waiting for him just outside the parlor. She'd wanted to give him the time he needed with Jor.

Jor saw her and smiled. "We'll talk again tomorrow. Catch up on each other's lives." He stood.

Reinn stood, too. They stared at each other, and then Reinn clasped Jor by the shoulders and hugged him—a brief embrace, but groundbreaking. Reinn didn't hug men. Ever. But a hug seemed right this time. He turned and walked toward Kisa, following her upstairs.

It seemed a lifetime since he'd last entered her room. He watched as she flung herself onto her bed and patted the spot beside her. He got rid of his shoes and joined her.

"What will the council do now that you've quit?" She didn't look at him as she asked.

He thought about lying, maybe saying that the council would simply appoint another Guardian and then let him go home. But he'd made a no-secrets pact with her. She wouldn't like the truth, though.

"Guardian of the Blood is forever. We aren't allowed to quit. That's why there haven't been many of us." Now for the hard part. "The punishment for quitting is death. The council will send hunters to take me out."

"They can't do that."

He heard the outrage for him in her voice, and something warm blossomed inside him.

"We have to stop them." With that *we*, she put herself firmly in his corner.

But beneath her determination he sensed fear. He didn't want her to be afraid. "Don't worry; I'm not going to sit around waiting for the hunters. Once we've found the person who has the formula, I'm heading for Scotland to take the fight to the council members. They think they're safe, but they'll find out what it feels like to be hunted."

"No, you're not leaving the Woo Woo Inn." Her

eyes gleamed with ferocity on his behalf, and her cat wasn't far beneath the surface.

Convincing her that he had to leave wouldn't be easy. He didn't want to walk away from . . . love? Was that what he really felt? *Yes.*

With that admission, a chapter in his life closed, and a new one began. Reinn hoped it wasn't his last one. At the end of his personal history, he wanted an epilogue with all the happily-ever-after stuff.

Whoa, slow down. Just because he'd discovered that he loved Kisa didn't mean she felt the same way. She would step up to defend *any* of her friends. And right now he had no proof he was anything more than one of those friends.

"I can't stay here, Kisa. Think. I won't go down without a fight, and the hunters could hurt innocents trying to get me. I don't want that on my conscience." Did he sound reasonable enough? He felt anything but. He wanted to scoop her up and take her somewhere far away where the hunters couldn't find them. He quashed that thought without blinking.

"You will *not* leave here to fight those bastards alone." Her glare was a thing of beauty. "And don't you dare try to sneak off when I'm not looking, because I'll find you wherever you go, and our reunion won't be pretty."

Reinn couldn't help it; he grinned at her. He'd be lying if he said all her fierceness on his behalf didn't make him feel good. "It's almost dawn, and I can't keep my eyes open any longer. So we'll have to continue this discussion later. You need to get some rest. It's been a long night, and you'll insult Billy Bob and Bubba if you fall asleep at their barbecue."

Without giving her a chance to continue arguing, he closed his eyes and let sleep claim him. Just before all awareness left him, Reinn felt the slide of her fingers along his jaw. Hey, that had to mean something, didn't it? He fell asleep smiling.

Chapter Fifteen

Kisa knelt on the kitchen floor glaring at Ganymede, who crouched under the table. "You're selfish, contemptible, and a real butthead."

Ganymede didn't bother to take his face out of the plate of mashed potatoes he was inhaling. "*And I have other wonderful qualities as well.*"

"Yuck, how can you eat just a whole plate of mashed potatoes?" Kisa wanted to dump the potatoes over his furry head and watch them ooze down his face and stick in his whiskers.

"*Talent, babe. Pure talent.*" Finished with the potatoes, he licked the plate.

Katie, once again queen of the kitchen, harrumphed. "Won't do any good appealing to his better nature. He doesn't have one." Her broom bounced once in agreement from its place of honor in the corner.

Kisa stood as Ganymede leaped onto a chair.

"*Look, my game is making trouble. If you want me to spread a little dissension, cause a little chaos, I'm your guy. But you're asking me to help save Reinn from his council. My question is: What's in it for me?"*

"You helped out at the Bare Truth. Why not now?" Kisa didn't know how to counter Ganymede's warped reasoning.

Ganymede yawned, showing small, pointed teeth. *"Self-interest, pretty kitty. I can't let anything bad happen to the Woo Woo Inn or else Cindy will be pissed. And Cindy is Darach Mackenzie's daughter. Darach and I have sort of a business deal. I run a tourist agency for time travelers. Once a year, Darach lets me take a group back to 1785 to visit the Mackenzie castle in Scotland. I cause problems for his daughter, and Darach cancels our agreement. Got the picture?"*

"Got it." No use beating her head against this particular wall.

Kisa had already started rounding up support for Reinn. She'd checked to see what time night fell in Scotland and then called Cindy and Thrain. After Kisa explained things, Cindy promised to talk to her father. Thrain was noncommittal.

Kisa didn't know if they'd show up to help, but Reinn could sure use a bunch of powerful Mackenzies at his back. Of course, Jor and Alan were on his side. That would mean a lot to Reinn.

Kisa had spoken to all the other nonhumans at the inn except for Sparkle and the harpy. She didn't think Ocypete would join in to save Reinn. In fact, if the harpy thought the council might kill him, she'd probably try to claim him for Hades. She was getting pretty desperate.

All the others had agreed to stand behind Reinn

when he challenged the council. After she talked to Sparkle, she'd figure out how to draw the council members to the Woo Woo Inn before Reinn went to Scotland in search of them. The final confrontation would be here, where all his nonhuman allies could fight for him.

"You win." Actually, he hadn't. Once Ganymede realized she planned to bring the battle here, where his precious inn could get nicked and dinged, he might have a sudden change of heart. Oh, wait. He didn't have a heart. Dumb her. "I'll leave you to your . . ."

Ganymede wasn't paying any attention to her. He'd leaped off the chair and onto the counter beside the stove, where Katie was frying bacon for breakfast.

Katie made shooing motions at him. "Get your fat-cat behind off my counter. If the board of health catches you there, I'm not taking the blame for it."

Kisa left them haggling over who could or couldn't sit on the counter and went in search of Sparkle. She found her in the parlor with Ocypete. The harpy looked steamed.

In human form, Ocypete didn't have her terrifying and totally gross vulture body, but her face made up for the loss. She had a strong face—supersized hooked nose, thin lips that turned down in perpetual bad temper, and small, beady black eyes. Okay, so it was more ugly than strong. Not that ugly was bad, but the harpy's face was scary ugly.

Sparkle smiled a greeting as Kisa joined them. "I was giving Ocypete a few fashion tips. Not all of us are blessed with a sensual nature, but everyone can make the most of what they have." Sparkle cast the harpy an assessing glance. "I'll need to meditate for a while before tackling this challenge."

"Interesting." Kisa didn't want to be dragged into the conversation.

Sparkle crossed her long bare legs and smoothed her short black skirt. Why bother? There wasn't enough material to make a decent wrinkle.

"Don't get me wrong, Ocypete; black is a sexy color. I couldn't function as an erotic being without my black clothes." Sparkle shuddered at the thought of life without the color black. "But there's sexy black and then there's . . . you. Sweetie, you're a complete disaster. Lumpy and dumpy dressed in shapeless black doesn't make a fashion statement."

Kisa widened her eyes. Wow, Sparkle was either very brave or very stupid. Ocypete didn't have a kind and gentle nature.

Ignoring all warning signs, like Ocypete curling her fingers into talons, Sparkle forged onward. "We'll get you into—"

"The hell with fashion. I need a freakin' victim for Hades before he takes a bite out of my butt."

Kisa winced. Clothes wouldn't make *this* woman. It would take a total body and soul makeover, and Kisa thought Ocypete's soul was already spoken for.

". . . some silky black pants and a revealing top, then put a pair of Manolo Blahnik stilettos on your feet—remind me to get your shoe size. Afterward I'll grab my makeup case and—"

"How about that pale puny human over there? Think he looks at death's door?"

". . . get rid of that pasty look." Sparkle grew

thoughtful. "Your hair is kind of wiry. I might have to straighten it a little."

Kisa sighed. As fascinating as this was, she needed to speak with Sparkle. "Uh, Sparkle, I have to talk to you for a few minutes."

Sparkle dismissed Ocypete with a wave. "We'll talk eye shadow later, sweetie." The harpy scuttled away.

Sparkle turned her attention to Kisa. "The shorts and top are cute in a country kind of way, but you need to pamper your body with cool silk if you want to project the image of a sensual woman to Reinn. I have an outfit for you that—"

Kisa held up her hand. "Whoa. Stop. We're not talking clothes, Sparkle."

Sparkle looked puzzled. "What else would we talk about? By the way, you might be ready for a few of my simpler sex toys. I'll go get—"

"I want you to help save Reinn from his clan's council. When the members find out that Alan is still alive, they'll send hunters to kill Reinn for not doing his job. I'd like everyone at the inn to make sure that doesn't happen. The council would think twice if they had to face all of us." Kisa waited tensely for Sparkle's decision.

The werecreatures and three vampires might not be enough to slow down the council, but add in a cosmic troublemaker, and the balance of power would shift.

Sparkle smiled. "Of course I'll help. I've worked hard to create a wonderful sexual relationship between the two of you. I won't let some stupid council ruin all my work."

Now for the tricky part. "I need the e-mail addresses or phone numbers of the council members. So I'll have to—"

"—get into Reinn's room while he's still asleep in your bed." Sparkle's expression turned sly. "Come with me."

Kisa followed her to the registration desk, where Sparkle retrieved the key to Reinn's room. She handed it to Kisa. "Get it back to me as soon as you're finished."

Kisa nodded. "One more thing. Reinn can't find out about this. He'd be totally ticked if he knew I was interfering with his plans to go it alone."

Sparkle widened her eyes. "I wouldn't say a word. I have a sneaky nature. It's a gift. You just make sure you keep your man happy with lots of hot sex, sister. It'll distract the hell out of him."

Relieved, Kisa hugged Sparkle. "I'll let you know the details when I have everything in place."

Sparkle nodded, her thoughts already elsewhere. "Ocypete needs a shadow that'll make her eyes look larger."

"Larger. Right." Kisa watched Sparkle scan the area for the elusive harpy and then hurry in pursuit as Ocypete tried to escape into the library.

Kisa glanced out the window. She still had time before Reinn rose. Now to find Jake.

Her brother was on the front porch talking to Seth. Kisa smiled as she joined them. "Getting lots of relaxation, Seth?"

The werebear turned his big, friendly smile on her. "Always."

"Jake, I need your help." She hoped he wouldn't give her a hard time about her request.

Seth lumbered off the porch. "Guess I'll take a short walk in the woods before breakfast."

No use putting this off. "Would you help me get some information from Reinn's laptop? I have to do it before he wakes up." She held up her hand to keep Jake from interrupting. "I know, I know: it's sneaky, underhanded, and illegal. And if Reinn catches us, he'll gift wrap us for Ocypete. But I need the e-mail addresses or phone numbers of the council members."

Jake was a technological wizard and the only member of her family who could help her with this. If he turned all upright and honest on her, she didn't know what she'd do.

He studied her for what seemed like a century, at least. "You really like this guy, huh?"

"A lot." She hoped her expression told him her feelings went way beyond *like*.

Jake raked his fingers through his hair. "Okay, if this is what it takes to keep his vampire butt alive."

Kisa swallowed hard and tried to keep her tears at bay. Her family had always been there for her, and she'd never appreciated it as much as she did now.

Neither spoke as they climbed the stairs and then let themselves into Reinn's room. Kisa stepped aside for the master. Jake did his magic with the laptop and made short work of Reinn's password protection. Once into the files, he found the e-mail addresses of the council members.

Then he turned to Kisa. "Anything else before I shut her down?"

She shook her head. Dusk was falling over the forest, and Kisa didn't want Reinn to catch them in his room. She glanced at the list she'd made. Five members. Tomorrow afternoon she'd start contacting them and hope they took her bait.

Reinn had only a few more people to check. He'd collected a short list of suspects—two zoologists and a cryptozoologist. All of them had a motive for wanting a live saber-toothed tiger. But then, almost anyone interested in making a fast buck would realize Kisa's potential.

Beyond a motive, the guilty party had to have inside info to know that Kisa shifted into a saber-toothed tiger. That would suggest a werecat like Harry. But all the werecats here were relatives or friends of Kisa's family. Was one of them a traitor?

He could faintly hear the voices of people enjoying the barbecue outside. Kisa had left a note on her pillow for when he woke up, explaining that she was helping Katie put together some side dishes to go with the barbecue. She should be safe with Katie, but he still wanted to be there to protect her.

Reinn was tempted to forget his Web search, go find Kisa, and spend the rest of the night outside having fun. Well, maybe not the entire rest of the night.

He felt more certain about his feelings for Kisa with every minute he spent around her. Not that he'd ever let her know about them. Reinn had a date with the council, and he wouldn't drag her into that mess.

But he *would* make love with her one more time before he left, if she'd trust him enough. And the next time they made love, there'd be nothing between them except the secret of how he felt about her. A necessary secret, and one he wouldn't feel guilty about.

Reinn pulled his attention back to his laptop. Okay, work first and then play. He started his search for Felicia Carter, even though he couldn't picture the wedding planner playing the part of master criminal.

A short while later, he wasn't so sure. The Felicia Carter he found wasn't a wedding planner at all. She was a paleontologist, and she didn't spend all her time collecting fossils. Good old Felicia had served time for extortion and assault.

Reinn didn't even stop to shut down his laptop. He knocked over his chair as he ran from the room. Kisa wouldn't suspect Felicia if the woman walked up to her. And even though he didn't think Felicia would attack Kisa in front of witnesses, panic was a living, breathing presence in him.

He hadn't felt this kind of fear since the night his family was slaughtered. Even during the carnage of battle he'd stayed cool and in control. Not now. He was on the edge. Reinn ran faster.

After checking Kisa's room, he barreled down the stairs, calling her name. By the time he charged into the kitchen, his control was slipping and he could feel the slide of his fangs.

"Where's Kisa?" He barely contained his urge to shake the information out of Katie.

Katie turned from the stove and then raised one brow. "Pull in your fangs, vampire. She took food to the slavering beasties outside. So what's your prob—"

Reinn didn't hear the rest of her sentence because he was on his way to the back lawn. He rarely used his preternatural speed for short distances. He did now.

It seemed as if everyone from the inn was in the mob surrounding the Badass Texas Barbecue team. Reinn could hear Billy Bob's voice above the murmur of the crowd.

"Ain't nothin' better than prime Texas beef in the hands of a master. Notice how the meat just falls off them ribs. And if heaven is all it's cracked up to be, then there'd better be Badass Texas Barbecue brisket there. If not, y'all leave and head for the other place. We'll be there raisin' hell and smokin' great meat."

Reinn didn't give a damn what anyone thought as he used his mental powers to shove the crowd aside. No Kisa. He scanned the area that bordered the woods and finally spotted her.

He froze when he realized Felicia was with her. Total stillness settled over him as fury bubbled just beneath the surface of his control. The need to destroy rose on a wave of bloodred, and death called him brother. Those who'd fought against him through the centuries would have recognized his expression now as he moved toward the two women.

The crowd behind him grew silent, shocked at being pushed aside by an unseen force.

Reinn ignored them. He also ignored their gasps as he took vampire form. The feel of his fangs filling his mouth gave a physical reality to the rage flooding him. No one attacked *his* woman. And Reinn didn't even question the *his woman* part.

He wouldn't reach them in time. The knowledge triggered a silent scream of denial. Felicia had seen him coming and recognized menace in his body language. Even as he watched, she pulled a sealed Baggie and a syringe from her pocket.

The woman knew her life was in danger, and she had only one bargaining chip: Kisa. Felicia would keep him at bay by threatening to fling the catnip in the Baggie at Kisa, and then inject her with the formula. Reinn could kill Felicia without touching her, but even in death the woman might stick the needle into Kisa in a final reflex action. He couldn't take that chance.

Kisa's back was to him. She hadn't seen the syringe or Baggie yet. He had to make her move before Felicia had a chance to grab her and press the needle against her arm. What would be the one thing that would make Kisa react instinctively, without pausing to think?

Suddenly he remembered. He got ready to

pounce as soon as Kisa moved. Then he shouted, "Kisa, giant spider overhead! Dropping fast."

With a frightened yelp, Kisa leaped away from Felicia. The woman cursed and lunged after her. Too late, much too late. Reinn smiled as he flattened Felicia with a mental left hook. He didn't think he'd killed her, but she wouldn't be getting up anytime soon.

Kisa looked confused, the people watching stood openmouthed, and Reinn tried to decide what to do with Felicia. If he'd had to kill her to save Kisa, he would have, but she wasn't a danger now. He could remove her memory of Kisa, but she would just come up with another scheme to take advantage of someone.

Ocypete took the decision away from him. Giving a delighted shriek and flapping her huge wings, the harpy swooped down to snatch up the unconscious Felicia. "Mine, all mine. And don't even think about trying to take her away from me. Hades, I've got a live one, soon to be a dead one, for you." With another happy whoop, she rose into the sky with Felicia grasped in her talons.

Everyone started talking at once. Dazedly, Kisa walked over to where Felicia had dropped the Baggie and syringe. She picked up the syringe, leaving someone else to handle the Baggie, and then moved to Reinn's side. "Is this what I think it is?"

He eased back to human form before answering. "Felicia Carter was never a wedding planner. She served time in prison, and I bet if we search her room, we'll find a laptop with messages from Lynch."

Dawning realization made Kisa's hands shake. *Oh, my God!* She gave the syringe to Reinn and then turned to her mother, who, along with everyone else, had run up to Reinn and her. "Did you hire Felicia?"

Her mother stared at Kisa with wide, shocked eyes. "Felicia moved into the condo next to ours about six months ago. She was only renting it. We got to talking one morning, and I told her about the wedding. She said she was a wedding planner, and she'd be glad to help out free of charge because we were neighbors. I believed her."

"She used you to get to Kisa." Reinn frowned. "It's not your fault. But someone in the werecat community has loose lips, or else Felicia wouldn't have known about Kisa."

Her dad snarled, his eyes going all catlike, and Kisa knew someone was in deep trouble. "Your cousin Phil came into a lot of money recently, and he had a convenient excuse not to be here." He nodded at Kisa's brothers.

Jake's expression didn't bode well for Phil. "He lives in Newark. We'll leave now. If he's guilty, we'll take care of him and be back in time for the wedding."

Kisa swallowed hard. This was one part of werecat culture that bothered her.

"He would've condemned you to a living death." Reinn's quiet words helped.

She nodded. "I know."

"Know what?" Seth held a huge plate piled high with ribs and potato salad. "I missed part of this story somewhere."

Kisa smiled at the werebear. "A family secret, Seth."

Seth still looked puzzled. "Reinn isn't family."

But I want him to be. The truth didn't change anything. Until Reinn confronted the council, nothing in his life was certain. She wouldn't put more pressure on him by telling him she loved him.

Bubba was still staring at the sky where Ocypete had disappeared. "What the hell was that? I never seen anything like it. Was that the Jersey Devil? Hell, I'm getting my ass inside before that thing comes back for seconds."

Billy Bob collared him just as he turned toward the inn. "Whoa, there. A true son of Texas wouldn't be spooked by a little ol' "—noisy gulp—"bird. We have people to feed."

Kisa looked around. The humans and Bernie the wereduck had all rushed into the inn. Only the carnivorous werecreatures had stayed to feed their faces. She glanced at Reinn. "Aren't you going to erase the memory of the harpy from everyone's mind?"

Laughter tugged at the corners of his luscious mouth. "I just did, except for your family and the Badass Texas Barbecue team. Billy Bob can twist it any which way he wants, but he won't find a bigger or badder harpy in Texas. I'd love to see people's faces when he tells them about this."

"You're evil, Mackenzie. Let's go inside. I have to

make sure Katie doesn't need any more help." Would he follow her inside? Would he follow her up to her bed? She'd better find out now, because once he discovered what she'd done behind his back, he might never speak to her again, let alone make love with her.

Ironic that she'd gotten all bent out of shape over his secret, but now she had one that would make him just as furious.

He nodded. They'd started toward the porch when Trouble raced up to them, ears flapping and tongue lolling.

"I almost caught one, I almost caught one!" Trouble bounced up and down like a demented pogo stick. *"There was this huge bunny, and I chased him all over the woods. I got close enough to grab him by his fluffy tail, but he jumped into this big hole."* He paused to make sure Reinn and Cindy were suitably impressed. *"I'm going back there after I eat. I'll wait by the hole. I'll get him when he comes out."*

Kisa smiled, thankful for the distraction of Trouble's silliness. "What would you do if you caught him?"

The dog gave her a blank stare before sitting down to scratch a flea. *"I didn't think that far ahead. I can only pay attention to one thing at a time. I have to catch him first."* The flea subdued, Trouble raced toward the platter of meat.

Kisa hoped one of the Badass team was close enough to fling himself across the ribs before Trouble reached them. Then she forgot about everything as she thought over what he'd said. So simple, yet so wise. She'd concentrate on just one thing tonight. Kisa wanted to make love with Reinn. Period.

As they climbed the steps to the porch, Kisa saw Jor following at a distance. *Good.* Jor would make sure the hunters Reinn worried about didn't sneak up on him. Reinn would hate knowing that Jor was now guarding both Alan and him. She smiled. *Too bad.* Reinn could just get over his anger and realize lots of people cared about him.

Once inside, Kisa deliberately bypassed the kitchen and instead climbed the stairs. Reinn climbed them beside her. He didn't say anything until they stood outside Kisa's door. Then he gently cupped her chin and raised her gaze to his.

"You have a decision to make, lady. If I walk into your room now, I'm going to make love to you." He let her see it all in his eyes—his hunger, his desire. His *love?*

Tonight. Only think about tonight. She wouldn't read more into his eyes than his need to be with her at this moment. It was enough for now.

Kisa couldn't decide whether the click as she unlocked her door symbolized a beginning or an ending. Would this be the only time they made love in her bed or the first time of many? She didn't know. What she *did* know was that wishing meant nothing. She'd make love as if tonight were all she had.

She smiled a sensual invitation. "Come on in and kick off your shoes. Then we'll make love. We'll do it hard and fast and then slow it down to make it last. When the explosion comes, it'll be Texas-sized, and tiny pieces of us will be raining down on the Woo Woo Inn for days. They'll be happy pieces, though, so that's okay."

Reinn walked into the room behind her, kicked off his shoes, and then scooped her into his arms. Leaning close, he whispered into her ear, "Yahoo."

Chapter Sixteen

Reinn carried Kisa to the bed and then dropped her onto the mattress. She bounced once before glaring up at him.

"The carrying was great, but I think setting me gently on the bed came next, not dropping me so you could see how high I bounced." She tried to look outraged, but the laughter seeped through.

"I don't know about that. If I'd had a bed like this when I was a kid, I would've spent a lot of time bouncing." The gaze he turned on her was hot, hungry, and all grown-up male.

She swallowed hard. With one look he'd flipped their mood from playful to sensual, reminding her that no matter how good a sexual game she talked, she hadn't spent much time on the playing field yet. "So what does a big, bad vampire do in bed when he isn't bouncing?" That was a leading question with a capital L.

He rolled onto his side so he faced her. "Makes love to his woman, just like any other man."

The word *his* hung between them. Did he mean *his* as in for only this moment, or did he have a long-term *his* in mind? Maybe she was reading too much into the word. It was probably only three letters in a casual sentence, meaning nothing. Kisa frowned. Did she know how to depress herself or what?

As the silence dragged on, Kisa realized he was waiting for her to respond to his last comment. She decided not to involve herself in a discussion of the true meaning of *his*. Time for a subject change.

"How did you get so much power? What exactly can you do that I haven't seen yet?" Lame, lamer, lamest. They were here to make love, and she was driving down every conversational side road instead of sticking to Main Street.

He shrugged. "When Mackenzies first become vampire, they don't have any real powers. They're immortal, but that's about it. We gain power as we grow older, but we have to guide that power in the direction we choose. Like any young vampire, I couldn't wait to get all the usual abilities—lots of physical strength, enhanced senses, and preternatural speed."

"But that wasn't enough for you," she guessed. He'd want to make himself totally invulnerable to an attack like the one that destroyed his family.

"I never had enough power. I was never safe enough." He almost sounded surprised by that revelation. "It didn't take long for me to realize my mind had no physical limits, so I spent centuries developing my mental powers." He leaned toward her, his smile a slow slide of seduction. "Let me show you what I can do."

Okay, she was feeling a little wary here. "Like what?"

He reached out to push a few strands of hair away from her face. His fingers lay warm against her skin, and the effect was a major wow. Whispers of heat spread like a brushfire, and her body clenched in anticipation of lots of red-hot sizzle and dangerous sparks.

"If you could choose, where would you like to make love?"

He probably thought she'd name someplace like Hawaii. Was he in for a surprise. "Mars."

"Mars?" He looked puzzled. "Why?"

"I've always wanted to explore other planets, but NASA isn't moving fast enough for me. The possibility that other civilizations once existed on Mars fascinates me. I'd like to see for myself." She shrugged. "Since I'm going to make spectacular love with you anyway, I may as well have the once-in-a-lifetime setting to go with it." Kisa smiled at him, letting him know she was fine with somewhere less exotic if he wasn't up to a trip to Mars.

He nodded, deep in thought. "I took you to my actual home last time. Only the winter part was illusion. This time the setting will be total fantasy." He grinned. "Don't worry, though. Our lovemaking will be real."

Reinn paused, and she got the feeling he was about to say something important.

"I'll have to join our minds again. Will you trust me to do that?" His expression didn't change, but tension charged the air around them.

"Will I experience your feelings along with my own, like we did last time?" The echo of that memory made her heart pound and her breathing quicken. Oh, yes, that was a good memory.

"Yeah." He waited.

She softened her smile and hoped he saw how much she wanted this. With him. *Only* with him. "So will we go to Mars with our clothes on?" She hoped not. "I like traveling light."

"We'll take only what we need. You won't have any use for this." He tugged at her top, and she lifted her arms so he could slip it over her head. "Or this." He unbuttoned her shorts, and when she raised her hips he slid them off.

Reinn bent his head to place his mouth over the spot on her throat where her pulse beat a wild rhythm of rising desire. He slid his tongue over her skin, leaving a trail of sensual promises behind.

"Last time I spent a weekend there, I think I saw a list of Martian laws carved into a boulder. One of them said that bras and panties are illegal. Guess they'll have to go." He did a rotten job of trying to look sad about the imminent loss of her black lace bra and even lacier black panties.

Once again she wouldn't get to wear Sparkle's sexy little nightie with the beaded thong. *Hmm, thong.* Maybe she could just bring the beads with her to experiment. . . .

He ran his finger under the edge of her panties and tugged. "Hey, if the Martians throw your cute behind in jail for wearing banned underwear, don't expect me to bail you out."

Kisa wanted to be a law-abiding citizen, so she let him unhook her bra and skim her panties down to her ankles. "I guess I'll have to leave them behind." She made a big production of flinging away her bra and kicking off her panties. Then she took a deep breath that gave her breasts maximum lift. "My cute behind won't do you much good in some moldy old cell."

From the direction of his heavy-lidded gaze, Kisa guessed that right now he was more interested in lift and thrust than anything her "cute behind" could do. But he'd soon learn that her behind had lots of latent talent.

He took a deep, steadying breath.

"Do you breathe?" *Dumb, dumb question.* Here she was, at a critical moment in her seduction scene, and she'd diverted his attention. But when questions popped into her mind, she had to ask. She wanted to know everything about him.

"What?" He blinked at her.

Damn. She'd pulled him out of the moment. "Nothing. Forget I asked. Let's get back to where we left off. I was taking a deep breath, and you were all glassy-eyed."

His wicked smile was hot enough to send scientists around the world into a frenzy over the sudden spike in global warming. "Not so fast. I *want* you to know things about me." His smile faded as his eyes darkened. "I want you to care enough to ask lots of questions."

She made a real effort to wipe the dopey grin off her face. He wanted her to care about him. That was a good thing, right? "Warning, incoming questions could strike at any moment." She thought about what they'd be doing on Mars. "Well, maybe not at *any* moment."

The gleam in his eyes said he knew exactly what moment she was talking about. "I didn't die when I became vampire; I just changed. Sort of like a tadpole when it becomes a frog. I'm physically different from when I was human, but I've never lost my human reflexes. I still take a deep breath to calm myself. And when I panic, like I did when Felicia threatened you, I can almost feel my heart pounding. Understand?"

Kisa could only nod, because she was busy pulling at his T-shirt. He obliged her by yanking it off.

If she lived out all nine of her lives, she'd never get over the hitch in her heartbeat every time she saw his yummy chest. She ran her hand over its broad expanse, enjoying the flex of hard muscle under warm, smooth skin. Kisa leaned over to flick each male nipple with her tongue.

The hand he laid on her arm wasn't quite steady. "Keep touching me like that and the spaceship will leave without us."

"Spaceship?" *Mmmm.* Sounded like fun. More than the force would be with her on this trip.

Kisa pushed Reinn onto his back and then unbuttoned his jeans. He helped her slide them far enough down his legs so that he could kick them off. That left white briefs. There was something so sensual about the stark white against his tanned skin that tremors of arousal made her fingers unsteady as she struggled to rid him of them. It didn't help that his erection grew larger with each fumbling attempt. Making an impatient noise, he helped her finish the job.

Kisa swallowed hard. She'd forgotten how much manhood he carried between his legs. Not that she judged a man by the size of his sexual equipment, but it gave her so much more to stroke, and hold . . . *Uh-oh*. She'd better lower her sexual thermostat fast or steam would start rising from under her hood.

"You're tanned all over." She'd probably noticed that the last time, but she couldn't talk when her tongue was hanging out.

"My natural skin tone." He clasped her hand before settling back onto the pillow. "Relax. It'll be a short trip."

She was more than ready. Still holding his hand, she lay back and closed her eyes. . . .

"'Tis time to put her into orbit around Mars, Captain." A large man with a mane of red hair and a Scottish kilt looked up at Reinn from his instrument panel.

Reinn nodded. "Good, Jock. You can beam us down whenever you're ready." It didn't seem strange at all that the captain was gloriously naked.

But then she was naked, too. "Why do you have someone from Scotland on every one of your ships?" she asked, falling into the fantasy with no effort at all.

He shrugged. "It's a galactic law. Every ship has to have someone aboard who can say, 'Aye, Captain.'"

She nodded. That made perfect sense to her. Relieved that the trip was over, she followed Reinn to the transport pad. Within seconds they were standing on the surface of the red planet.

Kisa drew in a deep breath of fresh Martian air and soaked up the warmth of the sun. She silently laughed at the stupid scientists who still thought Mars couldn't support human life. She made a face at the nearby rover, which had its camera focused on them.

Reinn shook his head as he drew her down to the ground with him. "It's not nice to tease NASA, sweetheart. All those scientists are probably calling the White House right now to let the president know there's life on Mars."

She smoothed her hand over his firm butt. "Mmm, if they wait a few minutes, they can also report there's hot sex here, too." Kisa offered a finger wave to the camera.

Kisa was just reaching for him when a discreet cough stopped her. She turned to see one of the big-eyed gray aliens immortalized by Roswell staring at them. He didn't look happy.

"You're on private property, humans. Didn't you see the damn sign?" He glanced around at the barren landscape. No sign. "It was here yesterday." His expression turned suspicious. "Did you take it down?"

Kisa smiled at him. He spoke English. *Cool.* "We

didn't see your sign. But we're only going to make love here in front of the rover camera to drive NASA crazy. Then we'll leave."

He frowned. "Uh-uh. Can't let you. If you make love here, pretty soon more of you will come. We'll have urban sprawl, pollution, and *Desperate Housewives*. You can make love in my spare bedroom."

Spare bedroom? Kisa thought that sort of took the adventure out of the whole thing.

Reinn glanced at the rover. It was making beeping noises and rolling closer. "We'll take you up on your offer if it can go with us." He nodded toward the rover, which was now almost camera-to-nose with him. "One of Kisa's fantasies is to make love in front of an audience."

It was? Kisa couldn't remember.

The alien gave an exaggerated sigh. "Okay. Bring it. But make sure it doesn't track in any sand. And get some of that dust off it."

Reinn and Kisa looked at each other and then down at their naked bodies. Reinn shook his head. "Sorry, nothing to dust with."

Much to the alien's disgust, they had to walk to his home with a dusty rover rolling behind them. The alien touched a key on the remote he held, and when the ground opened up he waved them onto an elevator. Kisa walked on ahead of Reinn. She could feel his gaze on her behind, so she did a little wiggling and a little waggling just for him. A glance over her shoulder assured Kisa that her effort moved him. Well, it moved at least one part of his body.

The alien wasn't much for small talk. He didn't have anything to say as they descended to his apartment and he led them to a large bedroom. He finally broke his silence. "Keep down the noise when you make love. The neighbor below me is a real butthead." When he left them he was muttering something about putting up another damn sign.

Kisa glanced around. The bedroom looked pretty ordinary—floating chairs, transparent bureau, and a white plastic bed.

Trying to ignore the rover's excited whirring noises in the corner, Kisa flung herself onto the bed. She beckoned to Reinn. "Time to play, my big, beautiful vampire."

He scowled at the rover. "This thing looks way too happy. I know you had your heart set on an audience, but I want my woman all to myself." Reinn went into the bathroom and came out with a towel. He draped it over the rover camera. The machine made angry bleeping noises, but Reinn ignored them as he knelt on the bed beside her.

"That's better." His gaze slid down the length of her body.

His hunger touched her breasts and between her legs with enough heat to make her stretch and arch her back in feline satisfaction. "I'm glad you did that. The power of our lovemaking would've shattered every lens in its little head, and NASA would've sent us the bill to fix it."

Reinn was way beyond thinking about the cost of a camera lens. He growled low in his throat before putting his mouth over one nipple.

Kisa made little noises of pleasure as he teased her nipple with his tongue, and when he scraped his teeth gently over it, she groaned.

"Oooh, yesss! That felt soooo good. Do it again."

Reinn released her nipple and stared at her. Kisa widened her eyes as she stared back. "Who was that?" It wasn't her. She didn't have a low, throaty purr like that.

Suddenly the bed rippled beneath them, and the white plastic turned bright red. "It's me. I'm your living bed. I share your sensory experiences and enhance them. We're going to have sooo much fun." The bed shivered with excitement.

Reinn muttered in a language Kisa didn't understand before flopping onto his back. "Can you do your enhancing without the sound effects, bed?"

The bed sighed. "Yes, but it's so much more fun when I express my enjoyment along with you guys."

Kisa thought it was amazing that the bed spoke English, too.

"Humor me. Enhance silently." Reinn was starting to look desperate.

"Your wish is my command, oh stupid master. If you want to pass on all my vocal input, it's your loss." The bed went silent.

Okay, Kisa was officially out of patience. "We're leaving." She climbed from the bed and headed for the door.

"Why?" Reinn looked puzzled. "I thought you wanted to make love on Mars." When she remained by the door, he swung his feet to the floor and stood.

"I did, and I still do. But I've decided I want you all to myself. *Forever.*" *Uh-oh.* She hadn't meant to say that out loud. Kisa watched him warily.

His gaze softened. "Me too."

He left her wondering what the *me too* referred to. Did it just mean he wanted her to himself right now? Or did it include the *forever* part?

While she was wondering, he was acting. Reinn walked over to the rover, took the towel from its camera, and then guided the machine to the bed.

"Hey, bed, I have someone I want you to meet. This is Rover. He's a stranger looking for some fun. How about showing him a good time?"

The bed rippled. "I looove strangers." Its plastic legs beat out a happy tattoo on the floor in time with its excited vibrations. Within seconds the downstairs neighbor was pounding out his anger on his ceiling. Together they made a great percussion duo. "Come closer, big guy, so you can see me in action. I'll tell you some great tales about the lovers I've shared hot times with."

The rover rolled closer, its camera focused on the bed as it made joyful little clicking sounds.

Kisa grinned. "That should keep NASA busy for a while."

Reinn joined her as they slipped from the room and headed for the planet's surface.

"Here." Kisa lay down on a soft sandy spot behind a boulder. She felt around to make sure there were no stones to poke her at an inconvenient moment and then sighed. *At last.*

Reinn joined her. He gazed across the empty Martian landscape. "The Martians have the right idea. Building down instead of up leaves the surface untouched and perfect for—"

"Loving." She watched him adjust his hips to the ground beneath him, his movements relaxed and so sensual she wanted to fling herself on top of his bare body. But she'd control the urge and wait for exactly the right moment to pounce. Cats were good at pouncing.

Kisa had never seen him in sunlight before. She propped herself up on one elbow so she could get a panoramic view. His golden skin looked warm, and so touchable that she couldn't help reaching out and sliding her fingers along one muscular thigh.

He turned his head to smile at her, a smile filled with erotic invitation that said, *Touch me again, in all the places that'll excite me and bring you pleasure.*

If they had any tomorrows together, she'd want to spend lots of hours lying side by side with him in the sun . . . *Sun?* "You're out in the sun and not screaming in agony. What's that all about?"

"I can do anything you want me to do while we're here, tiger lady." His gaze heated, telling her he was almost finished with talk and ready for action.

"Great. Can we stay here forever?" Oops, she'd said the F-word again. She should know better than to ask questions like that.

She saw the sadness in his gaze before he looked away. "As long as forever lasts for us."

Kisa couldn't stand the sorrow swirling around

them. Today was for happiness. "That sounds workable for now." She made her smile all perky and cheery. But it didn't matter what kind of fake smile she pasted on her face, because soon he'd wipe it away and replace it with one of genuine sexual repletion. "You're always trying to please me. What would please you the most?"

She expected him to smile. He'd didn't. There was something tentative in his expression, as though he didn't know what to say.

"Come on, tell me. If it's too weird, I'll just say no." Kisa didn't think he could come up with anything weirder than making love on Mars, but what did she know?

He nodded. "Close your eyes."

Sighing, she complied. What was the big deal? She found out fast. An image of Reinn looming over her, fangs gleaming whiter than white, formed behind her closed lids. He lowered his mouth to her neck, and she felt the slide of his fangs over her skin. She opened her eyes and gulped for air. "Okay, got the picture. Don't have to see any more."

He finally smiled. "Yeah. That's what I thought you'd say. Forget it."

She wouldn't forget it, but she'd have to think long and hard about whether she wanted to include that particular bit of vampire sex play in her repertoire of sensual experiences. It would hurt. A lot. A fun time would *not* be had by all if he attached himself to her neck in the heat of passion. Would he enjoy her thrashing around while she told the whole planet at the top of her lungs that his teeth were major owies? She thought not.

Reinn sat up and then leaned over her. He smoothed her hair away from her face before covering her mouth with his. His kiss was long and drugging, a master's course in all the ways his tongue could drive her wild. Kisa figured she'd passed her final with a straight A after exploring the heat of his mouth with passion and flair. It couldn't be anything but an A. She was good.

He pulled her to a sitting position as he covered her nipple with his lips and proved that his mastery didn't end with her mouth. She threw back her head and moaned while he circled her nipple with the tip of his tongue and then clasped it gently between his teeth and tugged.

Kisa lost track of what he did to her breasts after that because she was busy riding the giant waves of bliss on her personal sensory surfboard. The warm, wet flick of his tongue, the scrape of his teeth, and the wonderful power of a man's mouth to create suction drove her wild.

When she couldn't stand it anymore, she wrapped her arms around him and slid her body along his, reveling in the light sheen of sweat that made his skin all smooth and wonderful to touch. She glided her hands down to grip his firm and fantastic butt cheeks as she rubbed against his erection. *Mmm.* Tactile sensations with Reinn were always yummy.

Burying her face in the hollow of his throat, she

licked the tempting skin right where his pulse would've beat hard and strong when he was human. She hummed a low, husky note to signal how much she enjoyed the taste of aroused male and the scent that was his alone. The two senses combined were an erotic tease—dark, wicked, and wild. If only she could bottle his essence so she could take it out during long winter nights and remember.

As he laid her back on the sand and knelt between her spread legs, the fang thing poked at her consciousness. She pushed it aside and concentrated on every little detail of the moment. The sand was warm and a little scratchy against her skin. The sun was bright enough to blind her, but his bare muscular body shielded her from the glare. There was no sound, just her own harsh breathing.

Lowering his head, he put his mouth over the juncture of her inner thigh. Not where she thought he was going, but an erotic turn-on just the same. She tangled her fingers in his thick hair and tugged to get his attention.

"My turn to do fun things to your body, vampire." She paused between words to catch her breath. "You've done all the giving."

He lifted his head, and his gaze seared her. "Your life force flows hot and strong here. Feeling it beneath my lips arouses me more than is probably safe. So don't think you have to *do* things to me."

Her fog of sexual arousal parted for a moment of clarity. "Biting completes sex for you, doesn't it?"

The silence stretched on for so long that Kiss

thought he wouldn't answer her. Maybe she didn't want him to answer. She was still conflicted about the whole fangs-in-neck thing.

"Yeah." Just the one word.

Jeez, did he have to be so honest? "But you can have lots of fun without it, right?"

His smile was slow and oh, so sexy. "Yeah."

Okay, then everything was cool. He could have one fine orgasm without sinking his teeth into her neck. "Uh, when you bite someone, is it like major pain for the bitee?" Why was she asking? It wasn't going to happen.

"No."

"Look, I've had enough of the one-word answers. Elaborate a little." It didn't matter what he said; she wasn't going to let him sink his shiny whites into her neck.

"Our minds are joined, so you're sharing what I feel. When I . . . bite you at the moment of orgasm, my pleasure is so overwhelming that it suppresses any pain you might feel." She could tell he wasn't enjoying this little lesson on vampire mating habits. "Besides, you know from experience that I can take away pain."

Kisa nodded, but she still didn't think a bite was in her future.

Then she stopped thinking as he dipped his head between her spread thighs and used his talented mouth in a way guaranteed to bring her to screaming fulfillment.

He teased her personal orgasmic timer with the tip of his tongue and then slid his tongue inside her to create more magic until she arched and cried out. Her timer was ticking off the minutes—no, seconds—until detonation.

When he lifted his head, she took the opportunity to scoot down until she could dig her fingertips into his buttocks and hold him still for her mouth. She'd like the imprint of her fingers to stay on his beautiful behind forever as a reminder of how much she wanted him. But since he was a vampire, that was a no-go.

She felt him smoothing her hair while she cupped his heavy sacs. He groaned as she slid her tongue lingeringly over them and then took each into her mouth.

Emotion flooded her that had nothing to do with desire. The love she felt for this man who'd known only fighting and distrust during his long life, but who now made himself totally vulnerable to her, brought tears to her eyes.

Kisa shifted her attention to his powerful erection. She traced its length with the tip of her finger and then circled the head. A shudder worked its way through his body in anticipation of what she'd do next. Kisa didn't disappoint.

As he spread his legs to give her easier access, she massaged his inner thighs. Then she licked a meandering path of discovery along his shaft, swirling her tongue around and around until his body bucked beneath her. Driven by her need to taste and touch him in every possible way, she slid her lips over the head.

His inarticulate cry revved up her body's response.

She clenched her thighs, the heaviness low in her belly signaling that her sexual self was through waiting for its payoff. It wanted him, and it wanted him *now*.

Just a few more minutes. She'd never thought she had a talented mouth, but hey, she was apparently damn good. Kisa worked her way up and down the length of his hard flesh, teasing him with her tongue until, with a guttural cry, he lifted her on top of him.

"Ride me hard and fast, tiger lady." His voice was harsh with need.

Kisa thought it was amazing how two minds could think alike, although not much thinking was going on north of her belly button.

She straddled his hips, positioning herself above his erection. Lowering herself until his shaft just nudged her flesh, she paused to savor the feeling of her body opening to him, moist and ready.

Reinn lay with his thick hair a tangled glory around his face. His eyes darkened, hinting that he was having trouble holding back his vampire form. He wanted her that much. Kisa didn't fear his change. She trusted him *that* much.

Slowly, focusing on the sensation of being stretched and filled by the man she loved, Kisa lowered herself onto him.

He reached up to roll her nipples between thumbs and forefingers, and she flung back her head to keep from screaming her joy at the intense feelings flooding her.

Kisa took him deeper than she'd ever thought possible before lifting her body until only the head of his sex remained inside her. Pressing down once more, she experienced all over again the awesome feeling of him filling her completely.

Instinct took over as she withdrew and then impaled herself on him over and over again, faster and faster, until everything was a blur of driving sexual frenzy. She could almost feel the whoosh of air as she barreled toward that incomparable moment when everything in her personal universe stopped and pure pleasure burned through her.

He raised his hips, thrusting upward to meet her each time she ground herself against him. As she drove herself onto him harder and harder, she was vaguely aware that he'd become vampire. But the knowledge didn't change the incredible sensations racking her body.

Then she met his gaze. Beyond his sexual hunger, she saw something more—his acceptance that the final pleasure would be denied him. And she would do the denying.

There was no anger or accusation in his eyes, only acceptance. That wasn't right. She wanted this to be the greatest lovemaking he'd ever experienced because it was with *her*. Kisa loved Reinn enough to give him this, but did she have enough trust in him to ignore her fear?

She did. Leaning over, she allowed her long hair to slide across his skin. She absorbed his shuddering response as she put her mouth close to his ear.

"I want to lick every inch of your bare body, but since I'd explode long before I finished, I want you to bite me instead."

He stilled beneath her, his eyes widening with shock. "Do you mean it, Kisa? Are you absolutely sure?"

"I trust you, vampire." She nibbled on his earlobe. "And I want you in every possible way."

With a cry of triumph, he drove into her one last time. The thrust shoved her over the edge into a place she'd never visited before, not even during the first time they'd made love. Maybe it was knowing she'd have all of him today, maybe. . . .

She stopped thinking and became one with her senses. Kisa didn't feel the prick of his fangs, but suddenly their joined orgasms shattered around them. If pleasure could kill, she was dead. Spasms shook her body, drawing scream after scream from her until tears slid down her face. Her climax was a wind tunnel of escalating pleasure, tossing her around on currents of physical sensation she couldn't control, each one growing more intense as she was swept inexorably toward . . .

Oh. My. God! Her whole body shook with the power of her last spasm. And then she simply died. She knew she was dead because no one could live through that kind of ecstasy. She'd always thought ecstasy was sort of a silly word. No one experienced ecstasy.

As she lay with eyes closed, heart pounding loud enough to bring the whole Mars population to the surface, and breath coming in harsh gasps, she decided that *ecstasy* was an excellent word.

Beneath her, Reinn lay silent. Opening her eyes, Kisa met his gaze. And in the moment before he realized his emotions lay raw and open for her to see, she saw something there that made her heart pound even harder.

He quickly hid his feelings behind the mask that he wore for the world. But she'd seen.

She smiled her cat smile at him. The one that said, *You can run, but you can't hide.*

Because what she'd seen in Reinn Mackenzie's eyes had looked an awful lot like love.

Chapter Seventeen

Kisa stared at her laptop, bit her lip in indecision, and then looked over her shoulder at Ganymede, who'd stretched himself across the top of her couch. "Okay, this e-mail has to sound like it's coming from Reinn. So how about if I say, 'I refuse to kill Alan Mackenzie, and I challenge you to face me yourself instead of hiding behind the hunters. I'll be waiting for you at the Woo Woo Inn—insert address—at midnight.' Do you think they'll get here in time if they use their preternatural speed?"

Ganymede yawned. *"Probably not, because they'll be too busy laughing their asses off."* He leaped down to sit beside her so he could see the screen better. *"Babe, they'll know that crap isn't from Reinn as soon as they read it. You gotta write like a guy; use guy words."*

Kisa frowned. "Like what?"

Ganymede gave it some thought. *"What you want is to piss these suckers off so they'll come here to waste Reinn personally. You gotta understand how men insult one another to do that. You're a woman, so you have this kind of language barrier when it comes to guy talk.*" He narrowed his amber eyes as he decided on exactly the right words. "*Okay, get this down quick, because pure genius burns hot and fast.*"

She did a mental eye roll. "Ready."

His chuckle was pure evil. "*'Hey, assholes, I'm not doing your dirty work anymore. I get that you don't have the balls to come here to whack me yourself, but think about this. Before the hunters take me down, I'll tell them what dickless wonders you are. Your chickenshit council sucks, and you're fucking cowards. See you in hell, shitheads. Oh, and if you grow a pair before midnight tonight, I'll be waiting for you at the Woo Woo Inn. Respectfully yours, Reinn Mackenzie.'*"

Kisa winced as she typed the message. "Whoa, pretty confrontational, isn't it? I mean, these men won't be in any mood to listen to reason once they get here. And what's with the 'respectfully yours'? Sounds like you're into insult overkill."

"*The 'respectfully yours' is me being brilliant. Sarcasm is my forte. And yeah, it has to be confrontational. And yeah, I need to take the insults to the max. These men were Vikings and Highlanders. Lots of slaughtering and pillaging in these dudes' past. They're not gonna come here to make nice. They'll only respect someone bigger and badder than them. Reinn has to sound like that someone.*"

"I guess." As much as she hated to agree with Ganymede, what he said made sense. Kisa put in the Woo Woo Inn's address and then hit send before she could have second thoughts.

"*Why'd you wait until today to contact them? Cutting*

it a little close, aren't you?" He stared at the screen, and a photo popped up of a naked woman with lots of what made men happy.

Kisa decided against visiting violence on his fat little body as she calmly shut down her laptop. She needed him. "If I'd sent it yesterday, they might've shown up before I was ready. They have preternatural speed, so let them use it."

Now for a smooth segue. "By the way, have you changed your mind about helping Reinn? We'll meet the council on the front lawn, but if fighting breaks out, it could spread to the inn. Lots of stuff might get broken, and a bunch of humans would probably check out. Cindy might even tell her father who *didn't* protect her inn." The humans-checking-out part was a lie, because both Reinn and Ganymede could erase memories, but she chose not to remind him of that.

Ganymede looked startled. *"Didn't think about that. I was into the moment. Can we get that message back?"*

Kisa shook her head and tried to look regretful. "Uh-uh. It's popping up on someone's screen even as we speak." She hoped. If even one of the council members checked his messages soon, he'd alert the others.

"Sneaky. I like that in a woman. Guess I don't have a choice. Have to make sure the inn stays in good shape." He leaped to the floor and padded toward the door. *"This'll mess with my schedule, though. Gotta squeeze in a quick trip to town. A new burger place just opened. But I'll be back here by midnight."*

"Don't you like what Katie's cooking tonight?" Kisa looked at her list. Next she had to talk to everyone else involved in the stand against the council to make sure each understood his or her role. And she had to do all this before her big, bad vampire rose.

"Sure, but there's, like, four hours between lunch and dinner. A guy needs something to keep him going between meals." He stared at the door. It opened. He left.

Kisa shook her head. If Ganymede ever worked up the energy to care, he could rule the world. And wasn't that a scary thought. She forgot about Ganymede, though, as she went in search of Sparkle. Hal, the day guy, pointed Kisa toward Sparkle's room.

Sparkle answered the door wearing a black silk robe. "Hey, sister, come on in. I was just trying to decide what to wear tonight. Got to look sexy for the vampire council. Powerful men make me all tingly."

"How does Ganymede feel about all these tingly sensations?" Kisa glanced around the room. She blinked. Black dresses hung from all the doors. Black dresses were draped over every piece of furniture. Black dresses hung from the curtain rods and even from a hanging plant. "Let me guess, you're wearing a black dress tonight. Good grief, how many did you bring?"

"Twenty-eight." Sparkle reached for the dress swinging from the plant hanger. "I like lots of choices." She held up the dress. "Gucci. What do you think?"

Kisa chose her words carefully. "Beautiful. It's really . . . there." *Or not*. A gorgeous dress, but not a lot of it. "Umm, isn't it a little much for a casual night at the inn?" The dress would look right at home on a Paris runaway. But at the Woo Woo Inn? She didn't think so. "Why aren't all these dresses hanging in your closet?"

Sparkle's expression said that Kisa asked dumb questions. "Because I have other stuff in the closet. And no, the dress is just right for tonight. If all the council members are men, then this'll get their attention. Men are easily distracted, and a distracted man isn't going to be on top of his game. Ergo, this dress is perfect."

Other stuff in her closet? "All these dresses are black."

Sparkle blinked. "And your point is?"

What *was* her point? Kisa had forgotten. Oh, tonight. "I want everyone to meet on the front lawn at eleven thirty to wait for the council. As soon as the members show, every shifter will change into his or her animal form, and then I'll explain the facts of life to the council. I'll make sure Reinn is there, but he'll probably be a little grumpy." How about raging mad? Kisa wasn't looking forward to telling him what she'd done. "And I have some good news: Ganymede agreed to help us."

Sparkle nodded. "Fine. But I want to talk about black dresses. Black rules the night. A black dress makes every woman a sensual vixen. If more women wore black dresses, they'd have the world wrapped around their perfectly manicured fingertips." She eyed Kisa thoughtfully.

"Don't even think about it. Definitely not wearing one of your dresses tonight. I'll be shifting before the council can even get a glance at me, so I won't be a distracting force." Providing you didn't think a ticked-off saber-toothed tiger was a distraction.

Sparkle sighed her disappointment. "The dress might soothe the savage beast—namely your hot vampire—but I guess you wouldn't agree to take it off before you shift." She looked hopeful.

"Nope. Won't have time. And I'd tear it to shreds when I changed. I couldn't do that to one of these beautiful creations. I'd love to take a rain check on one of them, though." And surprise, surprise, she was telling the truth. She'd really like to see Reinn's expression if she showed up in that little Valentino dress hanging from the bathroom door.

"You're right. I'd hate to lose one of these babies. I only have forty more at home." Sparkle's gaze softened, and for one nanosecond, she seemed to forget about her personal agendas. "Don't worry; Reinn will be fine. If Mede has agreed to help, the council is toast." She dismissed Kisa with a wave of her hand. "See you tonight."

With that assurance spurring her on, Kisa went in search of the weres.

Something was wrong. Reinn sensed it in the way people glanced at him and then looked away. And Kisa hadn't met his gaze once tonight. Time to find out what was going on.

"So what's happening that no one wants me to know about?" He pushed the porch swing into motion as he stared across the front lawn at the darkened forest.

"What makes you think that?" She sat beside him, her tension making the air around them vibrate.

He looked at Kisa in time to see her glance at her watch. "It's eleven fifteen, and everyone's been real obvious about avoiding my gaze. I thought about slipping into a few minds, but I'd rather you tell me."

The moonlight did great things for her. It highlighted her hair, a rich, deep brown falling almost to her waist. He wanted to bury his face in the soft strands. The pale glow created shadows that played over her sexy lips and made her eyes gleam, mysterious and dark. Right now, though, mysterious translated to keeping secrets from him.

She bit her bottom lip and then released it. "Okay, here's the deal. I thought it was pretty dumb for you to face the council alone when there were people who'd stand with you. So I sent the members an e-mail, pretending it was from you. I called them some names and told them you'd meet them at midnight here."

He couldn't stop staring at the alluring shine of her bottom lip. He wanted to . . . "You did *what?*" Reinn never roared. Soft menace was more effective. Roaring indicated a loss of control. He roared.

Kisa looked at him from wide eyes, but she didn't back down. "Look, I have a vested interest in keeping you alive, so I did what I had to do. I know you like to play the I-don't-need-anyone loner, but dammit, you have people here who care about you. Let them help."

Reinn forced himself to ignore the sheen of tears in her eyes. "It's my life, so where the hell do you get off deciding what I should do with it?" People who cared about him? Why? He couldn't wrap his understanding around that.

Friends. It was a new and scary concept. Friends meant personal interaction—inviting them to his house, backyard cookouts, and admiring pictures of their kids. He shuddered at the thought.

I have a vested interest in keeping you alive. What did that mean? Did she just want him around to protect Alan when the new Guardian showed up? Or did his life mean something to her personally? Maybe she only wanted to help a friend. Cripes, he hoped not. Reinn wanted to be a lot more up-close than that. A lover? Okay, getting warmer. The man she loved? Hope sprang eternal and all that crap. She had to know how he felt. He'd called her *his* at least two times.

Reinn yanked his thoughts back to the present and the woman staring silently at him. Oh, yeah, he was steamed. At her. But it was hard to maintain a scowl when she was looking at him like that. Something warm and intimate shone in her eyes. Thinking about what that might mean made him forget his anger.

"Will you stick around to meet the council?" She sounded tentative, as if she expected him to climb on his bike and roar away into the night. Away from *her*. Lord help him, he didn't think he could do that now.

He ratcheted his glower down to a token glare. "You didn't leave me much choice. The council will kill Alan when they get here. Did you think of that?"

Her sudden sharp intake of breath told him she hadn't.

Kisa's stricken expression didn't make him feel as satisfied as he'd expected. "We'll keep Alan and Julie safe." He wanted to comfort her, a first in his long existence. Comforting wasn't what he did.

She nodded before glancing toward the inn's door. "Everyone should start coming outside now."

Reinn couldn't believe his eyes as all of the weres, along with Jor, Alan, and Sparkle, walked out of the inn to stand on the lawn. For once he was struck silent, and he swallowed hard against something in his throat that felt a lot like emotion. He took Kisa's hand and then went to join them.

Kisa stopped beside Sparkle. "Where's Ganymede?"

Sparkle looked upset. "He's upstairs puking his brains out. In other words, he has the dry heaves. The jerk was so busy stuffing his face at the new burger joint in town that he didn't realize he was scarfing down bad meat. Now he has food poisoning. He says he's dying, so I guess he won't be available to save our butts." She frowned at the toes of her shoes. "The grass is wet from the sprinkler. The dirt will stick to them."

The shoes or their butts? Sparkle hadn't been specific. Probably both, because without Ganymede a lot of their butts might be hitting the dirt.

Kisa patted Sparkle's arm. "They'll be fine." She led Reinn away before he could say anything.

Reinn rubbed his forehead, where a headache would be forming if vampires got headaches. "So we'll be facing a mob of the most powerful vampires in the Mackenzie clan with a few shapeshifters, three vampires, and a cosmic troublemaker who's worried about getting her shoes dirty."

"Mob? Five vampires don't qualify as a mob." She guided him toward the spot where Jor and Alan waited.

"You don't think they'll come alone, do you?" His nonexistent heart sank. She did. "The council will bring the hunters with them. There're ten hunters. That makes fifteen pissed-off immortals."

He watched conflicting emotions chase one another across her face, first panic and then determination. No matter how grim the situation seemed, he couldn't feel down knowing she'd done this for him. Reinn put his arm across her shoulders and pulled her close as they took the last few steps that brought them to Jor and Alan.

Reinn tipped up her chin and smiled at her. "Hey, we'll kick butt, sweetheart. I'm motivated, and I've had a thousand years of butt-kicking experience."

She returned his smile, but he saw the uncertainty behind it. "I've sent for more help."

"Who?" Who could make a real difference against fifteen of the Mackenzie clan's most powerful?

"Us."

Reinn swung around to see Thrain grinning at him. "A few of your friends have come to save your ass." The gleam in his eyes said he knew exactly what to expect from Reinn at the suggestion that he might have friends, and that those friends might care what happened to his ass.

Reinn glanced at Kisa. She grinned at him, proud that members of his clan valued him. He bit back the words of rejection that came so easily to his lips. Smiling at Thrain, he nodded toward the other vampires. "Thanks. I could use the help."

It was worth admitting that he needed them just to see the shock on Thrain's face. Reinn scanned the others. Five vampires altogether—Thrain, three men, and one woman. "Good to see you again, Darach." He acknowledged Cindy's father.

Darach offered him a wry grin. "Ye owe me, Reinn. Blythe is fashed at me because I left her behind in Scotland. But even though she is long-lived, she is still human. I refused to put her in harm's way."

"You did the right thing. I'll talk to her after this is over." For the first time he dared to believe that he'd be around when the battle was over. Reinn shifted his attention to the other vampires. They were strangers.

He paused to study two of them, a man and a woman. Reinn glanced at Thrain. "Aren't you going to introduce everyone?" His gaze returned to the strangers. He couldn't abandon the caution that had kept him alive over the centuries.

Sparkle slipped into the group. "I'm the one who asked them to come, so I guess I should introduce them." She turned to the big, dark-haired male with the blue Mackenzie eyes. "This is Eric. He helps run a theme-park attraction near my candy store in Galveston."

Reinn nodded at Eric. "I've heard your name before. We'll need your power if the council shows up."

Sparkle moved to stand beside the woman. "Reinn, meet Donna Mackenzie. Donna is Eric's wife."

Reinn smiled at the woman and then shifted his gaze to the last vampire.

"This is Taurin." Sparkle seemed at a sudden loss for words, not a Sparkle characteristic.

"Taurin?" The one word left it up to the vampire to introduce himself.

Taurin met his gaze. "Eric and Donna are my friends. I was at loose ends, so I offered to come along to help you out." He smiled, but a hint of unease touched his eyes. "I'm a night feeder."

The old familiar rage rose in Reinn. He felt the slide of his fangs as scenes from that long-ago night played across his memory. And if the visuals were a little fuzzy after a thousand years, the emotions were just as sharp; they sliced right to the center of his remembered pain. He gathered himself to spring at the other vampire.

Kisa put her arms around his waist. "Let it go, Reinn. It happened a long time ago, and you've hated long enough. Jor is alive, and this man didn't kill your family. Taurin wants to help you stay alive. Start looking for things in your life worth celebrating."

Like *her*. Reinn fought the bitterness that had

poisoned his entire life, fought his need to rend, to destroy, and slowly gained control of his hate. He closed his eyes and searched for calm. Kisa was right. He'd looked for, even expected, the bad in life up to now. But Kisa had changed that perspective. He was surrounded by people willing to go to battle for him. He opened his eyes.

Reinn figured his smile looked a little grim, but it was the best he could do right now. "Sorry about the fangs. Night feeders killed my family a long time ago, and you triggered an automatic response. I was wrong." Taurin would never know how few times in Reinn's life he'd said those last three words.

Taurin shrugged. "No problem. Eric can tell you how long I held a grudge against him for something he never did."

"So what's the plan?" Eric stared at Jor and Alan. "And who're these guys?"

"Alan's the bridegroom, and Jor is . . ." He'd never put a label to his relationship with Jor, but now he could look back and realize how events had bound them together. "My brother. Brother by Mackenzie blood and brother by the childhood we shared."

He felt Jor's hand on his shoulder and knew he'd said the right thing. But hell, the Reinn Mackenzie shaped by a thousand years of fighting was cold and unemotional. All this sharing of feelings embarrassed him. Time to steer the talk back to war.

"As soon as the council and hunters show, the shifters will do their thing and the rest of us will take vampire form." He studied Kisa. "You know, it might be better if you don't shift unless we really need you. I can't wipe memories from the Mackenzies." That settled, he returned to the battle plan. "Then we'll challenge the bastards."

"Then we'll *reason* with them." Kisa poked at him. "And who died and made you general?"

"I'm the oldest and most powerful vampire here, so I take charge. Besides, they've come for me, so it's my responsibility." Reinn narrowed his gaze on Kisa before addressing his waiting army. "We'll beat them to a bloody pulp."

"We'll calmly *explain* why their law isn't logical." Kisa glared at him.

Jor coughed. "Uh, hate to interrupt the strategy session, but I think the council's here."

"What?" Kisa turned to follow Jor's gaze. "Oh, boy."

If someone ever asked her to paint a physical representation of intimidation, she'd paint this scene. Against the backdrop of a moonlit night and the darker silhouette of the forest stood fifteen men in black. *Big* men. Really scary men who'd already taken vampire form. "Uh, I sort of thought the council would look old and doddering." Nope, no one in this group fit that description.

"All Mackenzies become vampire when they're in their late twenties or early thirties. That's the age they remain for as long as they live." Reinn sounded impatient with the need to explain.

"I knew that." She swallowed hard. The council members weren't smiling, and their grimness brought home to her exactly what she might have loosed on the Woo Woo Inn.

Kisa sensed movement behind her, and she glanced around. The shifters had taken their animal forms as they faced the invaders.

She sucked in her breath. *Whoa, would you look at Seth?* The massive grizzly rose to his full height and roared at the vampires. Kisa didn't know about the council, but she, for one, was totally impressed with Seth.

The council and hunters glided forward as one body. *Very cool.* Now that she'd gotten over her initial shock, Kisa studied them.

Great outfits. Sparkle would approve. They all wore long black leather coats, black shirts, and black pants. She could just see the gleam of their sword hilts.

Finally, when she couldn't put it off any longer, she looked at their faces. Big mistake. She assumed the council members were the five who stood in front. If someone had shown her a picture of them before she'd sent her e-mail, she might've toned down the insults. You didn't call men like these dickless wonders. Okay, so maybe Ganymede did, but he wasn't here to face the consequences.

"You've disappointed us, Reinn." The huge vampire with a mane of wild blond hair and long beard didn't look particularly crushed.

"Too bad, Valgard. Times have changed, but the council hasn't kept up. You're not a Viking raider anymore. You can't swoop down and kill anyone who doesn't agree with you."

Valgard's smile made Bernie the wereduck quack nervously. "Oh, but I can." He cast the weres a contemptuous glance. "These animals won't stop us." His gaze did rest on Seth for a few extra heartbeats, though.

A red-haired council member tapped Valgard on the sleeve. "He's recruited vampires to his side."

Eric's smile didn't reach his eyes. "Smart observation, Teilo. And none of us will be standing around contemplating our fangs when you try to take Reinn down."

Both sides glared at each other. Kisa jumped into the charged silence. "We can discuss this like rational people."

A council member with short dark hair hissed at her. "No, we can't, woman."

Kisa forged on desperately. "I don't know your name, but I'm Kisa. The Guardian of the Blood serves no purpose anymore. Your last Guardian was probably afraid to tell you, but lots of werecats have married Mackenzies and lived long, happy lives. Either he never found out about them, or the Protector kept him from making his kill. Your blood has been mixing with other species for centuries, and nothing bad has happened."

The vampire looked outraged. "You lie. No werecat could stop the Guardian of the Blood."

"But a Mackenzie could." Jor stepped forward. Angry and in his vampire form, he looked every inch the powerful thousand-year-old immortal that he was.

"A Mackenzie traitor." A fourth council member with shaved head and a diamond stud in one ear reached for his sword.

"I wouldn't reach for your weapon, Sceolan, because you'll be the first to die." Reinn's threat cut through the council's menace, and this time the silence was laced with the promise of violence.

Soft laughter shifted everyone's attention to the fifth council member, who, for whatever reason, hadn't taken vampire form. Kisa decided she had to rethink her definition of spectacular. Calling a man a sexual animal took on new meaning when applied to him. Shining hair that looked almost black in the moonlight fell to his broad shoulders and framed a face that only a dark god could have shaped. The brilliantly blue Mackenzie eyes seemed somehow wrong in that sinfully beautiful face.

As he met her gaze, he smiled, a slow, wicked lifting of his sensual lips that scared her more than the fierce Valgard's scowl.

"This is Declan, Kisa, and he looks like a dark god because his father *is* one." Reinn's voice held anger out of all proportion to the moment.

Startled, Kisa looked up at Reinn. His eyes were hot with emotion. Yep, he was angry. Wait, how did he know what she'd been thinking . . . ? "You read my mind. Maybe it's just me, but I could've sworn you promised not to—"

"I needed to know what you thought of . . ." Reinn spoke through gritted teeth, which looked pretty scary when fangs were part of the dental work.

He stopped before finishing, but it was too late. Kisa knew what he'd been about to say. He needed to know what she thought of Declan. Now why would that make him so mad? She started to smile.

Jealous? Was her gorgeous vampire jealous? Jeez, she hoped so.

She shrugged. "He's okay." God would forgive her for that tiny lie.

The anger faded from Reinn's eyes as he turned back to Declan. "If something's funny, let me know. I could use a laugh."

Declan's smile didn't fade as he glanced from Kisa to Sparkle and finally fixed his gaze on Reinn. "This whole confrontation is stupid. The council has better things to do than worry about the Guardian of the Blood. Who cares if a werecat marries a Mackenzie? Not me."

Kisa asked the obvious. "Then why're you here?"

"I wanted to meet the man who had the guts to call me a dickless wonder." Declan's smile never wavered, but there was a dangerous gleam in his eyes.

Reinn widened his eyes in shock and then narrowed them on Kisa. *Uh-oh*. Time for some damage control.

She smiled brightly. "Actually, I wrote that message . . . with a little help from a friend. Umm, I wanted to make sure you showed up." She held up her hands. "See, it worked."

Declan threw back his head and laughed, but a low growl rose from the rest of the council and waiting hunters. Reinn stepped in front of Kisa.

"It doesn't matter now what got you here. Let's finish this once and for all." Reinn tensed for battle.

Declan frowned. "Tell the two pretty ladies to go inside first. I wouldn't want to see them hurt."

Sparkle looked like she couldn't decide whether

to be outraged at being ordered inside or flattered by the pretty-lady thing.

Kisa popped her head out from behind Reinn. "Bring it on, guys. The pretty ladies can take care of themselves." Or not. The whole council and mob of hunters hissed as they pulled out their swords and then advanced on the good guys.

"Where's your sword?" Kisa didn't care how panicked she sounded.

"Up in my room. But the swords are just symbolic in this battle. Everyone will be using their powers." He turned away to deflect a flash of light, which hit with a mini sonic boom whatever invisible shield Reinn had thrown up in front of him. From Valgard's cursing, she guessed the light had come from him.

Suddenly the two sides flung themselves at each other. Howls, growls, and shouts of anger engulfed her. While the fight whirled around her, Kisa searched for someone who could stop the madness.

That was when she saw Sceolan rushing at Reinn's back with his sword lifted for a killing blow. Hello, hadn't anyone told him that his sword was merely symbolic in this fight? Reinn was busy battling Valgard and hadn't a clue what was behind him.

Only one thought flashed through Kisa's mind: *No. Not the man I love.* Then she shifted. Even as she roared her challenge before leaping at the vampire threatening Reinn, she remained coldly determined to stay in control of her cat.

She hit Sceolan squarely in the chest. As he

crashed to the ground with her on top of him, his sword flew from his hand. Through her killing rage, Kisa realized that everyone had frozen to stare.

Suddenly she sensed Sparkle and Reinn on either side of her.

Reinn laid his hand on Kisa's head. "Sparkle thinks she might be able to end this now."

Sparkle touched her shoulder. "I'm not powerful enough to take on all of them at once. But sex is my strength, so if I can draw extra power from two people who have an overwhelming sexual bond, I can do this."

Kisa's cat roared its need to sink its teeth into the vampire who lay pinned beneath her massive body, but she kept control.

"I love you, and the sooner we end this the sooner I can convince you to love me, too." Despite Reinn's awesome power, his whispered message in her mind resonated with uncertainty.

Even though the forces around her were recovering from the shock of finding a saber-toothed tiger among them and threatening to resume trying to tear each other apart, Kisa felt like laughing joyously. *"You haven't been paying attention, vampire. I already love you, but don't cancel the convincing. Sounds like something I might enjoy."*

Kisa took a deep breath and felt Reinn's fingers tighten in her fur as Sparkle drew the power she needed from them. The draining left Kisa trembling, but when she looked around, she would've whooped with joy if she weren't in her cat form.

Sparkle had done it, whatever "it" was. The

council members and hunters were screaming and stumbling in every direction. Except for Declan. He stood to the side looking amused, with a terrified wereduck hiding behind him.

Uh-oh. Kisa's body was reacting to the draining of power. She was returning to human form. *Naked* human form. With a muttered curse, Reinn ripped the long leather coat from a struggling Sceolan and had it ready to drape over her as soon as the change was complete. Sceolan took the opportunity to scramble to his feet and join in the running and yelling.

Sparkle put her fingers to her mouth and got everyone's attention with a piercing whistle.

"What did you do?" Kisa frowned. The council and hunters were all clutching the same place on their bodies.

"I temporarily moved their sexual packages to an undisclosed location known only to me." Her sly glance slid to Declan. "But I couldn't do that to a man who thinks I'm a pretty lady. I mean, who knows when he'll need all that wonderful male equipment? Could be soon."

Leaving Kisa with that thought, she turned her attention to the terrified vampires. "Lose something, boys?"

"What the hell are you? *Who* are you?" Valgard's eyes bulged in horror.

"I'm Sparkle Stardust, and I'm the cosmic troublemaker who has all your manliness tucked away for safekeeping." She glanced down at her shoes. "Now, see, they're dirty, and it's all your fault. That sort of makes me mad." She raised her gaze to Valgard, and Kisa shuddered at what she saw in Sparkle's eyes. "You never know what I'll do when I get really ticked off." She glanced at Reinn. "Want to tell them something before we begin negotiations?"

Reinn nodded. "The council will no longer appoint a Guardian of the Blood. Mackenzies will be free to marry anyone they choose." His gaze slid to Kisa, and he smiled a take-me-to-bed smile that said he'd already chosen.

"And the council will leave Reinn and everyone else here tonight alone to get on with their lives. No reprisals." Kisa wanted to make that perfectly clear.

The council and hunters stared from Reinn to Kisa to Sparkle with wide, unblinking eyes.

Sparkle reached down to wipe the toes of her shoes. "Just a suggestion, but if I were you, I'd vote in a few women council members. If some of you had been female, I couldn't have taken away all your . . . weapons so easily."

"You can't leave us like this." Teilo's whimper suggested he thought she could do just that.

Sparkle sighed as she studied her nails. "Sure I can. Here's the deal, guys. You agree to everything Reinn and Kisa said, and I'll return your body parts." She took a deep breath, calling attention to the fact that *she* still had all her body parts. "But remember, what Sparkle gives back, she can take away again. And there's nowhere you can hide where I won't find you." She frowned at her nails. "This shade is too dark by moonlight. I need something brighter, more vibrant."

Valgard had returned to human form and was looking about as pale as a vampire could look without qualifying as a ghost. "We agree."

Sparkle nodded and linked hands with Reinn and Kisa. Once again Kisa felt power draining from her. She must be about the same shade as Valgard right now.

The council members along with all their hunters gave a collective exhalation of relief before disappearing into the night. Declan was the last to go, and he turned to wink at Sparkle before following the others.

"Okay, I'm here to save all your asses. Where're the bastards you want wasted?" Ganymede padded to Sparkle's side. *"Pick me up, babe. I'm weak. It took all my strength to drag myself down those freakin' stairs. But a cosmic troublemaker's gotta do what a cosmic troublemaker's gotta do."*

Sparkle held her nails up to the light. "I took care of it, sugar lump, so you can go back to bed. I have to change nail color right now." She turned toward the inn and then stopped. "Oh, I know what you can do. You can take away the memories of all those humans running for their cars."

Kisa glanced toward the parking lot, and sure enough, people were clambering into their cars in a frantic effort to flee the Woo Woo Inn. *Go figure.*

With a mumbled complaint, Ganymede glanced toward them. Immediately the people started to climb back out of their cars. They looked around, confused. *"Now tell me how you took out the council without my power and experience, babe."*

Sparkle glanced over her shoulder. "I have hidden depths, Mede. Get used to it." Then she continued into the inn with Ganymede and everyone else trailing behind her.

Jor grinned at Reinn on his way in. "See you inside, bro. You'll have to invite me to visit you soon."

Reinn frowned. "See. I knew that's what would happen. Pretty soon I'll have people crawling all over my house."

Kisa had started to draw him toward the inn and hopefully into her bed when Trouble burst from the forest. His terrified yelps preceded him. He raced past them without slowing down, his tail tucked between his legs. A few strides behind him bounded a giant rabbit. As the two disappeared around the side of the inn, Reinn stared blankly at Kisa.

She grinned and shook her head. "Guess Trouble finally caught himself a rabbit, or maybe the rabbit caught him. Mel the wererabbit checked in this afternoon. Mel's a really big guy, so he changes into a really big rabbit. He's a professional wrestler. A pretty aggressive guy."

Reinn chuckled. "Did I ever tell you about the time the clan thought one of us had made a vampire rabbit and—"

"Shh." Kisa put her finger over his lips. "Don't think I need to know any more about rabbits."

His gaze darkened as he slowly licked her finger and then drew it into the warmth of his mouth. He slid his tongue around her finger before releasing it.

Sighing, she reached up and drew his head down to her. Then she kissed him, long and deep and with all the passion she'd stored up during their confrontation with the council. "So where do we go from here?" She hoped the kiss would give him a clue.

"We get married." He seemed pretty sure of that.

"At your house?" She held her breath.

He gazed at Kisa with his love for her shining in those blue eyes. "If mobs of people are going to be tramping through my house, it may as well be for something important."

"Mmm. Now that we've settled that, let's go to my room." She put her lips against his throat and savored his scent and yummy taste.

"And make love?" He pulled her close.

"On a comet. I've always wanted to make love on a comet."

And they did.

Night Bites

Nina Bangs

Cindy Harper has an ice-cream flavor for every emotion. But no sweet treat from her freezer is smooth, creamy, or tempting enough to cool down her dark fantasies about über alpha male Thrain Davis.

This is a man to be enjoyed on a strictly primitive level. Every woman who ever sees him smile wonders about the pleasure his mouth can give her. Too late she realizes the danger of inviting an ancient vampire into her inn. He forces her to examine her past when she is just fine with her present. He does have an upside, though. Who needs ice cream when you have a hot and yummy dark immortal in your bed?

Dorchester Publishing Co., Inc.
P.O. Box 6640
Wayne, PA 19087-8640

_____25614-X
$6.99 US/$8.99 CAN

Please add $2.50 for shipping and handling for the first book and $.75 for each additional book. NY and PA residents, add appropriate sales tax. No cash, stamps, or CODs. Canadian orders require an extra $2.00 for shipping and handling and must be paid in U.S. dollars. Prices and availability subject to change. **Payment must accompany all orders.**

Name: _____

Address: _____

City: _____ State: _____ Zip: _____

E-mail: _____

I have enclosed $_____ in payment for the checked book(s).

CHECK OUT OUR WEBSITE! www.dorchesterpub.com
_____ Please send me a free catalog.

NINA BANGS
Master of Ecstasy

Her trip back in time to 1785 Scotland is supposed to be a vacation, so why does Blythe feel that her stay at the MacKenzie castle will be anything but? The gloomy old pile of stones has her imagination working overtime.

The first hunk she meets turns out to be Mr. Dark-Evil-and-Deadly himself, an honest-to-goodness vampire. His voice is a tempting slide of sin, and his body raises her temperature, but when Darach whispers, "To waste a neck such as yours would be a terrible thing," she decides his pillow talk leaves a lot to be desired.

Dangerous? You bet. To die for? Definitely. Soul mate? Just wait and see.

Dorchester Publishing Co., Inc.
P.O. Box 6640   __52557-7
Wayne, PA 19087-8640 $6.99 US/$8.99 CAN

Please add $2.50 for shipping and handling for the first book and $.75 for each additional book. NY and PA residents, add appropriate sales tax. No cash, stamps, or CODs. Canadian orders require $2.00 for shipping and handling and must be paid in U.S. dollars. Prices and availability subject to change. **Payment must accompany all orders.**

Name: _____

Address: _____

City: _____ State: _____ Zip: _____

E-mail: _____

I have enclosed $_____ in payment for the checked book(s).

CHECK OUT OUR WEBSITE! www.dorchesterpub.com
_____ Please send me a free catalog.

reward *yourself* treat *yourself*

$10,000! Spring Fling Giveaway
TRUE STORY
SHE'S ONLY TEN—
LETTER TO TOBEY
LOVE

$5,000! Spring Fling Giveaway
TRUE STORY
I GOT A FOR VALENTINE'S DAY!
EMOTION

INSPIRATION & HOPE

$5,000! Summer Giveaway
TRUE STORY
STAR-SPANGLED SWEETHEARTS
SOFIA'S CHOICE
"PARADISE PLACE"
LIFE, LIBERTY AND THE PURSUIT OF HAPPINESS

It's like getting
6 FREE ISSUES

$10,000!
TRUE STORY
PASSION

ROMANCE

TRUE STORY
SUBSCRIBE & SAVE 50%

☐ YES, please enter my subscription to *True Story* for 12 issues at $24.00.
Make checks payable to Dorchester Media. Add $10.00 for Canadian & Foreign postage. (US Funds Only)

Name _____ (Please print) _____

Address _____ Apt. # _____

City _____ State _____ Zip _____ J6MOS.

PAYMENT ENCLOSED ☐ BILL ME ☐ Charge my VISA ☐ MASTERCARD ☐ DISCOVER ☐ AMERICAN EXPRESS ☐

ACCT.# _____

Signature _____

Expiration _____

For Credit Card Orders Call 1-800-666-8783
PLEASE NOTE: Credit card payments for your subscription will appear on your statement as *Dorchester Media, not* as the magazine name.

Please allow 6-8 weeks for
delivery of first issue.
Annual newsstand price is $47.88

Mail to: *True Story*
PO Box 2104
Harlan, IA 51593-2293

Tall, Dark & Hungry

LYNSAY SANDS

It bites: New York hotels cost an arm and a leg, and Terri has flown from England to help plan her cousin's wedding. The new in-laws offered lodging. But they're a weird bunch! There is the sometimes-chipper-sometimes-silent Lucern, and the wacky stage-actor Vincent: she can't imagine Broadway casting a hungrier singing-and-dancing Dracula. And then there is Bastien. Just looking into his eyes, Terri has to admit she's falling for someone even taller, darker, and hungrier. She's feeling a mite peckish herself. And if she stays with him, those blood-sucking hotel owners won't get her!

Dorchester Publishing Co., Inc.
P.O. Box 6640
Wayne, PA 19087-8640

_____52583-6
$6.99 US/$8.99 CAN

Please add $2.50 for shipping and handling for the first book and $.75 for each additional book. NY and PA residents, add appropriate sales tax. No cash, stamps, or CODs. Canadian orders require $2.00 for shipping and handling and must be paid in U.S. dollars. Prices and availability subject to change. **Payment must accompany all orders.**

Name: _____

Address: _____

City: _____ State: _____ Zip: _____

E-mail:_____

I have enclosed $_____ in payment for the checked book(s).

CHECK OUT OUR WEBSITE! www.dorchesterpub.com
_____ _Please send me a free catalog._

reward *yourself* treat *yourself*

LOVE

INSPIRATION & HOPE

EMOTION

It's like getting
6 FREE ISSUES

ROMANCE

PASSION

TRUE ROMANCE

SUBSCRIBE & SAVE 50%

☐ YES, please enter my subscription to *True Romance* for 12 issues at $24.00.
Make checks payable to Dorchester Media. Add $10.00 for Canadian & Foreign postage. (US Funds Only)

Name _____ (Please print) _____

Address _____ Apt. # _____

City _____ State _____ Zip _____ J6MOS.

PAYMENT ENCLOSED ☐ **BILL ME** ☐ Charge my **VISA** ☐ **MASTERCARD** ☐ **DISCOVER** ☐ **AMERICAN EXPRESS** ☐

ACCT.# _____

Signature _____

Expiration _____

For Credit Card Orders Call 1-800-666-8783

PLEASE NOTE: Credit card payments for your subscription will appear on your statement as *Dorchester Media*, not as the magazine name.

Please allow 6-8 weeks for
delivery of first issue.
Annual newsstand price is $47.88

Mail to: *True Romance*
PO Box 2107
Harlan, IA 51593-2293

SPECIAL OFFER
FOR NINA BANGS FANS!

READ ABOUT NINA IN THE MAY ISSUE OF

ROMANTIC TIMES

BOOKclub
THE MAGAZINE FOR BOOKLOVERS

Request your FREE sample issue today! (While supplies last.)

★ OVER 250 BOOKS REVIEWED & RATED IN EVERY ISSUE
Romance, Mystery, Paranormal, Time Travel, Sci-Fi/Fantasy, Women's Fiction and more!

★ BOOK NEWS & INDUSTRY GOSSIP
★ BESTSELLING AUTHORS FEATURED
★ PREVIEWS OF UPCOMING BOOKS
★ WRITING TIPS FOR BEGINNERS

Send to Romantic Times BOOKclub Magazine
55 Bergen Street, Brooklyn, NY 11201.
Please be sure to include your name, address,
day time telephone number and/or email address.

OR CALL TOLL FREE 1-800-989-8816
E-MAIL INQUIRIES TO: RTINFO@ROMANTICTIMES.COM
MENTION CODE: **S6NB**

Romantic Times BOOKclub is a magazine, NOT a book club.

ATTENTION
BOOK LOVERS!

Can't get enough of your favorite **ROMANCE**?

Call **1-800-481-9191** to:

✳ order books,

✳ receive a **FREE** catalog,

✳ join our book clubs to **SAVE 30%!**

Open Mon.-Fri. 10 AM-9 PM EST

Visit **www.dorchesterpub.com**
for special offers and inside
information on the authors you love.

We accept Visa, MasterCard or Discover®.
LEISURE BOOKS ♥ LOVE SPELL